THE
SWALLOWTAIL
LEGACY

Betrayal by
the Book

MICHAEL D. BEIL

PIXEL✛INK

PIXEL+INK

Pixel+Ink is an imprint of TGM Development Corp.
www.pixelandinkbooks.com
Printed and bound in December 2022 at Maple Press, York, PA, U.S.A

Cataloging-in-Publication information is available from
the Library of Congress.

Hardcover ISBN: 978-1-64595-050-9
E-book ISBN: 978-1-64595-166-7

First Edition

1 3 5 7 9 10 8 6 4 2

For Laura Lea, with all my love.
With apologies for the Oxford comma,
thank you for thirty years (!)
of infinite patience, inestimable support,
and unreserved love.
Oh, and one more thing: I'm listening. Really.

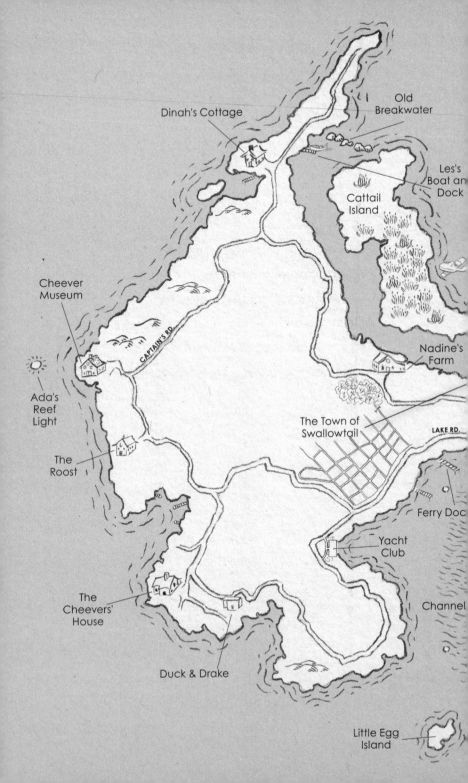

Dinah's Cottage

Old Breakwater

Les's Boat and Dock

Cattail Island

Cheever Museum

CAPTAIN'S RD.

Ada's Reef Light

Nadine's Farm

The Roost

The Town of Swallowtail

LAKE RD.

Ferry Dock

Yacht Club

The Cheevers' House

Channel

Duck & Drake

Little Egg Island

SWALLOWTAIL ISLAND

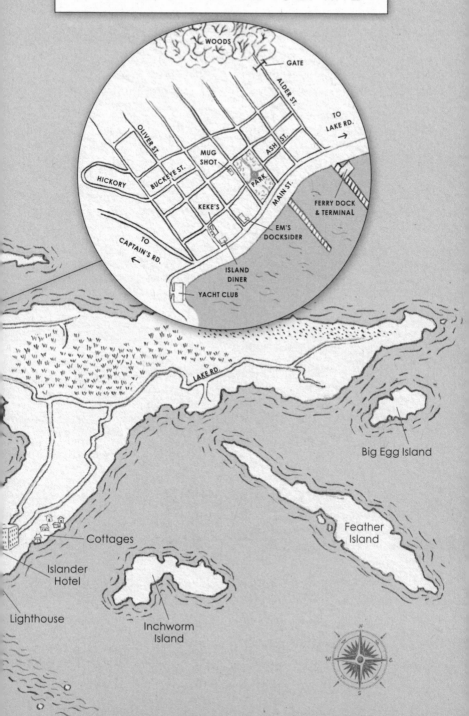

Prologue

ANN E. KEYHEART STANDS IN the front hall of the Captain's Cottage, her mouth still hanging open from the blood-chilling scream that brought me sprinting the seventy-eight yards back to her door. Not to brag, but if the 78-yard dash was a thing, I would have *totally* broken the world record. It's even more impressive when you add *these* details: it is after ten o'clock at night, the path is poorly lit, and I'm weighed down by the five pounds of plaster cast that's holding my broken right arm in place.

"*Whathappenedareyouokay?*" I say between breaths while I push the door wide open and barge inside. Captain Edward Cheevers's dark, intense eyes stare down disapprovingly at Keyheart from his portrait on the wall.

"Dead," she says in a voice that lacks *any* emotion. "She's dead."

You know, I'd better stop here, because I'm getting ahead of myself. If you understand soccer, what I need to do is back pass to the goalie and reset. So, let's back up a few hours so I can explain exactly *why* I was seventy-eight yards away from the Captain's Cottage, on the dark path between it and the Islander Hotel, at the very moment that my favorite author discovered a dead body on her living room floor.

CHAPTER
1

THERE IS NOTHING UNUSUAL ABOUT the way the day starts. Pip, my ten-year-old sister, is the first one awake, galumphing down the stairs and out to the barn to feed and say good morning to Tinker, her horse. Our stepfather, Thomas, is next, making coffee and ransacking the refrigerator for eggs and milk, when I make my appearance.

"G'morning, Lark. Perfect timing. Can you make up pancake batter with one arm? Good. Great. Bacon or sausage?"

"Bacon," I say, pouring the mix into a bowl and reading the directions.

Fifteen minutes later, as I'm flipping the last batch of pancakes, his three boys—my stepbrothers Blake, Nate, and Jack—stumble in, one zombie after the other, drawn to the smell of frying bacon.

Pip, as usual, chatters almost nonstop through breakfast, sharing stories of the previous day's UNBELIEVABLE and FANTASTIC adventures with Tinker, and outlining her (and Tinker's) plans for the new day. The rest of us nod or grunt occasionally so she doesn't think we're ignoring her. In our crazy, mixed-up family of six, Pip is the only true "morning person." After I've had my orange juice (in my favorite vintage Judy Jetson glass) and a stack of pancakes, though, I come to life.

It's a big day—another in a series, it seems—for me. It's the opening day of Swallowtales, Swallowtail Island's annual book festival, which promises to pack every hotel and B&B on the island with wannabe writers of every age. Two hundred aspiring writers are coming to take classes and to "workshop" their books, stories, and poems with other writers. It's also an opportunity to meet and discuss their work with publishers, agents, editors, and a handful of bestselling authors.

What does all this have to do with Meadowlark Elizabeth Heron-Finch, you ask? That's easy: Nadine Pritchard, the famous writer who was my mom's best friend when they were kids, just happens to be on the board of directors of Swallowtales. Right after we arrived on the island in June, she hired me to be her assistant, and together we solved the seventy-five-year-old mystery of her grandfather's murder. Along the way, we also stirred up a hornet's nest involving the wealthy and important (on Swallowtail Island, at least)

Cheever family and a few hundred acres of extremely valuable real estate.

When Nadine first asked if I wanted to be a page, which is sort of an assistant to one of the bigshot authors or other VIPs, I was less than enthusiastic, until I saw the list of authors.

"Can I be *her* page?" I asked, pointing at the name "Ann E. Keyheart."

"Ann Keyheart? Really? Why?" Nadine seemed surprised.

"She's, like, my favorite author. I've read *The Somewhere Girls* a million times. I know, it's not like me at all. All that teen drama. And you know, the really big secret that they all promise never to reveal. So cheesy. I usually hate that stuff, but I can't help it. It's so . . . good. Have you read it?"

Nadine shook her head. "No, but I know *of* it. I visited a girls' school in New York last year to talk about *my* books, and I'm pretty sure every girl there was reading it. Tough competition for a nonfiction book about the civil war in Somalia."

"Have you ever met her? Ann Keyheart, I mean."

"No. I understand that she used to be a Swallowtales regular, but stopped coming a few years back when her career really took off. We hadn't even asked her this year, figuring it would be a no, but then her people reached out to *us* a few weeks ago. Said she wanted to do it, and didn't even care about the money. She'd do it for free. Kinda hard to say no to *that*. You really want to be her page?"

"Uh-huh. Yeah. I mean, she's not crazy or anything, right?"

"Well, speaking as a writer, I think all writers are at least a *little* crazy. But if you want the job, you've got it."

It is the boys' turn to clean up after breakfast, and I have a half hour to kill before heading to the Islander Hotel for my first duties as an official Swallowtales page, so I return some texts. It wasn't until the second week of August that we made the family decision to stay on Swallowtail Island, and ever since I told all my old friends back in Connecticut, they have been freaking out. They can't believe that I am *choosing* to live on a tiny island in Lake Erie—with a year-round population of about two thousand, with no cars, and in *Ohio*, for goodness' sake. I might as well be moving to the moon as far as they're concerned. And now, with less than two weeks of summer vacation left, they're bombarding me with texts about how horrible my life is going to be. I have to give them credit for doing their research, at least. Thanks to them, I know that the average size of the graduating class at Swallowtail Island High School is forty-five, and that the soccer team hasn't won a game in more than two years. And that sometimes grocery stores run out of food because the lake is frozen and the ferry can't get to Port Clinton.

"Hey, listen to this," says Thomas, pointing to something in the *Swallowtail Citizen* that had arrived the day before. "It's a letter to the editor."

I roll my eyes at him. "So?"

I know, I know. What can I say? I'm twelve, I'm an orphan, and I live on an island. In Ohio. And sometimes the voice in my head (my mom's) telling me to be nice is too late for me to stop myself. At this point, though, Thomas knows me well enough not to take it personally.

"Trust me, you'll be interested," he says. "Some woman who read about you in last week's paper. Roseann Flaherty."

It's true. After Nadine and I solved her grandfather's murder and found Captain Edward Cheever's missing will—a will that, among other things, *might* make Pip and me the owners of about three hundred acres of valuable land on Swallowtail Island—the *Citizen* ran a big story about me. Now, before you start thinking I'm famous or something, you need to know that the *Swallowtail Citizen* is not exactly the *New York Times*.

"Does she want to buy some land, or is she offering to sell it for me?" It's a legitimate question. When word got out about the will and the land, we had to stop answering the phone because we were getting so many calls from real estate agents.

"It sounds to me like she's writing about the book you're looking for—the one from the English bookstore."

I sit up straight in my chair. Now Thomas has my undivided attention. Right after we arrived at the Roost, our house on Swallowtail Island, I found a tree swallow (*Iridoprocne bicolor*, to be precise) made of silver, along with a copy of *The Pickwick Papers* by Charles Dickens that had belonged to my mom.

Strangely, the pages were cut out in the center of the book to make a secret nesting place for the bird. Inside the front cover was a stamp from Crackenthorp Books in London, so I wrote to them to see if they knew anything about the bird. A few weeks later, I got a response from Mr. Archibald Crackenthorp, who wrote that he didn't know anything about the bird, but that a *second* Dickens book, *Little Dorrit*, had also been sent by his father to the same address around 1940.

When the guy was interviewing me for the story in the *Citizen*, he was kidding around at the end of his visit, calling me Nancy Drew and asking me about my next case. All I'd said was that I was looking for a book with a cutout for a little carved bird—that I'd heard there was a book like that some-where on the island, and I was going to try to find it. I *didn't* say why, or how I'd heard about it, or anything about already having one like it.

"I told you you'd be interested," Thomas says as I read over his shoulder.

"What does she say?"

Thomas continues: "Apparently your story triggered a memory of seeing a book with a bird hidden inside, like what you said you were looking for. She thinks that the bird was tan or brown all over, like a wren or a sparrow. It would have been around nineteen seventy-six, when she was in the fourth grade. A classmate brought it in for show-and-tell."

"Does she say anything about the book? The title?" I ask.

"Or the name of the girl who brought it in?"

"Uh, let me see. She doesn't remember the girl's name . . . the family moved off the island sometime afterward, but she remembers that the girl lived in a big house on Buckeye Street. A *yellow* house."

"There're no yellow houses there," I say. I cut across Buckeye on my bike on my way into town all the time and I would have noticed a yellow house.

"It's been forty plus years. Houses change colors. Change in *all* things is sweet, according to Aristotle." He looks closely at me, waiting for the inevitable eye roll, but I deny him the chance to be right. "Anyway, it's a clue, which is more than you had ten minutes ago."

"*Maybe* it's a clue. Maybe not."

"But you're going to look into it."

"Well, in the words of Larkus Maximus, *duhhh.*"

The job of a Swallowtales page is not complicated. In our training sessions, the organizers stressed a few key things. Number one, chauffeur the VIP from the ferry dock and help out with the check-in process. Deliver the information packet containing class rosters, schedules, invitations, and tickets. Then a quick tour of the Islander Hotel, where most of them are staying, and where all the classes and workshops will be held. We all received training on the photocopy machine and how to get VIPs connected to the Wi-Fi and a printer if they want. After that we're basically "on call," a text message away from whatever they want, whether it's a cup of coffee, a ride into town on one of the hotel's golf carts, or twenty copies of a handout for their class. "Be there if they need you, and stay the heck out of the way if they don't" we were told.

I'm supposed to meet Keyheart at the ferry dock, where she's due to arrive on the *Niagara* at eleven o'clock. Dressed in the official page uniform of khaki shorts and a peach-colored polo with the Swallowtales logo embroidered on the front, I take the keys to one of the hotel's electric golf carts and drive to

the lighthouse at the point. As I skid to a stop a few steps from the water's edge, the *Niagara* has just passed the outer channel markers and is heading for the red buoy that's no more than fifty yards from where I sit. From there, it has a straight shot to the dock, but I have plenty of time to get there. Once it reaches shore, there are lines to be made fast, ramps to be lowered, and gates to be opened before anyone can disembark.

The starboard railing is lined with passengers pointing at the lighthouse and, of course, capturing the moment of their arrival on Swallowtail Island on their phones. As the *Niagara* slips past me, a lone woman is standing in the shadows at the stern, leaning nonchalantly against the railing as if she's made the trip a million times. I think to myself, *Must be an islander— definitely not a tourist.* Then, while I'm reaching down to turn the key in the golf cart, she glances over her shoulder and casually tosses something overboard. I can't see what it is, but my brain registers a flash of black and white stripes, exactly like the ones on a can of CoffLEI, a coffee-flavored soda made on Put-in-Bay. (Its short for Coffee of the Lake Erie Islands, in case you're wondering.) Whatever it was, it *really* ticks me off, because, geez, there are trash cans and recycling bins all over the stupid ferry. Before I'm able to get a decent look at this Neanderthal, though, she disappears into the crowd along the rail. Annoyed, I step on the accelerator and kick up some gravel as I spin the cart around and head for the road to the ferry dock.

By the time the *Niagara* is tied up and passengers have begun to disembark, I have parked the golf cart in the lot and I'm standing outside the terminal holding up a sign that reads: A. KEYHEART. I know what she looks like, although I've been warned by more than one person that the author photo in all her books is several years old and "*definitely* Photoshopped." Passengers file past me, some making the expected jokes ("If I say I'm A. Keyheart, will you take me to my hotel?") but still no Keyheart. Finally, as I'm about to give up, a young woman clambers down the ramp, spots me, and waves. She's lugging three large suitcases and has a full pack strapped to her back.

"Hello! Thank you! I was worried you'd already gone," she says. She points to the sign. "That's me."

I'm not so sure; she looks like a college kid. I know they can do wonderful things with cosmetic surgery these days, but this is ridiculous. I look at the sign, then back at her. "Uh . . . are you sure . . . I'm waiting for the *author*, um, Ann Keyheart."

"Yeah, I know. I'm her P.A."

"P . . . A?"

"Personal assistant. Didi."

"Oh. Right." This is the first I've heard about an assistant, personal or otherwise. "I'm Lark, your, er, Ms. Keyheart's page for the week. I'm so sorry. I wasn't expecting . . . " I take one of the suitcases from her and stack it on the back of the cart.

"No problem," she says, pushing her sunglasses up and turning to take in the view of town from the dock. Her free hand goes to her mouth, but not before a quiet "oh" slips out, and her lovely green eyes turn watery.

"Are you . . . okay?" I ask.

She shakes her head quickly, as if to break out of a trance, and covers her eyes with her sunglasses. "Yeah. Good. Okay. I just . . . oh, there she is. Finally."

A woman in a lime-green linen pantsuit appears at the top of the ramp, stopping to pose as if she's waiting for the press to greet her on the red carpet at the Oscars. Her big moment is ruined, though, when a gust of wind takes her hat, and after a brief, swirling flight, deposits it in the harbor.

"Oh! My hat! No! That's from Harrods! Didi! Hurry!"

I run toward the ferry, thinking that I might be able to rescue the hat if I can find a boat hook, but it is not to be: the wake from a passing boat washes over it and it sinks before my eyes.

"*Annnddd* there it goes," says Didi. "Right to the bottom. Like the *Titanic*. I hope that's not an omen for the week."

"After I drop you off at the hotel, maybe I can come back and look for it," I say.

Didi shakes her head. "Don't worry about it. In fifteen minutes, she won't even remember that she had a hat. Harrods my *butt*. Marshalls, more likely."

Keyheart, barely five feet tall in her matching green espadrilles, slowly makes her way down the ramp, all the while staring sadly at the spot where the hat disappeared. I get my first good look at her, and mentally compare the woman before me with the younger, thinner, redder-haired, and somehow, but most definitely, *taller* person in the photograph that I was so familiar with.

"Hi, Ms. Keyheart, I'm Lark," I say, holding out my (cast-free) left hand, which she leaves hanging for a *long* second before giving it a quick shake. "Your page for the week. I just want to say how happy I am to be able to—"

"*You're* my . . . oh, that's just perfect. A one-armed page. Are you even old enough to drive that thing?" she asks, pointing at the hotel golf cart.

"Yes, ma'am. Don't worry about my arm. And you only have to be twelve to drive golf carts on the island."

"Good grief. I'm being chauffeured by a *child*. A child with a pituitary problem, apparently," she adds, backing up a step so she can take in all sixty-eight and a half inches of me. "Are your parents in the circus?"

Didi buries her face in her hands. "Actually, they're dead," I say, smiling sweetly. "But they *were* both tall."

"O-kayyy. On that note . . . Maybe we should get going," Didi says, guiding Keyheart into the seat next to me while she climbs into the back seat.

I press down on the accelerator and off we go, with Keyheart holding on for dear life and wondering aloud about the lack of seat belts.

When I pull up outside the hotel lobby, I say, "We need to

stop here to get you checked in, and then I'll take you to your cottage."

In addition to the main building, which has forty-eight rooms, the Islander Hotel has half a dozen "private cottages" for very special guests. Although she offered her services for free for the week, Keyheart had requested the Captain's Cottage, the newest and most luxurious of the bunch, with a deck that extends well out over the lake. It is named for Captain Edward Cheever, the famous sea captain—yes, the same one whose long-lost will I found, and whose land Pip and I *might* now own. His name and face are pretty much *everywhere* on Swallowtail Island.

"I'll take care of it," Didi says to Keyheart. "Can I have my phone back?"

Keyheart makes a face, sucking in a deep breath. "Oh. Riiight. Your phone."

"What?" says Didi. "Where is . . . no! You didn't."

Keyheart nods. "I'm afraid I did. I'm really, really sorry. I made my call, and then, I don't know what happened. One second I was holding it, and the next . . . "

"Did you leave it on the boat?" Didi asks. She starts to climb back aboard the cart. "Maybe we can get back before it leaves. Come on!"

I'm ready to make the drive back to the dock, but Keyheart is shaking her head. "It's not on the boat. I . . . it went over. The side. Ker-plunk."

"*No.* No, no, no!" Didi repeats. "How did you . . .that phone is my *life*. What am I supposed to . . . how can I even do my job?"

"Let's not be melodramatic, dear," Keyheart says, and I cringe, knowing how *I* would respond to somebody telling me not to be melodramatic. "You millennials and your phones! When I was your age, do you know what we had? Pay phones! You *did* bring your laptop, right? There you go. Problem solved. I would think you'd be happy to spend a few days away from all that technology. When we get back to New York, I'll buy you a new phone, anything you want. And myself a new hat."

Didi, eyes squeezed shut and hands folded atop her head, stamps toward the lobby, so I follow her inside.

"Sorry about your phone," I say. "That sucks."

"She's *killing* me," says Didi. "That's not even the first one that she's lost. She forgets to charge hers, and borrows mine. And then loses it. And did you notice, she won't admit that she *dropped* it. No, because that would be taking responsibility for her actions. No, *it went overboard*, like a fairy magically grabbed it out of her hands. She's such a *child*. Argh!"

"Do you want me to see if I can get you a phone?" I ask.

Didi takes a few calming breaths and leans her forehead against a varnished pillar in the lobby. "No. No. I'll survive. It's just the principle of the thing. Look, I'm sorry for ranting. That wasn't very professional. I shouldn't complain. She's really not *that* bad, and she's helping me with my own writing. Come on, let's get us checked in."

"There's a line at the check-in, so I'll just grab your keys for now. You can do the rest later, whenever you want. It will only take a minute. There's coffee and doughnuts and stuff in there if you want," I say, pointing into a small room off the lobby. "Help yourself."

"Yeah, maybe," she says. "I could use the caffeine."

When I return with the key cards, Didi has a large paper cup of coffee in her hand and is admiring one of the many sailboat paintings that adorn the walls of the Islander. Standing next to her is a woman sporting a name tag identifying her as Jean Morse from Lightwood Books.

"Hello! Welcome to Swallowtales," she says, turning to Didi. "I'm Jean Morse. I see you're already being taken care of by one of our terrific pages. It's great that they get so many kids from the island involved, don't you think?"

"It is. Really nice," Didi says. "Hi. I'm Didi. Didi *Ferrer*. It's *so* nice to meet you, Ms. Morse." She pauses, as if waiting for the name to ring a bell, and then adds, "Ann Keyheart's P.A."

Ms. Morse nods at the mention of Keyheart's name, silently mouthing an *ahhh*. "Wonderful. I was so happy to hear that Ann would be joining us this year. She caught me by surprise."

"Me too," Didi says.

Neil Derry, the hotel manager, appears at Morse's side. "I apologize for the interruption, Jean. We have a slight . . . logistical situation, if you will. I'm hoping you can help us sort it out."

"Certainly. Didi, it was a pleasure meeting you. I do hope to see you again. And tell Ann I'm looking forward to talking tonight," Morse says, turning and following Derry to the counter.

As Morse walks away, something about the way Didi tilts her head and twists her lips tells me she's confused.

"Everything okay?" I ask.

Didi's eyes follow Morse until she ducks into the room behind the check-in desk. "Yeah, I guess. That's Keyheart's new editor. Or she *will be* if she ever actually writes another book. I-I was under the impression that . . . I mean, Keyheart supposedly talked to her about my . . . maybe she didn't. Why would she . . . I'm so confused."

"I'm sure she has a million things on her mind," I say. "She's probably met a hundred people today. Maybe she just didn't make the connection."

"Yeah. Maybe," Didi says, but it's clear she doesn't believe it.

The Captain's Cottage definitely lives up to the hype. Lots of houses on the island have great views, but this is the first one I've been in that actually feels like you're *on* the water. It was designed by a naval architect, and the waterfront side resembles the front end of a ship, with the bow pointing out over the

lake. Pretty cool. Inside, it looks like the cabin of a yacht, with teak-and-holly floors, and lots of brass and built-in furniture. And overseeing it all are the dark, piercing eyes of its namesake, Captain Cheever, whose portrait hangs over the fireplace mantel.

"Yes, this will do nicely," Keyheart says, standing behind a wall of glass in the living room. "What is that Mark Twain quote? I have simple tastes. I'm always satisfied with the very best."

"That wasn't Mark Twain. It was Oscar Wilde," says Didi, dragging Keyheart's bags up the stairs to the master bedroom.

"What's that?" Keyheart says, scrolling through messages on her phone.

Didi stops momentarily and shakes her head. "Never mind."

"I'm supposed to tell you that there's a case of the sparkling water you asked for in the kitchen," I say. "I can show you how to use the coffee maker if you want. It's one of those with the little pods."

Keyheart waves off that suggestion. "I won't be making my own coffee. That's what Didi is for. Or room service."

I point to a rustic woven basket on the kitchen counter. "That's a welcome gift for you, of, uh, things from the islands. There's a bottle of wine and some taffy from Put-in-Bay, and a bunch of other stuff. Some lady here on Swallowtail wove all the baskets."

Keyheart doesn't even bother to look inside, dismissing it with a *whatever* wave of the hand. "That reminds me," she says. "There *was* one more thing I asked for. Something important." She opens the kitchen cabinets, slowly at first but then more frantically until she reaches into the last one and her hand emerges clutching a bottle of scotch. I recognize the bottle because it's the same one Thomas keeps around in case we have someone over who drinks it. "Figures. They didn't spring for the *really* good stuff, but I suppose I can make do."

"Anything else I can do for you before I go?" I ask as she twists off the cap and pours two inches of the brown stuff into a water glass.

"Didi!" she shouts. "This calls for a celebration. Where's that box of chocolates I packed? Our little broken-winged friend here *needs* one. You *do* like chocolate, don't you?"

"Yeah, I guess. I mean, unless it's got weird stuff in it," I answer, remembering the time that someone gave me a chocolate covered prune. Not cool.

"Well, these just might be the best chocolates in the world. And believe it or not, they're made right here on the island. Keke's Cocoas. I discovered them when I was here for my last Swallowtales. I'd almost forgotten how good they are, but when I signed on for this year's gig, I decided I couldn't wait till we got here, so I went ahead and ordered a few boxes. Didi and I have been gorging on them for weeks."

I point to the basket that she'd snubbed a minute ago. "There's a box of them in there, you know. I heard they're pretty good." I have looked in the window at Keke's, but have never been inside, because the chocolates are displayed under glass, like jewelry. It's not exactly the stuff people hand out at Halloween, if you know what I mean.

"They're not *pretty good*," Keyheart says. "They're to *die* for. They are the food of the gods." From the gift basket she lifts out the complimentary box of nine chocolate truffles, double-wrapped with green paper and cellophane. She reads the label and frowns. "These are milk chocolate. They're good, but trust me, not as good as the dark. Honestly, I think Didi's addicted to the dark ones."

Didi then reappears with what looks to me to be an identical box and hands it to Keyheart, who passes it on to me.

She checks the label and nods. "Yep. Seventy-five percent cacao. That's the stuff. Crack it open," she says.

I don't have much in the way of fingernails because I bite them, so I have a hard time finding a seam in the cellophane. Didi comes to my rescue by finding a paring knife in a drawer and giving it to me. I slice open the clear cellophane layer, remove it, and then turn the box over in my hands, looking for the edge of the wrapping paper so I can take it off in one piece—the way my mom taught me to open a present so the paper can be used again. ("Reuse, reduce, recycle" was like *religion* for Mom.)

"Good *grief*. Is this how you open presents on Christmas?" Keyheart asks. "It must be an all-day affair."

"I-I thought you might want to keep the paper," I say. "It's really nice."

"Oh, for crying . . . I don't give two *hoots* about the paper. Open it!"

I slide a finger under a loose corner of paper and tear the whole thing off in one motion. There's another layer of paper *under* the lid, covering the dark, almost black chocolates, so I set that aside and hold out the open box to Keyheart.

"My mouth is watering," she says, lifting out a piece with a perfect coffee bean stuck on top and handing it to Didi. "You first. Because I lost your phone. It's your favorite, right? The espresso ganache?"

Didi sets the chocolate on her tongue and closes her eyes.

"See! She's almost smiling. That's as close as you'll ever see. She can't help herself. They're *too* good. Your turn," Keyheart says to me. "And don't worry about nuts, in case you're allergic. The green boxes are guaranteed to be nut free. Didi and I are both *terribly* allergic."

"How do I know what's inside?" I ask. Fool me once, and all that.

"Oh, for Pete's sake! Ever hear of Forrest Gump? You never know what you're gonna get! Live dangerously!" She hands me a simple-looking one from the middle. I give it a good sniff that reveals nothing and bite off a corner.

Keyheart watches me closely. "Well?"

"It tastes like soap," I say, wondering if I can somehow make the rest of it disappear in my hand.

"Oh, you're lucky. You got one of the rose creams. It takes *fifty* rose petals to make each one. They're fantastic." Keyheart then makes a show of closing her eyes as she makes her choice. "I love to be surprised. Ooooh! It's spicy! Jalapeño and . . . cinnamon!"

Suddenly the bar of rose-flavored soap in my mouth doesn't seem so bad.

Keyheart replaces the lid on the opened box and sets it on the counter. "I'll leave the rest here. All yours, Didi. Well, maybe just leave *one* dark one for me, for later." She then tucks the other box back into the gift basket. "I guess *these* are all for me," she says, smiling. "Didi hates milk chocolate."

"I'm not going to eat a whole box," Didi says. "And for the record, I don't *hate* milk chocolate. I just *prefer* dark."

"Well, thanks for the, uh, chocolate," I say, wondering how long it's going to take to get the soapy taste out of my mouth. I set an index card with my phone number on the counter. "Here's my number in case you need me. Or you can call the main desk. They'll find me. There are copies of the schedule for the week in the living room."

"What time is the kickoff ratfest?" Keyheart asks, scrolling through messages on her phone.

"The VIP dinner," Didi translates, sensing my confusion.

The tradition at Swallowtales is for the writers, agents, publishers, and editors to have an elegant kickoff dinner together before joining the big party with all the workshop participants at around nine o'clock.

"Oh. Yeah." I reach into my back pocket and unfold my own copy of the schedule. "Cocktail hour starts at six thirty. Dinner at seven thirty. Are you both—"

"No, just me," Keyheart says. "Didi has her own plans. She's been invited to go *yaaachting* by some old friends of mine. So exciting! You're going to love it. I think I'll go rest my eyes for a minute." She toddles off toward her bedroom, glass of scotch in hand.

"I've been sailing before," Didi tells me, "and believe me, I'm *not* going to love it. It's so *boring*. Can you help me find the boat, at least? I *had* a text message with the name of the boat and the dock number, but . . . anyway, their name is Cheever. Roger. Or Reggie. Something with an *R*. I'm supposed to be there at four."

Of *course* it's Reggie Cheever. It just had to be the one guy on the island that truly despises me, and with good reason. Remember that three hundred acres I mentioned, the land that might now belong to Pip and me? Well, if I hadn't come along and ruined everything by finding that old will, all that land would belong to the Cheever family, the descendants of Captain Edward Cheever.

"The Cheevers," I say.

I must have made a face when I said the name, because Didi asks, "Do you know them?"

"You could say that. I know the dad, Reggie, and his son, Owen. Owen's . . . okay, I guess. I'll meet you back here around three thirty."

"Do mind coming by a little earlier, like maybe . . . two thirty?" Didi says. "There's something I'd like to . . . some-place I *need* to go. Will you still have one of those golf carts? Is that okay? I mean, you driving me around?"

"Totally cool," I say. "I'll see you then."

CHAPTER

2

AFTER LEAVING KEYHEART AND DIDI to enjoy the comforts of the Captain's Cottage, I check in with Nadine, who, as Swallowtales chairperson, is organizing and overseeing all the evening events—the dinners, the readings, the welcome, the last-night gala, that kind of stuff.

"Perfect timing," she says when she sees me approaching. "We finally got everything sorted out for tonight. The seating arrangements were rather complicated. You'd think that adults would be able to *act* like adults. It's more like middle school. *This* one doesn't want to be at the same table as *that* one. And *that* one refuses to sit next to this *other* one."

"You *did* say that writers are all a little crazy."

"That's true, I did. Between you and me, though, this group is especially *petty*. So, tell me about your day so far. How is your favorite author anyway? Is she settled in? And what do you think of the Captain's Cottage? Beautiful, isn't it?"

"Yeah, it's great," I say.

"And the celebrated Ms. Keyheart?"

"She's . . . *different*. Not what I expected."

"You know what they say about meeting your heroes," Nadine says.

"I keep telling myself that she wrote *The Somewhere Girls*, my favorite book in the whole world."

"That's a good way to think about it. Keep the art separate from the artist." As another girl in the page uniform comes into the lobby from the patio and walks toward us, Nadine says, "Have you met Gabby? Gabby Bensikova, Lark Heron-Finch."

"Hi," I say with a little wave.

Gabby, a head shorter than me and attractive in an uptight overachiever kind of way, looks me up and down. "Oh. So *you're* Lark. I've heard about you."

"Oh. Uh, okay," I say.

"It's a small island," Nadine reminds me. "Gabby lives in New York, but her family has had a summer place here for forever. All the way at the east end of the island, past the beach."

"The *nice* part," Gabby adds.

"I think *all* of the island is the nice part," says Nadine. "I'd forgotten that you were in Europe the week of the museum gala—you would have met Lark there."

"Oh, yeah," Gabby says. "I'm sure my dad would have signed

me up to work whether I wanted to or not. I heard it was a good party, though."

"This week," says Nadine, "Gabby is Howard Allam's page. Have you read his book *Final Edits*?"

"He's a *genius*," Gabby proclaims.

I shake my head with a little shrug. "Sorry, I haven't . . . "

"Lark is working with Ann Keyheart," says Nadine.

"Oh, right. *Young adult*," Gabby says with a smirk. "What was it, *The Somehow Girls*?"

"Some*where*. *The Somewhere Girls*," I say.

"Whatever. It was so . . . *predictable*, wasn't it? Like, I didn't see that twist coming from a mile away."

I try to speak, but no words come out, so I end up standing there with my mouth open and glaring at the snooty girl who has just insulted my favorite book. Inside my head, I hear Mom's voice: *"Let it go, Lark. Choose your battles."*

"Well, that's why we have events like *Swallowtales*," Nadine says, coming to my rescue. "Different strokes for different folks. There's something for everyone."

"Mom says the festival is becoming *too* democratic," says Gabby. "She says it used to be for *serious* writers."

"Gabby's mom is on the board, too," explains Nadine. "She's in the publishing business.

"Oh! There's my mom now," Gabby says. "I've got to run. It was nice meeting you . . . "

"*Lark*," I say.

"Right. *Lark*. That's . . . interesting. See you tonight at the thingy, I'm sure." She pirouettes elegantly and runs after her mother, who waved at Nadine before heading into the Oliver Hazard Perry, a large conference room that is the site of Swallowtales headquarters. It is also acting as a kind of teachers' lounge for the authors, agents, and editors, who are the reason so many writers are thrilled to snag one of the two hundred available spots in the conference. Well, that and the fact that Swallowtail Island is a great place to spend some time in August.

As the door shuts behind Gabby, I shake my head. "Geez. Pretentious much?"

Nadine laughs. "Don't let her get under your skin. She's grown up in a family that is, let's say, very artistic. Her father owns a big gallery in SoHo, and her mother's a senior editor at Lochmoor Books, like a real bigshot. She discovered Victoria Zabatsky, who just won the Weller Prize. Impressive stuff. And Gabby has danced with ABT and the New York City Ballet. A *serious* bunhead. She's incredibly talented. Of course, she knows that. You get used to her. So, what's next for you?"

"Didi, um, Keyheart's assistant, got invited to go sailing, so I'm gonna take her over to the marina at four. Guess who invited her? Reggie Cheever."

"Eek. Poor kid. How does she know him?"

"She doesn't. Keyheart does. Sounds like she knows

everybody. You wouldn't happen to know where he keeps his boat, would you? His *sailboat*, not the one I sank," I say with a grin.

"It's at the yacht club, not the town marina. Don't worry, you can't miss it. It's the biggest boat there."

"What a surprise," I say.

Didi is drinking a Coke on the patio of the hotel when I return from my little break at about two fifteen. She lowers her sunglasses and waves at me from a wicker couch that's placed to provide a perfect view of the lighthouse with the lake in the background.

"So, A.K. didn't scare you off. I wasn't sure I'd ever see you again. There's still time. Run!" she shouts, laughing. "Save yourself!"

"I'm good," I say. "Really. I mean, yeah, she's . . . different from what I expected. I don't really know what I . . . I love her books, so I figured she . . . "

"So, did you find out where this boat is? Please tell me it sank. There was a terrible fire. Or they left without me."

"Oh. Uh, no. I mean, yes, I know where it is, if you still want to go."

"I don't *want* to go. But *she* wants me to go, so I go. They're *her* friends, and I need her on my side right now."

"Why isn't she going?"

"Officially, or unofficially? Officially, because she's too busy. She'd *love* to, dahhling, but there's just no time in the schedule. Unofficially, she hates boats and she's not that crazy about her so-called 'friends.' So she sends me. It's not that bad. Part of the job."

"How did you get to be her assistant?" I ask.

Didi shrugs. "Good question. I'm not really sure. I've only been out of college for a couple of years. I'm going to be a writer, so I figured that working in publishing would be a good way to learn about the business, what kind of books they're looking for, that kind of thing. Anyway, it was kind of random. I'm in the middle of interviewing for this editorial assistant position at Keyheart's publisher when *she* just barges into the office and starts telling the guy interviewing me how much she needs an assistant. I didn't even know who she was. She sees me and starts asking me all these questions. Can I do social media stuff? Do I know how to book flights and hotel rooms? Do I live near her, so I can basically be on call 24/7? Somehow the food allergy thing comes up and turns out that we're both super allergic to nuts, but nothing else. Next thing I know, I'm learning how to make a soy milk latte, cleaning her cat's litter box, and posting pictures of boxes of Keke's Cocoas on her Instagram account. That degree from Columbia is really coming in handy."

"It must be cool, though. I mean, you get to read what she's writing *way* before anybody else."

"You'd think so, wouldn't you?" she says. "The fact is—between you and me—I've been with her a year and she hasn't written a single word."

"Really? I thought writers wrote every day. Isn't that what they're always saying?"

"I know, right? I thought I'd be helping her with research and reading her early drafts and making suggestions . . . Ha! What a joke. As far as she's concerned, I'm a gopher. I make coffee and pick up her dry cleaning and answer her emails and make restaurant reservations for her—not that I ever get invited to go along. This week is the first time. The good news is that I have lots of time to write. And unlike her, I follow Epictetus's advice: 'If you wish to be a writer, write.' So I *do*, every day."

"Geez, you sound just like my stepfather. He quotes that Epictetus guy all the time."

"Oh, yeah? Well, he is the go-to guy for us Stoics." She stands, slips her backpack on, and takes a deep breath. "Okay. You're still cool if we take a little detour?"

I nod. "Nowhere I have to be for a long time. The cart is in the parking lot."

"Awesome. Now all I have to do is remember where we're going."

When they get to the cart, Didi takes out a map of the island and, with her finger, traces the road from the hotel up to Lake Road, and then east almost to the very end. "Somewhere around *here*," she says, pointing to the last fork in the road.

"That's where you want to go?" I ask. "There's, like, nothing out there."

Didi taps her finger on the spot on the map and nods, so I step on the accelerator. Like Thomas is always saying, *"Mine is not to reason why,"* and all that. We rumble down the gravel road for a few minutes in silence until Didi finally breaks the spell.

"So, have you lived here all your life, or what? What's it like in the winter? Pretty dead, I'll bet."

"We just moved here, this summer," I answer "From Connecticut. We had a house here, though, for a long time. My mom's family. This is gonna be my first winter here, though."

"Oh, yeah? Where in Connecticut?"

"Essex. You know it?"

Didi nods. "Sure. One of my roommates at Carton was from there."

"You went to Carton Academy? I'm thinking about going there. Or, I was before we moved. Now I'm not so sure. I guess I'll wait and see what going to school here is like."

"If you have the chance, you should *definitely* go to Carton," Didi says. "Are you, like, a basketball player or something?"

At twelve years old and five-feet-eight-and-a-half inches (and still growing), I get that a lot. "Soccer."

"Well, then you *have* to go. The soccer team wins *all* the time. The girls' team is one of the best in the *country*. One of my best friends played. She went to UNC, and now she's playing for a team in England. Crazy. If you want to talk to her about what it was like, I could totally help you out."

"Y-Yeah, definitely," I say. "Omigosh. I would love that."

"I'll call her this weekend. I owe her a call anyway."

A moment later, as we're passing a spot where we have a view of the lake, she points out at the deep blue water with Feather Island in the background. "I guess this isn't bad, though. It's prettier than I remember."

"Oh. I didn't . . . You've been here before?"

"Not for a long time. My grandmother had a summer house here." For the second time, I see Didi's eyes grow watery, but this time she doesn't try to hide it. "She . . . died a few years ago, and they sold it. I want to see the house, but I'm not ready . . . *yet*. Maybe tomorrow. I'd *really* love to go inside, but I doubt that's gonna be possible. I probably won't have time anyway. I'm at the mercy of A.K.," she says, sniffling and wiping away the one tear that had escaped. "There's a lot going on. She might need me."

A mile farther along, I slow down as we approach the fork that Didi had pointed to. "I think this is it."

Didi looks ahead down the road—now just a grass path, actually—and smiles broadly. "Yes! This is it. I remember. Keep going!"

It's a short trip, as the path ends at the shore, a couple hundred yards away. Didi hops out of the cart and points out at Big Egg Island, which, in spite of its name, is quite small. "That's where we're going. Big Egg."

I look up and down the footpath that runs along the shore for a boat, but there's nothing in sight. "Ummm . . . how are we getting there?"

"Follow me." Didi takes off down the path ahead of me, stopping at a large flat rock right at the water's edge. She sits on the rock and starts to take off her shoes.

"We're *walking*?" I say.

"Yep. Carry your shoes. You'll need them."

"You've done this before? It seems kinda far." Despite my doubts, I kick off my sneakers. She wades out into the lake, feeling the bottom with her feet. "I did it the last summer I was here, when I was twelve. There's a sandbar—it's kind of narrow, though. I seem to remember my shorts getting a little wet. But then, I was a lot shorter than you."

I follow her into the warm, smooth water, my toes digging into the sand, and together we wade across the narrow channel, holding our shoes over our heads. Only once, when I got distracted by a noise on the island and took a step off the sandbar, did the water reach the bottom of my shorts.

"How did you find out about this?" I ask when we are standing on the rocky shore of the island.

"It was a summer camp thing. You could pick some of your activities. Most kids picked sailing or kayaking, but a couple of us went with this lady on these birdwatching hikes. The one here was the best. It was kind of a secret, I think. I don't know if it's still here, but there used to be an eagle's nest up in one of the tall trees on the far side. We got to see a baby bald eagle. The lady made us swear not to tell anyone. She was afraid too many people would come out here and bother it. But there's something else that's pretty cool, too. Follow me."

She climbs up and over a fallen tree and leads the way to the center of the island. There is a small clearing where there are no trees, only rocks, including one that juts up about ten feet, with a flat top. Didi circles it, examining it from all angles. "I know there's a way up because we did it. Yes! There. See this curvy ridge? It's wide enough for your feet. You just have to hug the rock on the way up."

Once again, she leads and I follow in her footsteps, fingers rubbing along the limestone all the way. With only one good arm, it's a challenge, but nothing I can't handle. When I reach the top, I stop to admire the view of the lake to the south, with Perry's Monument standing tall and proud on Put-in-Bay. At my feet are rows of deep, curving grooves cut into the stone.

"Glaciers did this," says Didi. "The last ice age, about twelve thousand years ago."

"So cool," I say, feeling the grooves with my hands.

"Actually, it was freakin' *cold*," Didi says with an apologetic smile. She turns her attention to a spot near the south edge. "Look over here."

I join her, kneeling over a shallow indentation in the stone.

"Do you see it?" she asks, running a finger around its outline.

It's eight or ten inches across and about an inch deep. The

edges are worn smooth and part of it is difficult to make out because of moss or lichen, but I have no trouble recognizing the general shape.

"It's a swallow!" I say. "In flight."

"I'm impressed," Didi says. "You even know what *kind* of bird. That's more than I knew the first time I saw it."

"What's the story? I've never heard of it."

"I don't think anyone knows for sure. *Kate* said it could be a petroglyph, carved by Native—"

"Wait. *Kate?*" I say, my heart skipping a beat.

"Yeah, the lady I told you about. Her name was Kate . . . something. She taught at—"

"Kate *Heron?*"

Didi nods. "Yeah, that's her. What's going on?"

"She was my *mom*," I say. "I'm Lark *Heron*-Finch. She was an ornithologist."

"Whoa. That is weird. Omigosh. This is crazy, but I actually think I met you before. You're about twelve, right? It would have been . . . eleven years ago. You were just a baby. Your name, though . . . I thought it was something with an *M*. Madison. Or Melanie. Or—"

"*Meadowlark*," I say.

"That's it! It was you! We stopped by her house one day on the way out to Rabbit Ear Point. I remember this one room—"

"The bird room. It looks exactly the same. She was obsessed, in a good way."

"So . . . you still . . . live there?"

"Yeah. I, uh, kind of own it now. Me and my little sister inherited it from Mom. We're with my stepdad now. And his kids."

"*Inherited* . . . So she really did . . . When you said that earlier to Keyheart about your parents being . . . that was true."

"Uh-huh. Afraid so. My dad died a long time ago, when I was five. Mom . . . This spring."

"Omigosh, I'm so sorry. She was . . . *amazing*. So smart—no, more than that. She was *brilliant*, and funny and inspiring. I've never forgotten something she said when we were right *here*, on this rock. There were only four or five of us that day, and we were talking about whether it was some random accident of nature that just happens to look like a swallow, or if had been carved by Native Americans, or somebody else, and why . . . you know, why a swallow, why *here*, where no one can see it. Next thing you know, though, somehow we're talking about the meaning of life, and philosophy, and mortality. . . . It was the first time in my life I was part of an actual, *adult* conversation, and I was absolutely spellbound."

"Sounds like Mom. She never really treated us like kids."

Didi continued: "She was saying how people really haven't changed in thousands of years. That we have all wanted basically the same thing all along—to be remembered, to leave some kind of a mark on the world, a legacy. We want to believe that, in the end, somehow our short little lives *mattered*. We carve our names in stone and line them up in cemeteries and hope—*hope*—that the letters and numbers on our stone will mean something to *somebody* in the future. But the reality is, most of us are going to be forgotten pretty quickly."

"I can hear Mom now," I say. "She always said that just because something is carved in stone doesn't mean it's going to last forever. Sooner or later, those letters and numbers start to fade, just like this little bird."

"Exactly. After camp that day, I walked over to the cemetery on the island and looked around. Your mom was right; I couldn't even read the old stones—and they're not even that old. I knew right then and there that I was going to be a writer. That's how I was going to leave my mark. It's been a long, weird journey—and I've made a million mistakes along the way—including one really big one—but I'm finally there. And that's why, when Keyheart told me we were coming to Swallowtail for the book thing, I just knew I had to find this place again, and put my hands on this little indentation—and remember the person, the day—that got me started."

"That's so cool. I have, like, goose bumps."

"Weird, huh? My path in life determined by a dent in a rock that may or may not be a carving of a bird. And how crazy is it that it was *your* mom. I don't even want to think about what kind of Twilight Zone-y twist of fate brought you and me together. The mind boggles. Anyway, thank you."

"No, thank *you*," I say. "Seriously. I love hearing stories about my mom from before I was . . . And you know, I think maybe she did tell me about this place once, a few weeks before she died. Or she tried to, at least. She was talking about Swallowtail, and all the things she used to do and her secret places. She said something about a rock, and a swallow—it wasn't really clear, and she was having trouble staying awake and then . . . "

I turn my head away from Didi as tears stream down my face, but she wraps her arms around me, squeezing me tightly. We stand there for a few seconds without speaking until she finally releases me.

"You okay?" she asks.

I do my best to compose myself quickly, sniffing and wiping my eyes with the bottom of my shirt. "Y-Yeah. I'm good—it's just, you know, sometimes . . . "

"I *do* know," Didi says. "All too well."

"We should probably get going," I say.

Didi lifts my wrist for a moment to read my watch, and then drops it, frowning. "I suppose you're right. Not that I'd mind missing this boat."

We clamber down from the rock and retrace our steps back to the shore, where we remove our shoes once again and wade out into the lake. When we're about halfway between Egg and Swallowtail Islands, I say, "Back on top of that rock, you said that you were going to be a writer, and now you're finally there. Does that mean that you're writing a book?"

Didi turns around, smiling slyly. "Past tense. *Wrote*. Or present perfect. *Have written*." She glances all around us to make sure no one is listening. "Don't tell anyone, but I finished my first novel a few weeks ago."

"Wow! Congratulations! That's amazing," I say as we reach the other side and head down the path for the waiting golf cart. "That must be so . . . What's it about? Is it going to be published?"

"Thanks, but remember, shhhhhh." She puts her index finger to her mouth.

"I don't get it. Why is it—"

"I don't want to jinx things by talking about it. Hopefully, I'll get some good news this week. Remember Jean Morse, back in the hotel lobby? Keyheart's new editor? Well, after I finished the book, I asked Keyheart to read it. Of course, she made me print it out; she refused to read it on her computer. Anyway, she swore that she liked it, *and* she promised to send my book to her editor, Jean Morse. That's why I was confused when we ran into her. I was hoping that she'd recognize my name, at least. But then I started to think: maybe she never got my book. It got lost in the mail. Or, the more likely scenario, Keyheart never got around to sending it. I had offered to box it up and everything, but she was like, no, I'll take care of it. And when I asked if she'd heard anything from Morse, she got annoyed and called me an impatient millennial. First of all, I'm *not* a millennial. And second, like it's *bad* to want to get things done. So a couple of days ago, when I never heard back from her editor, I went ahead and sent the first three chapters to an agent without telling Keyheart. She would *kill* me if she knew."

"How come? I mean, isn't that what you're supposed to do? I work for a writer, too, and she's always on the phone with her agent."

"Well, I *swear* I didn't know this until *after* I sent it, but I found out that the guy I sent it to used to be *Keyheart's* agent. Something happened and she switched to a new agency before I started with her. I'm pretty sure she fired her last P.A. because of something to do with her old agent, so she will definitely fire me if she finds out I sent him my book. Anyway, he got back to me right away, and *seems* really interested, but I don't want to count my chickens, you know?"

"Wow. So, this might be a big week for you, too. You must

be so *psyched*. I can't wait to read it. Come on, give me a hint. What's it about?"

A small pendant—two interlocking *D*s—hangs from a silver chain around her neck, and she rubs it between her fingers. "For now, all I can tell you is that it's a *very* personal story. It's kind of *my* story, but a whole lot more. Going back to that whole 'leaving your mark' thing, I honestly don't know if anyone's ever gonna remember me because of this book, but it doesn't matter. I put my heart and soul into it. That day on Egg Island, your mom said there are two kinds of baby birds, ones who wait to be pushed out of the nest by their parents, and those who stand up at the edge of the nest, look around, and say, 'I'm ready,' and then make the leap. Well, I'm the second kind."

I laugh, remembering Mom telling me that same story.

Didi unhooks the clasp at the back of her neck and slips the pendant and chain into her pocket. "Can't afford to lose my lucky charm on the boat. It holds all the answers." She pauses, watching the gulls circling overhead, and adds, so quietly I barely hear the words, "Even if I don't always know the questions."

3

THE YACHT CLUB IS ON the far side of the harbor, tucked into a corner where the boats are protected from the wind and waves. I park the golf cart, and the security guard buzzes us in at 4:07.

"Maybe I'll get lucky and they'll be gone," Didi says, holding up her crossed fingers. "I really don't feel like doing this."

But the Cheevers are sitting in the cockpit of their boat. Nadine was right. *Winsome* is by far the biggest, flashiest, newest boat in the harbor, and sits in the perfect slip for a show-off like Reggie Cheever: all the other boat owners have to walk right past it to get to their own (smaller and older) boats.

I stop beneath the clubhouse awning, having no intention of getting any closer. "That's it," I say, pointing. "The big white one. Sorry."

"Oh. Bummer. They don't look like they're in a hurry. *Quel* nightmare." She looks at me and gets an idea. "Hey! Why don't you come, too? At least I'll have someone to talk to. *Trust* me, my boss can find the cocktail hour without your help."

I take two steps back, toward the gate. "Uh, no. I can't. I-I don't do so good on boats. Even if I wanted to—" I hold out my cast.

"You can stay in the back, where it's dry," Didi says. "Trust me, Keyheart will find the party, she can sniff out a bottle of scotch from a mile away. And besides, there's this guy, Irwin, he shows up at all her events. He's a superfan, which is a nice way of saying that he's *this* close to being considered a stalker. Flies his own plane, supposedly, so I'm sure he'll be here. Always trying to get Keyheart to go flying with him. Fat chance of *that* happening. He's harmless, though, and Keyheart takes total advantage of him. He'll make sure she gets to the dinner and always has a fresh drink in her hand."

Before I can respond, Owen Cheever, who had been standing on the foredeck with his back to us, turns and spots me. Worse, he raises his hand a few inches as if he's thinking about waving. I quickly turn away, insisting, "I *really* have to go."

"What's wrong? Who is that kid waving at you?"

"It's . . . complicated," I say, hating myself for using such a cheesy cliché. Meanwhile, my mind flashes back to earlier in the summer—Owen and me at soccer camp, and at the beach where I punched him after he called my stepbrother Blake a really bad word, and finally at the museum gala, where we became . . . friends. Or did we? It really *is* complicated. "Me and the Cheevers are . . . not a good mix. But I'm sure you'll have fun. Call me if you need a ride back to the hotel." I turn and run before she remembers that she doesn't have a phone, or the Cheevers decide to chase me off yacht club property with torches and pitchforks.

Once the yacht club gate slams behind me, I don't look back until I'm almost to the hotel. When I park the cart in the lot, I realize that my arm hurts like crazy under the cast. I was still a little out of it in the hospital, but I'm pretty sure the doctor told me to try to keep it as still as possible. Just a guess, but climbing rocks and going pretty much nonstop for hours at a time is *probably* not what she had in mind.

When I reach the hotel, I check in at the desk and breathe a sigh of relief when there are no messages waiting for me. With a little over two hours to myself *and* a hotel golf cart at my disposal, I take the long way home. Pip is in the backyard brushing Tinker, her piebald, half-Chincoteague pony, while Nate and Jack are kicking a soccer ball back and forth and arguing about who would win a fight between two superheroes that I've never heard of. I look around for Blake before remembering that he's off with some friends from the summer theater camp he took part in while the rest of us played soccer.

"Hey, guys. Who wants to go for a ride and help me with something?" I say.

Nate shouts, "Shotgun!" and jumps into the front seat. I could tell him that we're going to drive off the end of the pier and he would still be first aboard.

Jack is naturally more cautious. Of all of us, he's the one most concerned with following the rules. Unfortunately for him, as Thomas has pointed out, poor Jack has four older siblings to steer him away from the "straight and narrow path."

"What do we have to do?" he asks.

"What do you mean?" I say.

"The last time you wanted our help was when Nate had to jump off that porch. And you broke your arm."

"Don't worry, little man. It's nothing like that," I promise. "I need your help solving a little puzzle. It's like detective work, but nothing dangerous. No broken bones this time. And then, ice cream. Thomas gave me some money. C'mon, Pip. Put Tink in the barn. Her coat is perfect."

"Whoa! Look at that!" Jack cries, pointing up at a strange airplane, barely above the treetops.

"Cool! It's a Seabee!" says Nate, who has built enough model airplanes that I trust him to know what he's talking about. "Let's follow it!"

"It looks like a VW bus with wings," I say. "Kind of sounds like one, too."

"Where is he going?" Pip asks. "I hope he's not going to crash into the lake."

"Okay, let's go," I say. "Everybody in!"

Pip quickly leads Tinker into the barn, closes the door, and jumps into the back seat next to Jack.

"Hold on!" I say, and speed away. The plane has disappeared behind the trees, but at the end of the drive, I turn left onto the road to the museum and Rabbit Ear Point, and catch a quick glimpse of it.

"There it goes!" cries Jack. "Go faster!"

"The pedal's on the floor, buddy," I tell him.

As we bounce along the unpaved road as fast as the cart will go, Pip sweeps her arm from left to right in front of her and asks, "Is all this our land?"

"It's not ours yet," I say. "But, yeah, it might be someday. The line starts up at the cove by Dinah's house and goes all the way down to the little harbor. Everything on *that* side of the line."

"What are you gonna do with it?" Nate asks. "I would turn it into a go-cart track. And a baseball field. And one of those paintball battlefields."

"I think it should be a home for retired racehorses," Pip says. "And rescued dogs. Can you just *imagine*?"

"Don't get ahead of yourself," I warn. "Thomas and Nadine say that sometimes cases like this take *years*. And the Cheevers have a *lot* of money for lawyers."

"That's not fair," Nate says. "I hate that Owen kid. He thinks he's so *great* at soccer. That's why it was so cool when you punched him."

"It's not nice to hate," says Jack.

"That's right," Pip says. "I don't *hate* Owen Cheever. I just . . . despise him. I *loathe* him. I *abhor* him."

"Wow. Thesaurus much, Pip? Anyway, it's not Owen's fault who his dad is."

"I can't believe you're sticking up for him," Nate says. "He's the *enemy*."

Eager to change the subject, I angle my head to the side to listen for the plane as we reach the fork in the road a short distance south of Dinah's cottage. "Okay, where'd he go?"

Nate points to the right. "There it is! Turn!"

I turn the wheel hard to the right. From the road, the land

slopes gently down to the shore of the narrow channel between us and Cattail Island, which is the marshy home to thousands and thousands of birds (and *lots* of bugs) but no people.

The airplane circles over Cattail and then turns back toward us, maybe fifty feet over our heads.

"What is he *doing*?" Pip asks as the plane drops lower and lower. "He's going to crash!"

"He's not going to crash," Nate says. "It's a *seaplane*, you guys. He's gonna land in the lake."

"I can't bear to watch," says Pip, covering her eyes as the plane makes its final approach.

"Open your eyes. This is *cool*," says Nate.

"C'mon, Pip," I say, pulling her by the arm out of the cart. We race to the shore, arriving just as the plane skips once on

the water right in front of us and then skims across the lake surface, slowing to a stop near the bottom of Cattail Island. The pilot then turns the plane around and motors past us going the other direction, waving at us from the open door of his cockpit.

"Now where's he going?" Jack asks.

"I'll bet I know," I say. "There's a dock up by the old breakwater. Les keeps his boat there. Let's go see."

Sure enough, that's exactly where he's headed. He ties his plane up at the dock, throws the strap of a duffel bag over his shoulder, and follows the path to the road, where the driver of an Islander Hotel golf cart is waiting for him.

"When I grow up, I'm getting one of *those*," says Nate. "That's awesome."

"Are you serious?" I say. "No offense, but don't expect me to fly with you. You couldn't *pay* me to go up in that thing. All right. The show's over. Let's go look for a yellow house."

I drive us into town, stopping right in the middle of a street lined with old houses.

"Why did you stop here?" Nate asks. "What street is this?"

"Buckeye," I say. "There are, let's see, fourteen, fifteen, *sixteen* houses."

"Oookayyy," Pip says. "Now can we get ice cream?"

"Not yet. Here's your challenge. One of those sixteen houses used to be yellow. Whoever finds out which one can have my ice cream, too."

Nate looks me straight in the eyes. "You swear?"

"I swear," I say.

He takes off without another word, racing down the street to the last house.

"I don't get it," Pip says. "How are we supposed to . . . why do you need to know which house was yellow?"

"I don't care how you do it," I say. "I mean, don't *damage* anything. Maybe I should have mentioned that to Nate. Knock on the door and ask if you want. It's just something I need to know. It's the house where the girl I told you about used to live—the one who had the book with the bird inside, like mine. There's just one *little* problem."

"Now you tell us," Jack says.

"I don't know when it *stopped* being yellow," I say. "It might be a long time ago. All I know is, it was yellow in 1976. Nadine says most people get their house painted about every ten years, so there might be a *lot* of paint on top of the yellow. Hey, I didn't say it would be easy. Just go take a good look, like Nate's doing. See, he's smart, looking *under* the porch, where there might be some of the old color. I'm totally betting on him."

"What do we do if somebody asks what we're doing?" Pip asks.

"Tell 'em you're looking for your cat," I answer.

"What does she look like?" asks Jack.

"Who?"

"My cat," he says.

"Jack! Go!" I say.

It's a good thing that people on Swallowtail Island aren't overly suspicious because we definitely look like we're planning burglary on a massive scale as we dart in and out of hedges and crawl on hands and knees around foundations.

In the end, it's Pip who solves the mystery and she does it by following my advice: she knocks on the door of a house near the center of the street. An elderly woman with hair the same shade of blue as her sweater set answers the door and steps outside.

"Lark! Come here," she shouts.

I join them on the porch and smile at the old woman.

"This is Mrs. Pawlowski," says Pip, who introduces me, and then Nate and Jack as they straggle in from their mission.

"Your sister says you're looking for the yellow house," Mrs. Pawlowski says.

"Yes, ma'am. You're Mrs. Pawlowski? Are you related to the police officer?"

"My grandson," she says proudly. "Dennis. Do you know him?"

"Only a little," I say, which is technically true. Officer Pawlowski and I—well, let's just say we *got acquainted* earlier in the summer. If Reggie Cheever is the president, then Officer Pawlowski is probably the vice president of the Not-Fans-of-Lark Club. "Have you lived here for long?"

"Oh, my, yes. My late husband bought the house in 1968. We moved in on our tenth wedding anniversary."

"Wow, that's a long time ago. Do you remember, was there

ever a yellow house on the street? Like, in the seventies?"

"There certainly was. The Laslows." She points at a house down and across the street. "The one with that lovely spruce in the front yard. It used to be buttercup yellow."

"Thank you," I say. "That's really helpful."

"Oh, there's more," Mrs. Pawlowski says. "Yellow was a popular color for a while. There was the Handemans, on the corner, on this side of the street. Theirs was a pale yellow, very subtle. And the pretty house three doors down. The white and green, number twenty-two. For a time, it was a little brighter yellow."

"The people in the house we're looking for probably moved away around nineteen seventy-six," I say. "Maybe a little later."

"If it was nineteen seventy-six," Mrs. Pawlowski begins, "that rules out the Laslows. They bought in seventy-two. I remember because we were *very* surprised to see a McGovern sign in their yard. And the Handeman house has been in the family for *generations*. So I guess that leaves the Murray place, three doors down. Sorry, I still call it that even though Mrs. Murray died almost ten years ago and the house was sold." She steps off the porch to point down the street at a white house with sage-green trim. "She lived there for, oh, more than thirty years. She was a lovely woman. Exquisite taste."

I do the math in my head. "Do you remember anything about the people who lived there before her? Like, did they have a daughter? She would have been about ten in nineteen seventy-six."

"They did! A pretty little thing, with two long braids. Barrie. Unusual name. Unusual girl. She came over to say goodbye. Isn't that funny? Until this moment, I'd completely forgotten about her." Mrs. Pawlowski squeezes her eyes shut as she tries to summon more information from her memory. "Oh, what was their name? It was something with an F . . . Francis! Yes, that's it. I remember now. They moved to South America. Argentina, I think. The father worked for a German company. They left rather suddenly. If you want to be certain of the dates, you can always go to the registry of deeds and ask for Mrs. Linn. She'll help you. Tell her I sent you."

As *fascinating* as the registry of deeds sounds, it's going to have to wait till during the week, and besides, I have to get back to the hotel. Even though Didi has assured me that Keyheart wouldn't dream of missing the cocktail hour before dinner, it's my job to make sure she's there. At 6:20, I knock on the door of the Captain's Cottage and wait. There's no answer and I can't hear anything inside, so I knock again. Still no answer, so I call the main hotel number and have them connect me to the cottage number. Strangely, I can hear ringing in my phone when they make the connection, but when I press my ear to the door, I can't hear anything. I knock again, a little louder, and finally, at 6:28, Keyheart, with wet hair and dressed in a fluffy white hotel robe, opens the door.

"Lucy!" she says. "Come on in. I'll be ready in two shakes. Don't wanna miss out on the free cocktails. Grab yourself a water from the fridge and take the load off." She downs the last of her drink and hands me her empty glass. "Here you go. Put that in the sink, will you."

She disappears into the bathroom, where a hair dryer roars into action.

I take a good whiff of the empty glass on my way to the kitchen, burning my nostrils. Seriously, do people actually *like* that smell? After I rinse the glass and leave it in the sink, I notice that the bottle of scotch is on the stone countertop. The level of liquid inside, however, has dropped considerably, so I'm guessing that the answer to my question is *yes*.

Next to the sink is something new: a bottle of champagne in a clear crystal bucket, along with two champagne glasses and the green box of Keke's Cocoas, all on a round silver tray. The lid is not on the box, so I can see that it's the box of dark truffles that I had opened earlier in the day, and there are still just three pieces missing. There's a handwritten note on the tray, and curiosity gets the better of me. Because she's the famous author Ann Keyheart, I assume that the champagne is for her, but I'm wrong. And just when I start to think that maybe there's something to all that stuff about not meeting your heroes because you're bound to be disappointed, she gives me hope for the world;

the champagne is *from* her—a gift for Didi. After checking that the bathroom door is still closed, I read the note:

DD—

Thanks for being the best P.A. ever! Sorry about your phone (I'm such a klutz!) and for being such a pain in the you-know-what. This bottle is for our <u>special</u> celebration——we'll crack it open tonight after the shindig. <u>Please</u> help yourself to the chocolates——you earned them, and my hips certainly don't need them!

Hope you had fun sailing!

Cheers!
-AK

So, maybe she's not perfect, but clearly she's not the devil in a linen pantsuit that Didi led me to believe she was. I take a bottle of water from the refrigerator and slowly push open the door into Didi's room. Except for the laptop, closed and charging on the desk by a window, a book of poetry on the bedside table, and the carry-on-sized suitcase against the wall, the room looks exactly like it must have when she first set foot inside. There's not a wrinkle in the bedspread, a dirty sock on the floor, or a half-full water glass on the bedside table. I don't know why I'm being so nosy, but I can't stop myself from peeking inside the dresser drawers where her *perfectly* folded clothes are stacked. I mean, it's like a picture from a Pottery Barn catalog. The bathroom, too, is neat and organized; the towels are still folded neatly on a chrome rack and the basket of soaps and lotions is on the glass shelf above the sink. A contact lens case and a bottle of saline solution on that same shelf are the only signs that Didi has been there.

"Hellooo? Lucy?" Keyheart calls out from the living room. "Are you still here?"

I hurry to join her. She has changed into a new pantsuit, navy blue with white piping, and is wearing more makeup than she wore earlier in the day.

"You look nice," I say.

"Not too nautical?" she asks. "I figure, it's an island. And look at this place. It's where nautical motifs come to die. Like it was decorated by Captain Stubing. If I can't wear it here, where can I?"

I have no idea what she's talking about—motifs? Captain who?—but I nod and smile.

"Speaking of nautical, did Didi make the boat on time?" Keyheart asks. "She said you were going to walk her over."

"Yeah. We, uh, the boat was still there when we got there."

"Well, better her than me. I *hate* boats. It's like being in prison, but with a chance of drowning. I think Shakespeare said that. If Didi were here, she'd tell me I'm wrong, I'm sure. Sometimes she's too smart for her own good. And from what I hear, Reggie Cheever's record isn't so great this summer. He's already sunk one boat."

I check my watch and ask, "Are you ready to go?"

She points to the door. "Onward and upward." Then her heel catches in the rug and she almost does a face-plant. On her way down, though, she grabs hold of my broken arm and somehow pulls herself back up to vertical. "Oopsie-daisy."

It's all I can do to keep the scream of pain and accompanying tears inside as I guide her to the door with my good arm. "Don't forget your key card," I say, gritting my teeth. I'm back to thinking that Didi may be right about her boss's true identity.

In her heels, Keyheart walks at the speed of a slug on dry ground, so the pain in my arm is almost gone by the time we make it to the hotel patio where the VIP cocktail hour is in full swing. I have done my duty, so I point her toward the bar and look for a friendly face.

The only person my age who I recognize is Gabby Bensikova, the pretentious bunhead, and unfortunately, we make eye contact, so I have to nod. She glides across the patio as if she's on ice skates and joins me.

"Is this going to be a long night, or *what*?" she says.

I guess our friendship has progressed beyond *Hi, Lark*.

"Yeah. Seriously," I say.

"How's it going with Ann *E.* Keyheart?" She *way* over-emphasizes that capital *E*, pronouncing the whole name in a mocking tone.

"She's *great*," I say. "Super nice. And funny."

"Huh. That's not what *I've* heard," says Gabby. "I hear she's a *nightmare*."

"Really?" I say, pretending to be truly surprised.

"My mom tells me things," she says, leaning in close to me. Like a sponge that has soaked up too much water, she is waiting desperately for me to give her just the slightest squeeze.

I'm determined not to give her the satisfaction of spilling whatever publishing world gossip her mother shared with her, so I try changing the subject: "So you're, like, into dancing."

"I'm into *ballet*," she says, her nose high in the air. "Although I've never heard it put quite that way."

"Do you go to school for that, or what?"

Gabby looks at me sideways, as if she can't decide if my utter lack of knowledge of ballet is real, or if I'm pulling her leg.

"Uh, ye-ahhh, I go to school for that. And I practice three or four hours a *day*. At a *minimum*. While all my friends are sitting on their butts watching TikTok videos or posting selfies on Instagram or whatever, I'm in dance class."

"Sounds kinda like me and soccer," I say.

"Um, no offense, but I think it's a *little* different. Ballet is about *discipline*. It isn't just some *game* where you're running

around chasing a stupid ball. I'm going to dance profession-
ally. I *should* be in the last week of a summer program in *New
York* right now, but I tore a tendon in my foot and had to drop
out."

I ignore the part of my brain that is saying in a loud, clear
voice: *Don't engage. Walk away, Lark.*

"It's a lot more than chasing a stupid ball," I say, feeling
the blood rush to my face. "I'm gonna get a scholarship and
play . . . if you knew how many miles I run every day, or the
hours I spend in drills, or just practicing dribbling . . . trust
me, you couldn't handle it, not for one day."

"I suppose you think you could handle a day in my life?
That's a laugh. Ballet is *way* harder."

I scoff. "Yeah, right."

"There's really no point in arguing. I mean, you actually
think Ann Keyheart is a great writer. What chance do I have
in convincing you that ballet is harder than soccer?"

As I open my mouth to respond, Nadine waves to me from
across the room and makes her way toward us through the
crowd.

"Ah, good, you two found each other," she says. "Having
fun yet?"

"Time of my life," I say, smiling through clenched teeth.

"Have you seen your brother Blake?" Nadine asks. "We had
a last-minute addition to the presenters and I asked him to help
out. Lucky for me, today was the last day of theater camp."

I scan the room, spying him near the bar, talking to a man in a badly wrinkled plaid sport coat. "There he is."

He sees me and waves quickly before holding up a finger to say he'd join us in a minute.

"That's your *brother*?" Gabby says, staring wide-eyed and struggling to lift her jaw from the floor.

"Uh-huh. Well, technically my stepbrother."

"He's *gorgeous*, isn't he?" Nadine says to Gabby. "And he's only a year ahead of you in school."

I roll my eyes dramatically. It's not the first time that a girl has gone gaga for Blake's boy-band looks. "Who is that with him, in the plaid, with the bushy hair? Man, he looks *terrible*. He has *got* to be a writer."

"Jordie Holloway," answers Nadine with a laugh. "He's an agent, but you're right. He looks more like a writer. He's got that whole 'rumpled genius' look down. He's the last-minute addition. Just got here. Drove all the way from the city. Incidentally, he *was* Ann Keyheart's agent until a year or so ago."

"Ohhh, I know about this," Gabby says. "She totally *dumped* him for some young, flashy agency. And the word is, when she was just starting out, she was broke and all, but Jordie over there believed in her and let her live in his house for free for more than a year. *And* did all kinds of other stuff to help her out. So after she gets famous, *that's* how she repays him: she dumps him."

"I don't know about any of that," Nadine says. "And the

reporter in me says there're two sides to *every* story."

"Oh, there's definitely more to the story," Gabby says. "She ran him over with another bus last *week*. He had a deal for film rights for the author of some mystery series, but then somehow Keyheart sticks her nose in. Next thing ya know, the guy fires Jordie and signs on with Keyheart's new agent. But that's nothing compared to what she did to Howard Allam. Or Wendy Eppinger."

Nadine holds up her hands. "Whoa. Gabby, stop right there. This week is about the beauty of books, and writers, and how they make our lives *better*. For a few days, let's all forget that some of them might be flawed human beings and focus on the *good*. Deal?"

CHAPTER

4

WHILE THE SWALLOWTALES participants are in the main dining room enjoying an all-you-can-eat dinner of fish and chips featuring a local favorite, Lake Erie perch, Nadine ushers the VIPs into a private dining room for a four-course dinner with, Keyheart has been assured, an ample supply of excellent wine. After the dinner, both groups will meet in the spacious hotel lobby for more drinks, and the aspiring writers will have their first opportunity to meet and schmooze with the presenters.

Meanwhile, the pages and other Swallowtales helpers retreat to the patio for burgers and hot dogs. Blake and I fill our plates and then look for a quiet spot to sit and eat. We're on our way to an empty table well away from the others when Gabby's voice rings out: "Lark! Over here!"

"Great," I say under my breath. "Thanks. Sure."

Blake follows me, whispering to the back of my head: "Who *is* that?"

Gabby rearranges the chairs around the table, greets me like we're BFFs, and holds out her hand for Blake to shake. "Hi, I'm Gabby."

As Blake shifts his plate to his other hand so he can shake Gabby's, one of his hot dogs falls out of its bun and to the ground.

"Oh, no!" she cries. "Wait here, I'll get you another one."

I bend down to pick it up, but she runs off toward the food line before I can invoke the five-second rule. Trust me, Blake totally would have eaten that hot dog. I mean, the patio floor was *pretty* clean. A little wipe with a napkin and it's good to go.

Gabby's back in a matter of seconds, looking quite proud of herself as she sets a plate with a new hot dog in front of Blake. "There you go."

"Thanks," mumbles Blake.

"So. You've got Jordie Holloway, huh? The agent," Gabby says. "What's he like? My guy, Howard Allam, is super quiet. But he's brilliant, you can just tell. I'm just in awe every time he opens his mouth. I am *so* lucky. I mean, I don't know what I would do if they matched me up with a *YA* writer." She shoots me a look to make sure I understand exactly what she's saying.

Blake half shrugs. "Holloway's okay, I guess. Seems a little . . ."

"Depressed?" offers Gabby.

"No, not really. More like preoccupied. Like he's looking for somebody. I don't think he heard a word I said."

Gabby smirks for my benefit. "Gee, I wonder who."

"What am I missing?" Blake says.

"Nothing," I say. "Let's talk about something else."

"There are the Cheevers," Gabby says, pointing, as a couple disappears inside the hotel bar. "They own the hotel. Did you know that?"

"No, but I'm not surprised," I say. "Seems like they own everything else on the island."

"You know *Owen*, don't you?"

She knows perfectly well that I do. "Yes. I know Owen. Isn't there anything else . . . Blake, did you know that Gabby's a dancer? You know, like on *Dancing with the Stars*."

"*Ballet*," she says, shooting me a dirty look. "Not at all like that."

"Blake's going to be an actor," I interrupt.

"I-I never said—" Blake stammers. "I took one class."

"I'll bet you're really good," Gabby says, touching his arm. "I can tell from your eyes."

Pardon me while I find someplace to vomit.

Half a minute later, she has turned the conversation back to her, regaling him with a story about her first time in *The Nutcracker* and it's like I'm no longer there. While they ignore me, my mind wanders back to the Cheevers. Now that I know they own the place, I'm not surprised they're here (making sure everyone sees how rich they are), but I want to keep track of them so I can keep as much distance as possible between us. And if they're here, does that mean Didi is back, too? It seems odd that they would be back from sailing so soon, but a glance at the glasslike surface of the lake explains it: I don't know much about boats, but even I know that no wind means no sailing. If she is back, I hope she'll change her mind and come to the party for a while. The fact is, I have lots of questions for her about Carton Academy, and not the kind you find answers to in the brochure.

The dinners wrap up at about eight thirty, and everyone heads for the lobby bar. There's still no sign of Didi, and by the time I finally track down Keyheart, she is perched high on a barstool holding court for a cluster of fans—a fresh drink in one hand and a pen in the other as she signs copies of books that fans have brought with them, and agrees loudly with the guy standing next to her, who is outraged that Hollywood has yet to make a film based on *The Somewhere Girls*.

I wriggle my way through the crowd until I reach her side, catching her by surprise.

"Sweet home Alabama!" she cries, tilting her head back to look up at me through glassy eyes. "You're very, very tall. Ladies and gentlemen, I present my bodyguard, Lana."

"How was dinner?" I ask.

She leans toward me, spilling some of her drink on my

sneakers. "Oopsie-daisy. Sorry 'bout that. Between you and I? It was *terrible*. There was definitely something *off* about that beef."

"I'm *pretty* sure the menu said it was lamb," I say.

"Huh. That might explain why it tasted funny," she says, and then gulps down the rest of her drink and waves the empty glass at the bartender. "Robert, my good man. Another. And this time maybe not quite so stingy."

The bartender, whose name tag clearly identifies him as Richard, makes eye contact with me and I give him a helpless shrug. He takes a bottle from the top shelf and pours a full two inches of scotch into a fresh glass and hands it to Keyheart.

"That's more like it," she says.

A mid-thirtyish guy decked out in equal parts denim and denial (about his age and the state of his receding hairline) approaches, grinning idiotically. "There she is!" he announces. "Future Nobel Prize winner for literature, Ann E. Keyheart."

"Hello, Irwin," Keyheart says, holding her hand out for him to kiss while I look on, suppressing my urge to gag. "I was beginning to worry that your plane went down in the middle of Lake Erie."

Ah. *Irwin*. So this is the guy that Didi told me about, the superfan who flies himself to all Keyheart's events.

Irwin laughs as if he's just heard the world's funniest joke. Tears are literally running down his cheeks when he recovers enough to speak. "You kill me, Ann. How can it be legal to be so danged funny?"

"Um, yeah," I say. "She's a hoot. Ms. Keyheart, can I get you anything? Do you want me to find you a table and chair? It would be easier for signing books," I say. What I'm thinking is: *Sit before you can't stand anymore. Because if you drink that pint of scotch that Richard just handed you, that's where you're headed.* "Where's Didi? Still shailing? *Sai-ling.*"

I explain that I've seen the Cheevers at the party, which means that Didi *should* be back on dry land.

"Call her!" says Keyheart. She points at a tasteful hunter-green phone on a table next to the wall. "Use the house phone. Tell her to get her butt over here. I'm going to buy her a drink. Go!"

I pick up the phone and ask to be connected to the Captain's Cottage, and then listen as it rings over and over. After about fifteen rings, I hang up and return to the bar.

"No answer," I say. "Maybe she's here already. Or maybe she went out . . . someplace else, you know, to get something to eat."

"Bah! She never goes out. She's completely antisocial. All she does is sit at that laptop all day."

"Oh! Right. She told me that she's writing, er, *wrote* a book. She's probably talking to somebody here about it. I mean, that's why people come to this thing, right?"

When I mention Didi's book, Keyheart sits up straight, her eyes narrowing. As I try to back away a few inches, she grabs my arm and pulls me even closer. "What did she say?

Tell me, *exactly*," she demands, her face uncomfortably close to mine.

I'm afraid to breathe because I might get drunk from the fumes. "Nothing, really. Just that she, um, finished it a couple weeks ago and you're helping her out, looking for a publisher. She wouldn't say what it's about."

"Hmmphh," says Keyheart. "I hope she's not holding her breath. I didn't promise her anything. I said I'd do my best, considering that it's amateurish, millennial gobbledygook. A lot about the narrator's *feelings*. But what do I know? All *I* did was sell two million books."

"Two point one seven five million, to be exact," Irwin says. "I checked Bookscan the other day."

Keyheart pokes my arm with her index finger. "There. See? That's why I like you, Irwin."

Irwin looks as if he might float away on a cloud.

Across the room, Nadine, standing in front of several Swallowtales VIPs, taps on a microphone until the room quiets down.

"Good evening, everyone! I'm Nadine Pritchard, the chairperson of the thirteenth annual Swallowtales Bookfest. On behalf of the many, many people who have made it all possible—welcome! Our reputation as a premier literary festival grows every year, and helps us attract a truly wonderful group of writers, agents, editors, and publishers, a few of whom are standing here beside me."

As Nadine introduces them, I keep track of Keyheart's reactions. For the most part, they consist of snickering, snorting, and downright *snarling*.

"Bunch of has-beens," she says, turning back to face the bar before Nadine even finishes. "And never-was-ers. I guess the A-listers weren't available."

"Well, except for *you*, that is," says Irwin, clearly disappointed when he doesn't get the hoped-for reaction from Keyheart.

"There's one more name I'd like to mention," Nadine says. "We're lucky to have bestselling author Ann Keyheart with us again, after a break of a few years. Ann? Come on up."

Keyheart spins on her barstool at the sound of her name, her face breaking into a huge smile. Her hand, still holding on to that drink for dear life, goes to her heart, as if she's honestly moved by the callout. She hops down from her perch and totters across the floor in her high heels to Nadine, with the crowd, led by Irwin, of course, cheering her every (unsteady) step. Meanwhile, the VIPs standing behind Nadine step back out of the spotlight, sharing pained looks and eyerolls.

"Thank you *so* much, my dear," Keyheart says, hugging Nadine.

I'm mid-cringe in expectation of what's to come when Gabby slides into the space next to me.

"Well. *This* should be interesting," she says with a wag of her perfectly shaped eyebrows.

"Tell us what brings you back to Swallowtail," Nadine says, handing the microphone to Keyheart.

"Oh, my. So many things," says Keyheart. "I have *such* fond memories of this place, and the people . . . old friends. *Dear* friends." She blows a kiss in the direction of the suddenly baffled-looking group behind Nadine.

"Boy, she's laying it on thick," says Gabby.

"After all my success—the awards, the bestseller lists, the money—I guess the Swallowtales festival slipped my mind. But then when you called and made such a generous offer *and* gave me the absolute *best* cottage, well, I just couldn't say no, could I?"

Nadine's face registers the slightest degree of bewilderment as Keyheart speaks; it's obvious that the version of events that she remembers is *quite* different from Keyheart's.

Another problem: now that Keyheart has the microphone, she's like a shark with a mackerel in its jaws—she's not letting go. She rambles on for a few minutes about how inspired she is by the beauty of the island: the sailboats in the harbor, the rows of pristine Victorian houses on Main Street, even the smell of the horses. There are *oohs* from the crowd (and a look of genuine surprise from Jean Morse, her editor) when she drops a hint about a new book. Luckily for all the rest of us, a busboy drops a full tray of wineglasses and there is a tremendous crash that goes on for several seconds.

Nadine knows an opportunity when she sees one and

snatches the microphone from Keyheart's death grip.

"I think that's a sign that we should let everyone get back to enjoying themselves and making new friends," Nadine says. "Have a great night, and, as E. M. Forster might say, *connect* with your fellow writers. We'll see you all bright and early tomorrow morning for breakfast and the start of the seminars and lectures."

"Well, that was fun," Gabby says. "Time for a final check-in with my writer and then I am out of here. See ya tomorrow. Tell your brother I said bye."

"Uh, sure," I say.

When she's gone, I find Nadine, who is gathering empty glasses and straightening chairs.

"Hey, kiddo," she says, smiling broadly. "Well, *that* was interesting. I knew she had a . . . reputation for being a bit difficult, but nobody told me that she was *this* bad. I mean, *yikes*. I wasn't sure I'd ever get that mic out of her hands. I don't think anyone would blame you if you called in sick for the rest of the week."

"Ha. Tempting, but no, I'll be back for more tomorrow. She's kind of . . . she's like a boat that broke loose from its mooring out in the harbor. You know it's going to crash into *something*, you just don't know where or when, or how much damage it's gonna do."

"But you have to keep watching," Nadine says.

"Exactly! 'Cause I wanna be there when it happens. I have a feeling it's gonna be *awesome*. I've never met anybody like her.

You look at the faces around the room, and everybody—everybody except her fans, that is—*hates* her."

"Nadine nods in agreement. "It *is* impressive how universally disliked she seems to be. Do the best you can."

"I've got this," I say. "It's only a few days, and most of the time, she'll be in classes or meetings. Besides, I think she likes me. She tells people I'm her bodyguard."

"Uh-oh. On your toes. Here she comes," Nadine warns.

"There she is!" says Keyheart. "My very own pet giant. Nadine, do you know Lila?"

Nadine winks at me. "As a matter of fact, I've known *Lark* all her life. Well, it looks like most people are calling it a night. Tomorrow's a big day. Whenever you're ready, *Lark* will walk you to your cottage."

Keyheart looks around the room. "In the old days, this party woulda gone on all night. Writers *used* to know how to party. What a bunch of lightweights. Bah!" With a backhand flip of the hand, she's off, toddling toward an exit on the wrong side of the building.

I breathe a sigh of relief and mouth a thank-you to Nadine before catching up to Keyheart and spinning her around and aiming her at the right door. *Five more minutes,* I tell myself. I'm looking forward to crawling into my bed with my dog, Pogo, and getting a decent night's sleep.

The outside light is off when we arrive at her cottage, so I light up the lock with my phone. "You still have the keycard?"

"What? Oh. Key. It's in here, somewhere." She opens her handbag and shoves it toward me.

Luckily, when I shine the light inside the bag the card is sitting on top. I stick it in the slot, cheering internally when the lock clicks and the little green light comes on. There are no lights on in the living room when I push the door open, so I find the wall switch before letting Keyheart squeeze past me.

"Sheesh. Didi could have at least left one light on in here," she says.

"Do you want me to come by in the morning, to show you where breakfast is?" I ask. "It starts at seven."

She stops and turns to look up at me. "You're very tall. Have I mentioned that already? What did you say? Breakfast. No. No, no, no. Didi will make me coffee."

"Okay. Well, have a good night."

"Toodles," she says as I pull the door shut.

It's exactly 10:08 when I start up the path to the hotel, stopping for a few seconds to let Thomas know that I'm on my way home. Less than a minute later, I hear Keyheart's scream.

CHAPTER

5

WITH KEYHEART'S SCREAM, AND MY record-breaking sprint back to the cottage door, you're all caught up.

"Dead. She's dead," Keyheart said.

"What! Who's dead?" I say, looking past her into the room, where everything appears normal.

"Didi. She's . . . she's dead." Keyheart, not looking so great herself, faints and falls to the floor with a thud before I can catch her.

My heart thumps against my ribs and I have to remind myself to breathe so I don't end up on the floor like Keyheart, who is out cold. Her chest is rising and falling, so I put off dialing 911 for the moment, at least until I figure out what's going on with Didi.

The moment I see her, I know that Keyheart is right. There's no doubt about it: Didi is dead.

She's on the floor in front of a loveseat in the cottage's living room, the left side of her face against the hardwood, eyes staring out at a spot across the room. The pendant with the two interlocking *D*s is in her left hand, its thin silver chain broken, probably when she fell. Her right hand holds the telephone receiver, with the long cord stretched tight. The phone base has been pulled from its home on a polished wood table and is wedged beneath one of the chairs. And on the floor are some chocolates and an empty box from Keke's Cocoas.

The God's Honest Truth is that I gasp when I see those blank, unblinking eyes. And I have to say, I'll be just fine if I never have to see another dead body. One is enough. More than enough. And then the cold, hard reality of what I'm seeing hits me like a speeding locomotive. My mouth is suddenly uncomfortably dry, my stomach feels like I've been punched, and my chest tightens so much that it hurts to breathe. How is this *possible*? Six hours ago, Didi Ferrer was *alive*. More than just alive. She was *thriving*. A living, breathing, beautiful young woman, drinking coffee and complaining about her boss, and laughing, and crying. Standing on top of that rock on Big Egg Island, telling me the story of the day that changed her forever, she was so *full* of life and hope. Her dream of becoming a writer was coming true.

This isn't right. It doesn't make sense. It isn't *fair*.

The beep-beep-beep-beep-ing of the phone in Didi's hand finally snaps me out of my trance, and I kneel down next to

77

her. Keyheart is still completely out of it as I call 911 on my own phone.

"911. What's your emergency?"

"Yeah, I'm calling from the Islander Hotel, one of the cottages. There's a . . . a dead girl here." As you may have noticed, I'm a big believer in straight talk. No sugarcoating it or lame euphemisms for me.

"Okay, are you certain that she's deceased? Have you checked her—"

"She's dead. I'm sure." I put my phone on speaker and set it on the table while I slowly extend my hand and place the palm against Didi's cheek. It is cold to the touch, and a chill runs down my arm and all the way to my toes. I pull my hand it away, breathing rapidly through my mouth. "Can you just send someone, 'cause I'm here with my, with this lady and she fainted, and, well, just *please* hurry."

The operator gets my name and exact location and tells me to remain calm until the police and an ambulance arrive. Weirdly, that's not a problem. Yeah, the initial shock of seeing a dead body was like someone pressing the fast-forward button on my heart, but while I'm listening to the operator, I hold out my hand before me and it's rock steady.

I've seen enough episodes of *CSI* to know a few things. Number one, secure the scene, even if you don't know if a crime has been committed. But just because I'm not supposed to touch anything doesn't mean I can't take a good look around (and take some pictures) while I'm waiting for who-ever's coming. A glance at Keyheart confirms that one, she's still breathing, and two, she's not going anywhere. First stop is the kitchen, which looks exactly as it had at six thirty. The glass that I rinsed for her is right where I left it, next to the bottle of scotch, and beside that, on the silver tray, the crys-tal bucket with the unopened bottle of champagne and two champagne glasses. At the end of the counter is the wicker gift basket, with the bottle of Put-in-Bay wine and the other box from Keke's—the milk chocolates, still unopened. The only thing missing from the scene is Keyheart's note to Didi, but that seems easy enough to explain: Didi probably read it and then stuck it in her pocket, or threw it away, or put it in her room as a keepsake.

I stick my head in Didi's room, where at first glance, every-thing also seems to be as it had been a few hours earlier. The covers on the bed are untouched, her suitcase is on the floor against the wall, and Didi's laptop is still on the table, plugged into the charger. But the chair has been pulled out from the desk and the laptop is open. The wallpaper image on the screen is a photograph of an old woman waving from the ferry dock on Swallowtail Island.

"I wonder if that's her grandmother," I say aloud, and then turn to see if anyone has heard me. I snap a few pictures of Didi's room and do the same in the kitchen, and then retrace my steps back to the foyer, where Keyheart, still on the floor, is mumbling and shaking her head back and forth.

"Hey. Are you okay?" I ask. "You wanna sit up?"

"Nroayed. Throoomspinning." The combination of alcohol and the rush of adrenaline she must have gotten when she discovered Didi has clearly done a number on her.

"All right. You can stay there."

I get a pillow from a nearby chair and prop up her head. Then I turn my attention back to Didi, counting the chocolate truffles that fell to the floor alongside her. It had been a box of nine, but I'm able to find only three. When I opened the box earlier, each of us had taken one. That makes six, so either Keyheart or Didi ate the other three.

"Jacquesalot. Thazwha appen."

"What?"

"Jacquesalot!"

"Jacques's a lot of what?" I ask.

"Najacques! Jacquesalot."

Great. My first day on the job. One dead, one clearly having a stroke or something.

That thought is interrupted when I look up to find Officer Pawlowski of the Swallowtail Island Police, all six-foot-four and two hundred and twenty pounds of him, staring down at me. He must be off-duty, because he's not in uniform.

"She's not dead," he says.

I think it, but bite my lip to keep from saying *duhhh* aloud.

"Yeah, I know that," I say.

"Whoa!" Pawlowski says, wrinkling his nose. "She's *drunk*. Why did you say she was dead? I left a poker game for this. I was *winning*."

"Over there," I say, pointing past the loveseat. "She's on the floor."

"Jacqueshalot!" Keyheart says. She sits up for a moment, but her neck doesn't seem to be able to support her head and it drops back onto the pillow.

"Oh. Geez. She *is* dead," Pawlowski says when he gets his first look at Didi. "Who is she?"

"Her name's Didi Ferrer. She's *her* assistant," I say, motioning in Keyheart's direction. "That's Ann Keyheart. She's here for the book thing. Swallowtales. She's a writer."

"She find the body? That why she's . . . "

"Yeah. At 10:08."

"Howdya know *that*?"

I tell him the whole story from the time we left the party in the hotel lobby, and when I finish, two paramedics, a man and a woman with enough medical equipment to outfit a small hospital, bustle into the room.

"Hey, Cal. Annie," Pawlowski says. "There's no hurry. And you're not gonna need any of that stuff. The stiff's over there."

"She has a *name*," I say. "Didi. I just met her today, but she was nice. And funny. And talented. I can't believe she's . . . "

The female paramedic kneels down next to Didi and

confirms the obvious. "Couple of hours, I'd guess. Looks like she was trying to call for help. Definitely some swelling in the face and neck. Probably an allergic reaction. She may have tried to call but wasn't able to talk."

"Thejocksareots," says Keyheart without raising her head from the pillow.

"I *really* need you to get her out of here," Pawlowski tells me. "Can you take her back to the hotel and wait there? I'll come up and get a statement from you in a few minutes. She's going to have to find someplace else to stay tonight. The hotel should be able to help you with that."

Suddenly, Keyheart sits up straight. Her eyes are puffy and red and she's having trouble keeping them open and focused, but somehow she pulls herself together enough to say, "It. Was. The. Choc. O. Lates. The box. Is on. The floor. Next to her. There. Must. Be. Nuts. She's. Allergic."

Pawlowski turns to the paramedics. "Is that possible?"

The guy nods. "Sure. Some people are super allergic. Anaphylaxis, almost immediately."

"Don't people like that carry one of those injector thingies?" Pawlowski asks.

"EpiPens," says the woman. "I don't see any sign of one around the . . . around her. Could be in her bag. She may not have had time to get it. She's alone, she's scared. People don't always think straight. Or maybe she just doesn't have one. Not everybody who's allergic does."

Keyheart frantically digs in her purse, her hand finally emerging with a brightly colored plastic tube that I recognize immediately as an EpiPen. "Always. Have mine. You. Never know."

"Shame you weren't here," says the female paramedic. "Good chance you could have saved her life."

Keyheart wails loudly as her head drops back onto the pillow.

Meanwhile, Pawlowski picks up the box of chocolates and reads the logo printed in one corner: "Keke's Cocoas. Hey, they're here in town."

"Um, shouldn't you be, like, wearing gloves or something?" I say. "I mean, just in case there's—"

Pawlowski smirks and waves me off, but he sets the box on the coffee table. "You watch too much TV. This ain't a crime scene. An accident, that's all."

"Technically, that's up to the medical examiner to decide," the female paramedic says.

"It's just . . . I thought you said that there were no nuts in those," I say to Keyheart, who has risen to her feet and is starting to regain some color in her face.

"They *are* nut-free," she says. "They guarantee it. The green boxes. Oh, my—that could have been . . . *I* ate one from that box." Her hand covers her mouth with that realization, and she starts to sob and wail again, her whole body shaking so violently that a picture hanging on the wall shifts and ends up crooked.

I'm really not good in this type of situation, so I'm relieved when more people show up. First inside is the hotel's manager, Mr. Derry, followed by Nadine and, unexpectedly, Thomas and Blake.

"What's going on? Is someone hurt?" asks Derry.

Officer Pawlowski, with both arms extended to make a wall, moves toward the crowd that has just entered. "Folks, you can't come in here. Wait outside. I'll be out in a minute." He points at me. "You, too. And get . . . *her* out. I can get your statement tomorrow. I know where to find you."

I get Keyheart to her feet and we follow the others out the door where I explain what's going on.

When I finish, Thomas pulls me into his arms and squeezes.

"Just . . . *horrible*," Nadine says. "The poor girl. She must have been terrified."

"Let's get you home," Thomas says. "You've had a long day."

It's well after midnight by the time I crawl into my bed and snuggle up next to Pogo, our English setter, named for her habit of imitating a pogo stick whenever anyone mentions going outside. Moonlight streams into the room through the French doors as I lie there staring at the ceiling and listening to the slow rhythm of Pip's breathing.

In my mind, I replay the time I spent with Didi, trying yet again to understand a world that clearly does not *want* to be understood. What force of the universe conspired to cast our fortunes together for a few hours, just long enough to reveal the bond that we shared, and then tear us apart in such a bizarre— and permanent—manner? And, more important, *why*? There *has* to be a reason, and as the sky to the east begins to glow in a lovely predawn shade of orange, I realize that it is up to me to find it.

With that settled, my body finally decides that it has had enough for one day, and I fall into a deep sleep. I have a vague memory of Thomas coming into the room and chasing Pip downstairs for breakfast, telling her that I'd had a rough day and needed the rest. It isn't until my phone buzzes with a text from Nadine at eight fifteen that I open my eyes.

Hey Kiddo. Hope you're still sleeping. Let me know how you're doing when you wake up. They found Keyheart a room in the hotel and she's settled in. She's insisting that she's going to teach her classes today, but no worries— take the day off. I'll make sure she's taken care of.
xo,
N

I text: I'm fine. cu in 30.

After a shower and three thick slices of Thomas's *excellent* French toast, I am ready to face the world—and Keyheart—again.

Thomas hovers around the table while I eat, offering to make me something else if I'm still hungry.

"No thanks," I say. "I'm good."

"Listen, Lark, if you need to talk to somebody . . . somebody other than me—"

"Like a shrink? No. I'm fine. Really."

"It had to be . . . upsetting for you," he says. "The whole situation, especially after you spent the afternoon with her. Why don't you hang out here today, maybe give your therapist a call. When's the last time you two talked?"

After the Incident on the Soccer Field (known within the family as the ISF) a few months back in Connecticut, I had to talk to a therapist to work on my "anger issues" if I wanted to be let back on the school soccer team. Now that we'd decided to stay on Swallowtail Island permanently, I had stopped calling in for our weekly chats.

"I dunno. Couple weeks ago."

Thomas knows I'm lying, but doesn't press it. "Might be nice to talk to her."

"Yeah. Maybe later. I've got to get to the hotel. Keyheart's going to teach her classes today, so I need to be there."

Thomas tilts his head. "But . . . I thought you said that Nadine told you to take the day off."

"She said I *could*, but I *want* to go in." Then I use his own words against him: "You're always telling me that the best way to get over something hard is to keep busy. If I sit around here all day . . . "

Realizing that he's beaten, he smiles and hands me a granola bar. "Well played. You're so much like your mom. Just promise that you'll call if you need anything."

Back at the hotel, I ask around and learn that Keyheart has not been down for breakfast yet, so I knock on her door at nine fifteen. Forty-five minutes should be enough to get a cup or two of coffee in her and steer her in the direction of the conference room where a dozen eager-to-learn writers will be waiting for her words of wisdom starting at ten.

"Ms. Keyheart," I say to the door when there's no answer. "It's Lark. If you want to grab some coffee and something to eat before your class, I can show you—"

The door swings open. Keyheart is standing there in yet another linen pantsuit, this one coral with turquoise trim. Her hair and makeup aren't perfect, but they're better than I would have expected considering the condition she was in when I last saw her.

"Oh. It's you," she says. "I'd *kill* for a cup of coffee. Didi usually does that."

"Oh. I'm sorry. You must be . . . I still can't believe that she's . . . "

"Yeah, yeah. It's the same thing every time. One way or another, Didi always manages to leave me in the lurch. Last time we did one of these ratfests, she ate some bad clams and got food poisoning the first night. Spent the next twelve hours projectile vomiting instead of doing her *job*. And now she goes and dies on me. It's really, *terribly* inconvenient." I must have a look of pure horror on my face, because she rolls her eyes and sighs loudly. "Oh, great. I've offended you. Well, join the club, LeBron."

"There's coffee downstairs," I say. "You still have time before your class, even if you want breakfast."

She groans. "Don't remind me. The *class*. Uuuggghhh. Well, come on. Lead the way. If you're not gonna *bring* me coffee, the least you can do is show me where to find it."

In the hotel restaurant, the other guests whisper and point, no doubt talking about Didi's shocking death and Keyheart's decision to carry on as if nothing happened. Meanwhile, she complains nonstop about how long it takes the waitress to bring coffee and a cinnamon roll, then about the size of the cup ("Too small!"), the temperature ("Too hot!"), and the freshness of the roll ("This is older than you.")

Two refills later, the restaurant empties as Swallowtales participants scatter throughout the hotel conference rooms for the start of the first class. Keyheart is oblivious to it all, and I tell myself that it's because she's in a state of shock over Didi's death. I mean, she has to be a *little* upset, right?

When the clock in the lobby starts to chime the hour, I smile hopefully at her. "Guess it's time. I'll show you where your classroom is."

She gulps the last of her coffee and rises to her feet. "I suppose I can't put it off any longer. Tell me again, why did I agree to this? That sea of eager faces, so bloody *sincere*, and hanging on my every word. Like I can *teach* them to write. And the stuff they bring in for me to read. *Atrocious*." She shivers and her face looks as if she's just eaten a spoonful of cocoa powder.

"Isn't that what they're paying for, though?" I ask. "They want to learn from you. I mean, you wrote *The Somewhere Girls*. That means something to a lot of people. It means something to *me*."

"Pfffttt. That was a long time ago."

She follows me up the stairs and down the hall to her room. I peek inside, where twelve hopeful faces peer up at me, their notebooks open and pens at the ready. "This is it," I say. "Good luck. I'll see you in a couple hours."

She goes inside and closes the door. I stick around outside the door for a few minutes—long enough to be amazed by her transformation. Gone is the surly, sarcastic devil in a pantsuit that I'd had breakfast with, replaced by an almost unrecognizably charming and caring teacher. She's giving them exactly what they paid for.

I can't figure her out, and the GHT is that I'm not sure I want to.

As I'm passing through the lobby on my way to see what's going on at the Captain's Cottage, I spot Nadine at a table in the hotel restaurant with Officer Pawlowski and a woman I don't recognize, wearing a white lab coat. I move closer, staying out of their line of sight while I pretend to read a plaque on the wall about the role of Swallowtail Islanders during the Battle of Lake Erie in the War of 1812.

"That's the medical examiner," whispers Gabby, who catches me in the act of snooping thanks to her ability to cross a room without making a sound. "She's from the hospital in Port Clinton."

"Oh."

"Were you really there last night? You saw . . . her?"

I nod. "I went in right after Keyheart found her."

"I think I would have freaked out. I've never seen a dead person before. Was she, like—" Gabby strikes a zombielike pose with her mouth and eyes gaping.

"I-I don't think I should talk about her," I say.

"Oh. I'm sorry. That was . . . in case you haven't noticed, I have a habit of saying the wrong thing. It just . . . comes out. I didn't mean to upset you. It must be so weird. I mean, I saw you guys hanging out yesterday. She seemed kinda cool, and, like, so *not* a fit for Keyheart. What happened, anyway?"

"Nobody's sure, yet. It could be because she accidentally ate something with nuts. She was crazy allergic, I guess. But they didn't know for sure. I guess that's why *she's* here," I say, pointing at the medical examiner.

"Yeah, probably. Keyheart must be *really* upset. She's probably still in bed, huh?"

"Um, actually, she's teaching. She wanted to."

Gabby grabs my arm. "Wait. What? I need to process this. Her assistant *dies*, and twelve hours later, she's teaching a writing class? Have you seen her?"

"Yeah, a few minutes ago. At breakfast—"

"She had *breakfast*? Man, that is *cold*."

"Well, coffee. And a cinnamon roll." As the words leave my mouth, I hear how crazy it sounds. "I guess it is a little strange."

"A *little* strange? That's like saying Misty Copeland is a little bit talented."

I have no idea who Misty Copeland is, but I get her point. "Okay, so it's a *lot* strange."

"I'm starting to see why . . . come with me. Let's go for a walk. I want to tell you a story. You need to hear this. Let's get a soda first."

She leads the way to the temporary break room that the hotel has set up for all the volunteers, where she takes two cans of diet soda from the refrigerator.

"Diet?" I say. "Don't they have regular?"

"Oh. Sorry. I don't *do* sugar." She makes the switch and hands me the new can. "Let's sit outside."

We park ourselves on a bench by the lake, and Gabby takes a swig of her soda. She makes a face when that perfect nose of hers catches a good whiff of fish funk from the flat, calm lake. "Eww. What *died*?" When she sees my raised eyebrows, she cringes at her insensitive choice of words. "See? I can't help it. It's a real problem. My mom says that somebody's gonna punch me one of these days. I'm so sorry. Again."

"It's okay," I say. The GHT is that I can totally relate to somebody with impulse control issues.

Gabby looks over her shoulder to make sure no else is listening. "You have to hear this, 'cause Ann Keyheart is not some naive hick. She's done some things." She holds up her index finger. "Item number one: her old agent, Jordie Holloway. I already told you that story, what she did to him after he basically supported her for a year. Number two: Wendy Eppinger, Keyheart's *former* editor at Horace Books, who, incidentally, was also her college roommate."

"She's here, too, isn't she?" I say.

"Oh, yeah, she's here," Gabby says. "Right after college, Wendy started as an intern at Horace and worked her way up to publishing director of the YA division. She published all Keyheart's books, including *The Somewhere Girls*, and made sure that she got perks that no other author got. Eppinger's life was perfect. She loved her job, met this great guy and they get engaged. But then her fiancé starts sneaking around town behind her back with . . . guess who. *Keyheart*."

"Really?" I say. Obviously, I don't know anything about the fiancé, but based on what I've seen so far, I'm having a hard time understanding why anyone would *choose* to spend a lot of time with Ann Keyheart.

"I'm telling you, she's *rotten*. To the core. Anyway, eventually, Eppinger finds out about them and she goes ballistic, like you'd expect. There's this huge fight at Horace and some publishing genius decides that it's more important to side with Keyheart than with their loyal employee. So, Eppinger gets sent packing and Keyheart gets a new contract, even though at that point she was already a year late delivering a book. Luckily, Eppinger did find another job with another publisher, but according to my mom, she's making a lot less than she was. Plus, you know, all those people gossiping about her."

People like you, I'm thinking as Gabby takes another swig of soda.

"All right, all right," I say. "I get it. She's not gonna win the nicest person in the world award."

"Not gonna . . . have you been *listening* to me? She's *horrible*. You're defending her because you like one stupid book she wrote."

"I'm not defending her. Geez, I'm just her page for the week. What do you want me to do?"

"If it was me, I'd quit," Gabby says. "I couldn't work for someone like that. And now that you *know* . . . okay, one more story, then I'll stop. Howard Allam. You know who he is, right?"

"He's the guy . . . you're his page. Some writer."

"Not just some writer. A *brilliant* writer. The next F. Scott Fitzgerald."

"Sor-ry. What terrible thing did Keyheart do to *him*?"

"It was a few years ago, when Allam's first novel was just coming out. He'd gotten this big advance and everybody in the book biz was talking about it. So, a few days before his book hits the stores, it's the cover review in the *New York Times Book Review*. Do you *know* how big that is? *Especially* a debut."

"I'll take your word for it," I say.

"One problem. They hired Keyheart to write the review and she *savaged* it. She didn't even know the guy, but if you read it, you'd think he killed her dog or something. She went full John Wick on him. It was the meanest, nastiest, snarkiest review *ever* and it totally went viral. Once it came out, nobody cared about the book itself, or Howard Allam—the review was all anyone could talk about, and Keyheart becomes some kind of folk hero. She even gets invited onto Jimmy Fallon and Colbert to read the review aloud, like it's some great piece of poetry or something."

"But . . . c'mon. Did it really make that big of a difference? My mom told me that lots of great books got bad reviews when they first came out. I mean, who cares what one person thinks? If the book is good . . . people will still buy it, won't they?" I ask.

"Sure, some people will, but in this case, a *lot* of people didn't, based on that one review. So, the book that was in the running for awards and a movie deal totally fizzled out. The book tour went from fifteen cities to two and the three-book contract that the publisher had offered Allam suddenly became a one-book deal. And that's when Keyheart stuck the knife in again."

I cringe, waiting to hear what terrible thing she did next.

"Because he was expecting a big check from the publisher when he signed the contract, Allam had put down a big deposit on a house in upstate New York for his mom. She worked two jobs all her life to support him and was still living in this cruddy little apartment. When he didn't get the check, he had to back out of the deal . . . *after* telling his mom that he was buying it for her."

"Ouch. Yeah, that's pretty bad."

"Hold on. I'm not done. You want to know the *worst* part?"

"Y-You haven't gotten to that yet?"

Gabby purses her lips and shakes her head. "Nope. It was all a lie. Keyheart didn't hate the book at all. In fact, she *loved* it. A few months later, her assistant—who got fired—leaked some emails between Keyheart and somebody in the media. She said that the book is probably the best first novel written by an American since *To Kill a Mockingbird*. But she was so jealous of it, and Allam's talent, that she went out of her way to wreck it. I'm telling you, there's a trail of dead careers floating belly-up in her wake."

"And let me get this straight. All these people that Keyheart has . . . "

". . . screwed over?" Gabby offers.

"*Fine*, the people she's screwed over. They're all here this week?"

"Well, I'm sure there are more out there, somewhere, but three of them are definitely here: her old agent, Jordie Holloway; publisher and former friend Wendy Eppinger; and rival author Howard Allam. Publishing is a small world."

Something about all three of them being on the island sends up a tiny flare in the back of my brain. "Hmm. Eppinger was her college roommate. And Keyheart lived with Holloway for a year. They would have known . . . " My voice trails off as more brain cells start to do their job.

"Would have known what?"

"I'll tell you later," I say, getting to my feet. "I need to do some thinking. And a little digging."

CHAPTER
6

FIRST STOP: KEKE'S COCOAS. THE original store is on Oliver Street, a few doors off Main. It's a postcard-perfect shop with an awning striped in the same shades of green and blue as the paper that they wrap their boxes of chocolates in. I lock my bike to the rack on the sidewalk, and as I go inside, the bells hanging on the door jangle noisily.

A high school girl who I recognize from the big party at the museum earlier in the summer greets me unenthusiastically: "G'morningcanIhelpyou?"

"Hi, I'm looking for . . . Keke? Is she—"

"Hold on. I'll get her," says the girl, who clearly doesn't remember me.

While I'm waiting, I get a good look at the boxes of chocolates on display under the counter and in the various glass

cabinets around the room. The green boxes, guaranteed to be nut-free, are kept separate from the blue boxes that contain chocolates with nuts.

Still, accidents happen, right? If Keyheart and the paramedics are right, nuts were the likely cause of Didi's death, and obviously she ate a bunch of chocolates from one or both of the green boxes in the cottage. Two plus two equals four, right?

"Hello there. I'm Keke. What can I do for you?" She's early thirties, athletic looking, and stands a solid five-ten or eleven.

"I-I have a question about the boxes without nuts. Is it possible—"

Keke cuts me off. "No. It's not possible for there to be nuts in the boxes that say no nuts. Is that what you were going to ask? You allergic?"

"Me? No. I'm, I have a friend who . . . I just want to make sure."

"Well, you can trust me," Keke says with a grin. "I get it. My little brother's allergic to peanuts. It was hard, growing up, because I *love* peanut butter, know what I mean? When I opened this place, I wanted to make truffles for *everybody*. That's why I have two kitchens. Everything in the green boxes is made—and packaged—over on Swan Street. The only time a green box is allowed inside this building is after it's wrapped in cellophane and ready for sale. The empty boxes, all the green paper, the chocolate, the fruit, *everything*—if it's going to end up in a green box, it *never* sets foot inside here. Never. Never ever ever. Even the people who do the dipping and wrapping are different. If I've been in the kitchen here and have to go in the nut-free zone, I wear a freaking hazmat suit. It's a pain in the neck, but it's . . . Sorry, that's probably *way* more than you wanted to know."

"No, no, thanks. Really. That's good to know," I say.

"Are you visiting somebody on the island?" she asks. "I haven't seen you around."

"We just moved here. From Connecticut."

"That's why you look familiar! You were in the paper! That thing with the Cheevers. Sinking the boat and all that."

"That's me. I'm Lark."

Keke shakes my hand. "Well done, you! You didn't hear it from me, but it's about time somebody brought them down a peg or two. Unfortunately, Reggie Cheever is my landlord. My lease is almost up and of course he's threatening to raise my rent because I've been successful. Well, you don't want to hear about that. Poor kid, you're probably still recovering from my lecture on food safety. How about some chocolates?" she asks. "What do you like?"

"I'm not really a chocolate person," I say, the taste of soap still lingering in my mouth twenty-four hours later. "But my stepdad does, and his birthday's next week. How about one of those nine-piece boxes, the blue ones. Are those dark or milk chocolate? He likes dark better."

"Those are dark. These over here are milk. Or, if you want, I can make you a custom box with some of each. You can choose whatever you want."

"No, that's okay. All dark is good."

"Excellent choice," Keke says as she hands me the bag and refuses to take my money. "Keep it. These are on me."

"Wow. Are you sure?"

"Yep. Anybody who sinks one of Reggie Cheevers's boats gets a free box."

"Oh, ha! Thanks, that's really nice." I turn to leave, but stop in my tracks. "There's something you should know," I say. "I wasn't *completely* honest when I came in. There's a good chance

I won't be the only one asking about the nut thing."

"Oh? Why's that?"

"You probably haven't heard yet, but a girl died at the Islander Hotel last night. She was there for the book festival. Anyway, she was allergic to nuts and it looks like that's why she died."

"Oh, my. That's awful. But . . . what does it have to do with me?" Keke asks. "Oh, the gift baskets for all the VIPs. But those were all nut-free. That's what they asked for. And like I said. It's impossible. Maybe she got another box from, who knows . . . or there were nuts in something else she ate. Wow. That is so sad. I'm really sorry—did you know her?"

"A little. She was the personal assistant for Ann Keyheart, the writer I'm assigned to help out."

"Hey, I know that name," Keke says. "She ordered a bunch of boxes a couple of weeks ago. *Big* order. New York address. Six with nuts, a dozen without. She said she gave them for gifts a few years back and everybody loved them so much she figured she'd do it again."

Behind me, the doorbells jangle and when I see who it is, I'm really glad I decided to warn Keke. It's Officer Pawlowski, and he is *not* happy to see me.

"What are *you* doing here?" he says. "I really hope you're not butting in where you don't belong. *Again.*"

I hold up my bag. "Um . . . it's a chocolate shop." I'm proud of myself for not adding *duh* to the end of that sentence.

"Hmphh," he says.

Keke turns and gives me a nod of respect. "Let me know how your stepdad likes them."

"Yeah, I will. See you around. And, uh, good luck," I add, glancing at Officer Pawlowski, who is picking up boxes of all sizes and colors and reading their labels.

Keke hands me a business card and walks to the door with me. "Thanks for the heads-up," she whispers. "That's my cell number on the back, just in case of . . . whatever. You have yourself a good day."

As I'm unlocking my bike, Officer Pawlowski sticks his head out the door. "Still need to get a statement from you. Come by the station later. How about two o'clock?"

I walk into the hotel lobby just as Keyheart steps off the elevator.

"Ah. Speak of the devil," she says, looking right at me. She shoos away superfan Irwin, who's talking nonstop in her ear and grabs my good arm. "Well, that was brutal, but at least I'm done for the day. What's next. Lunch. Good, I'm starving. Lead the way."

"I, uh, you're . . . not exactly done for the day," I say.

"What are you talking about? Of course I'm done. I taught my class. Now it's time to eat. And relax. With any luck, the sun will come out and I can lay out on that fancy deck."

I unfold the copy of her schedule that I've been given.

"According to this, you have another class at one. You have time to get something to eat—"

"What! *Another* class? That must be a mistake. I just *came* from a class. I never teach more than one class a day."

I show her the paper and point at the time in question. "See? Right here. Don't worry, like I said, you have time for a quick lunch."

"This is ridiculous," she says. "I need to talk to whoever's in charge of this ratfest."

Fortunately for me, Nadine happens to walk into the lobby at that moment. With my eyes, I signal for help and she comes running.

"Hello, Ann," she says to Keyheart. "I'd like to say again how sorry we all are about your assistant. She seemed like a lovely young woman. If there's anything we can do—"

Keyheart shoves the copy of her schedule under Nadine's nose. "According to *this*, I am supposed to teach a *second* class today. I am *quite* sure I never agreed to anything like that."

Nadine, who has dealt with warlords and roving bands of guerrillas in her career as a journalist, remains totally calm. "Actually, Ann, you did. If you remember the conversation we had, when I told you the number of students who were interested in YA fiction, you suggested breaking them into two groups . . . and that you would be thrilled to take on both sections, *especially* if we were able to get you the Captain's Cottage. You were very keen on that detail."

"I-I don't remem—"

Nadine continues, "That being said, I understand that, well, circumstances have changed. I'll admit to being surprised this morning when you insisted on going ahead with your class. But you know what? I ran into one of your students on the way here and she said that you were, quote, *brilliant and inspiring*. She said that even if the festival ended today, she feels like she got her money's worth."

I swear on the copy of *David Copperfield* that Dinah Purdy gave me that Keyheart's head actually begins to swell.

"Yes, well, I see. That's very nice," she says. "We'd better get a move on, then, if I'm going to be on time for my next class."

"Right this way," I say, nudging Keyheart toward the door to the hotel restaurant. Over my shoulder, I mouth *thank you* to Nadine.

Inside the restaurant, a table of students from her first class invite Keyheart to join them, and to my surprise, she agrees. A guy with a goatee moves a chair from another table and the ever-present Irwin orders the others to squeeze together to make room for her.

"I'll be in the lobby if you need me. Have fun," I tell her. Then I turn and *run* before she changes her mind.

Back outside on the patio, Blake is sitting at a table by himself with his eyes closed and face tilted up to the sun. When I pull out a chair and sit, he opens his eyes.

"Oh. It's you," he says, and then closes his eyes again.

"Nice to see you, too," I say, giving his chair a kick. "You eat yet?"

"Nah. I'm waiting for my guy. I have to give him a ride to . . . I dunno, someplace in town. He should be here any minute."

Jordie Holloway, looking much less rumpled than the last time I saw him, waves at Blake from across the patio and walks toward our table. Meanwhile, Gabby the ballerina is chatting with Howard Allam at the hotel entrance. When she sees us, she gives Allam a gentle push through the door and makes a beeline for us.

"Man, that girl is everywhere," I say to Blake. "Whatever you do, don't tell her any of your secrets."

"I wasn't planning on it," he says. "I just met her yesterday."

"Well, trust me. She's very . . . interested."

"Get out. No way."

"Fine. Don't believe me. Here she comes."

Holloway greets Blake as if they are best friends who haven't seen each other in years. "Blake! How ya doing today, old sport? Enough about you. Let me tell you, *I* feel like a new man. I slept like the *dead*." He holds out a hand for me to shake. "Wait a minute. Is this your girl—"

"*Sister*," Blake interrupts.

"Now that you say it, I see the resemblance," says Holloway.

Blake and I share a look, and under my breath, I say, "Let it go."

I shake Holloway's hand. "Hi, I'm Lark."

"Ohhh. Now I remember," he says. "I've heard that name. You're assigned to the dragon lady."

"He means Ann Keyheart," Gabby says with a knowing grin.

"Yeah, I got that," I say.

"Hey, it's all water under the bridge," Holloway says with a wave of the hand. "Ancient history. We've all moved on. I wish her nothing but the best."

"Did you hear about her assistant?" Gabby asks.

"Did she fire another one?" Holloway says with a little laugh. "That job should come with an expiration date."

"It did, kind of," Gabby says.

"She *died*," Blake says, shooting a look at Gabby. "Last night, in her room."

"Oh, my—I'm *so* sorry," Holloway says. "That's terrible. Oh, man. You must think I'm the most insensitive jerk who ever . . . I swear I didn't know. When I got here yesterday, I hadn't slept in two days, so I went straight to my room and crashed. Slept for twelve hours. And then I've been on the phone all morning with a client who's having a breakdown. What *happened*? Do they know?"

Blake glances over at me. "Lark was there . . . right after that Keyheart lady found her. They think it was an allergic reaction."

"To nuts, most likely," I say. "Didi was super allergic."

Jordie Holloway's face goes stark white and his lips quiver as his body sinks into a chair. "D-Did you say . . . Didi?"

"Yeah. Didi Ferrer," I answer. "Did you—"

And then the pieces of the puzzle come together in my brain: Holloway used to be Keyheart's agent. Didi sent the chapters of her book to *him* without knowing that little fact, and then was worried that Keyheart would find out and fire her.

"I didn't know her, but we had emailed a few. . . She's the reason I came. I was hoping to talk to her—"

"—about her book," I say.

"You know about it?" he asks. "She emailed me the first three chapters. I wasn't even supposed to be here, but after I read those pages, I just *had* to meet her in person. She said she'd be here, so I drove all the way. That poor kid." Still pale, and shaking his head in disbelief, Holloway slowly rises from the chair.

"Do—do you still want a ride into town?" Blake asks him.

"What? Oh. No. There's been a change of plans," says Holloway. "That's what I was coming over to tell you. I'm, uh, having lunch here . . . with some friends."

"Okay. I'll check in with you later," Blake says. "In case you need anything."

"Yeah. That, uh, that sounds good. Sorry, I'm still processing. I'll let you know." With a halfhearted wave and a mumbled, "Have a good day," he heads for the hotel.

"Wow. Did you see his face when he heard about that girl?" Gabby says. "Like he saw a ghost. He was *totally* flustered."

From my vantage point, I can see through a set of sliding glass doors into the restaurant. Holloway approaches a table where a woman and a man are seated with their backs to me. When they stand to greet him, I see who they are: Wendy Eppinger and Howard Allam.

Gabby sees it, too. "Well, will ya look at that. Like a meeting of the Ann Keyheart fan club."

"The three of them are doing a workshop together," Blake says. "He told me about it yesterday. It was put together at the last minute, when they found out he was coming."

"I guess that makes sense," says Gabby. "A writer, an agent, and an editor. Still, it seems funny that they all know each other. Oh, well. Time for lunch. They have a lovely *salade Niçoise* here. See you later."

"Let's go into town for lunch," I say to Blake as soon as she's gone. "Unless you'd rather have a sa-LAAD niss-WAZZ, whatever that is, with your *girlfriend*. Then maybe we pick up Pip and the boys and go to the beach. How often do we have a free golf cart to use?"

"We're only supposed to use them for official stuff," says Blake.

"Don't be such a teacher's pet. Live dangerously for once. Besides, I want to pick your brain about something."

"*My* brain?"

I shrug. "I-I'm working on something and I need to talk to somebody. I'd talk to Nadine, but she's crazy-busy and I don't really know anybody else. Not that I trust, anyway. C'mon. You drive. My arm is killing me."

We take the golf cart into town and I tell Blake to park in front of the Island Diner, where we slide into the red vinyl seats of the booth next to one of the front windows.

"I'm sure they have a chicken sandwich," I say, answering the question Blake asks about every restaurant before he has a chance to ask it. "But try the grilled cheese. It's just like Mom used to make." Mom was the first to tell anyone that she was not a great cook, but she did make a killer grilled cheese.

"Do they use—"

"Mayo on the outside? Yep. And a little dijon mustard inside. I toldja."

"Oh, shoot," he says, patting his pockets. "I don't have any money."

"My treat," I say. "I think I owe you anyway."

"Uh, *yeah*. Like a hundred bucks."

"No way. "Fifty, maybe."

"I don't get it. You make all that money working for Nadine."

"Yeah, but Thomas makes me put it all into savings."

"Why? You're not gonna need money for college. You're *so* gonna get a soccer scholarship."

"Maybe," I say. "There're a lot of good players out there."

The waitress takes our order and when she's gone, I lean over the table toward Blake, making sure no one else can hear me. "It wasn't an accident."

"*What* wasn't an accident?"

"Shhh! Didi. The chocolates."

"So . . . you're saying . . . "

"It was murder."

"That's crazy. Why would anyone want to murder *her*?"

"Well, that part was an accident."

"You just said it *wasn't* an accident."

"I mean they didn't mean to kill *Didi*. They meant to kill Keyheart."

"Who is *they*?"

"I'm working on it. I already have three suspects, and it's only lunchtime."

Over grilled cheese and french fries, I repeat Gabby's account of all the gory details of Keyheart's history with Wendy Eppinger, Jordie Holloway, and Howard Allam.

"Wow. She sounds *crazy*. What is wrong with people?" Blake is, seriously, one of the nicest people in the world, and he can't even *imagine* doing the things that Keyheart has done over and over in her life.

"So, you agree that they all had the motive to kill Keyheart?"

"I don't know. There's a long way between being really *mad* at somebody and, you know, actually committing *murder*."

"But what if you could do it in a way that looked like an accident?" I ask. "They would know things about Keyheart. Important things. *Medical* things. Eppinger was her college roommate and Keyheart lived at Holloway's house for a year."

"Ohhh. You're saying they *knew* she was allergic to nuts."

"Uh-huh. I haven't figured out how they did it yet, but it has something to do with chocolates, the ones from Keke's Cocoas. The first time I was in the cottage with Keyheart, she said that she had ordered a bunch of boxes online right after she found out she was coming to the island. Said she remembered how good they were from the last time she was here. And she made a big deal about saying they didn't have nuts. *Anyway,* I talked to Keke herself this morning and she says there's no way the chocolates got mixed up at the shop. Somebody must have messed with them later, but instead of killing Keyheart, they killed Didi . . . who unfortunately was *also* allergic to nuts. Omigosh, that reminds me. Can't go to the beach. I have to talk to the cops at two. I guess because I found the body—although, technically, I didn't, Keyheart did—I have to make a statement."

"But . . . isn't it possible there were nuts in something *else* Didi ate, and it really was an accident? 'Cause I don't see how somebody could have tampered with a box of chocolates that Keyheart ordered online and were delivered to her in New York."

"They could have done it yesterday, during the day," I say. "Didi was gone. She and I went to. . . well, that's a whole 'nother story. Maybe somebody snuck into the cottage while Keyheart was sleeping. It would only take a second."

"It's *possible,* I guess," Blake admits.

"I'm not done yet." I flatten a crumpled copy of the official Swallowtales program on the table. "Check it out. Here're the suspects. Eppinger. Holloway. Allam. They all hate Keyheart. They all live in New York City. And they all know each other. And at least some of them had to know about the nut allergy thing."

"What are you gonna do? You're gonna tell the police, right?"

"Not yet. They'll never believe me anyway. I have an idea, though." I snap pictures of the headshots of my three suspects from the program and text them to Keke with this message:

Thanks for ur help this morning. And for the chocolates!!
Did any of these peeps buy chocs in the past few days?
Esp boxes w/nuts.

"Just because they bought chocolates with nuts doesn't mean they're murderers," Blake notes.

"Yeah, but it's another piece of the puzzle," I say. "I'll bet you a week's worth of babysitting Pip and the boys that at least one of them went to Keke's."

"No thanks," Blake says. "I'm not betting against you."

"Finally. You're learning."

CHAPTER

7

I SHOW UP AT THE police station right on time and find
Thomas sitting on a bench outside waiting for me.

"Hey, Tomás. What's going on? Why are *you* here?"

"Ah, there's that Lark charm I've come to love so much," he
says, smiling. "They called to say that you were coming by for
your statement. Apparently, since you're not a suspect, they *can*
talk to you without me around, but they're trying to be nice. I
thought that, well, with your history, it might be a good idea."

"What, d'you think I'm gonna punch Pawlowski? Have you
seen how big that guy is?"

Thomas's left eyebrow rises a fraction of an inch and he fake
coughs to cover up a smile.

"I saw that," I say, but I laugh because deep down, I know
he's right.

"It's up to you," he says. "I can leave if you want."

"Nah. It's okay. He'll be nicer if you stay. And I'll get out of here faster."

Officer Pawlowski takes his good old time, and calls us into his office at two fifteen. Right off the bat, it's crystal clear that the whole thing is strictly a formality. He's simply waiting for the coroner to confirm what he's already one hundred percent certain of: Didi Ferrer's death was an accident. When I point out—again—that the box of chocolates was green and therefore nut-free, he waves me off.

"Those aren't the only nuts on Swallowtail Island," he says.

Thomas sees *my* raised eyebrow and says, "Lark. *Don't* say it."

"But it's so . . . oh, *fine*," I say, crossing my arms in a huff at being so . . . *oppressed*.

The light finally switches on for Officer Pawlowski: "*Ohhh. I see what you're . . . ha ha. Very funny. What I was thinking was, maybe she ate a Snickers bar.*"

"She didn't eat a *Snickers* bar," I say. "She wasn't an idiot. And what about the fact that Ms. Keyheart is also incredibly allergic to nuts? Geez, how can you be so . . . *obtuse*?"

"La-ark," says Thomas.

"I think we're done here," Pawlowski says, closing his notebook and getting to his feet.

Outside, Thomas pats me on the head. "Well, *that* was fun. *Obtuse*? You are something else."

"What can I say? I do my best," I say. "And you *know* he's looking it up on his phone right now. We should get out of here before he figures it out."

"What are you up to, anyway? What's this about green boxes?"

"Kind of a long story. I'll tell you later. . . what's for dinner?"

"Oh, you're going to grace us with your presence? I thought there was another big bash at the book thing."

"Eh. Nothing really special. Now that Keyheart is in the hotel instead of the cottage, my job got a lot easier. I don't need to escort her around as much. Supposedly, she's having dinner at the yacht club with the Cheevers. Lucky her."

"Lucky you," Thomas says.

My phone dings; it's Keke, replying to my text:

Yes! Saturday morning. Eppinger, 3 w/nuts, 2 no nuts, Allam, 2 w/nuts, 4 no nuts. They came in together. Never saw the other guy.

So, Blake and I are both right. And that makes a total of five boxes with nuts bought by two people who know about Keyheart's nut allergy and who knew she was coming to Swallowtail, *and* where she would be staying. Thanks to social media, the whole world knows that she loves Keke's Cocoas, so that all somebody had to do, I reason, is sneak into her cottage and switch a few chocolates in a box she already had.

"Well, *that's* interesting," I say after reading the text. "Ya know, I gotta go, Thomas. I'll see you later."

"Still on for dinner?"

"Yes. I mean, probably. You know what? I'll let you know."

Based on our history, I'm pretty sure that Officer Pawlowski would laugh me out of his office if I tried to explain my theory of the crime that he doesn't even believe *was* a crime. What I need is something to connect a suspect to the scene of the crime. Which means I have to do some old-fashioned snooping, starting with Jordie Holloway. I text Blake the news from Keke, but (no surprise) he doesn't respond. He's probably sleeping, which is how he spends most of his free time.

A few seconds later, though, my phone dings. It's not Blake; it's Nadine, asking me to meet her in the hotel lobby ASAP.

She's waiting for me at the main desk, standing next to a cute, college-age girl who is a mix of preppy and punk, and somehow making it work. Her hair is mostly hot pink and her ears and nose are well-pierced, but from the neck down, her plaid, sleeveless sundress and quilted cotton bag would fit right in with the ladies-who-lunch at the yacht club.

Nadine looks relieved to see me. "Lark! Thank goodness. You must have been close."

"Yeah, the cops wanted to talk to me about last night . . . what's up?"

At the mention of the word *cops*, the girl with pink hair looks me up and down, much as I had done to her a few seconds earlier. In my peach shirt and khaki shorts, I'm not exactly at the cutting edge of fashion and certainly don't look much like a criminal.

"Lark, this is Suzy," Nadine says. "Didi's roommate. From New York."

"Oh." I feel the blood draining from my head. "Um . . . hi. I'm Lark."

Nadine continues before I can say anything else: "She's on the island for a . . . she's a musician. She's playing at one of the bars in town."

The expression on Nadine's face tells me that Suzy has no idea of what's happened to Didi.

Nadine glances around the nearly empty lobby. "I think we should sit. You can leave your bags there. They'll be fine. Please."

"Um, what's going on?" Suzy asks, dropping into a comfy chair.

"I'm afraid I have some terrible news," Nadine starts. "About Didi."

Suzy sits up straight in her chair. "Didi? What's wrong? Is she okay?"

Nadine puts her hand on Suzy's arm. "I'm so sorry. Last night, it looks like Didi ate something with nuts and had a bad allergic reaction. She was alone in her room . . . by the time the paramedics reached her, it was too late."

Suzy's head tilts slightly to the left and she stares at Nadine, waiting for her to say that she's being punked, that it's all a joke, that Didi's fine and in fact, it was *her* idea to play this little trick. As reality sinks in, Suzy looks like an inflatable swimming pool toy that someone has let the air out of. She leans back in the chair, her eyes watery and mouth wide open in disbelief.

"Oh. Poor Didi. Just when everything was finally . . . what about her parents? Do they know? I don't even know where they are. Half the time Didi didn't know. They're always traveling. They just got back together. They were separated for years."

"The police were able to track them down," Nadine says. "Not sure how. Unfortunately, they're somewhere in Asia. They're trying to get back, but it's going to take some time."

"Did you know her for a long time?" I ask. "Were you guys . . . "

"We met at boarding school," Suzy says. That memory hits her hard, and she buries her face in her hands for several seconds, rubbing her eyes and temples and then burying her fingers in her shocking pink hair.

"Can I get you anything?" Nadine asks. "A glass of water?"

Suzy stands, collecting herself and taking several long, deep breaths. "No. Thank you. I'll be okay. It's still . . . sinking in. I just need a minute to process it. It doesn't seem possible. When did she . . . "

"It was about ten last night. Her employer, Ann Keyheart, found her. Lark was there, too. She's the one who called 911."

Suzy nods at me. "I was about your age when I met her. The thing is, back at Carton, we weren't really friends. Ran in different circles, I guess you'd say. After college, we both ended up in New York, and reconnected. It's not like we were best friends or anything, but, you know. It worked. Two people sharing an apartment in a crappy neighborhood, you get to know each other, look out for each other. That's why it doesn't seem *possible*, what you said about her eating something with nuts. She was *way* too careful. She drove me crazy. Everywhere we went, everything she ate, she asked a million questions. How could she make such a . . . "

"Nobody knows for sure yet, but it looks like some chocolates with nuts got mixed up into a box that wasn't supposed to have any," I say, deciding for the moment against sharing my theory that her death was a murder gone wrong. "I'm really sorry. I just met her yesterday, but we spent a couple hours together. I drove her out to a place on the island she wanted to see. She told me about . . . all kinds of things about her life. She seemed really nice."

"I tried to call her yesterday," Suzy says, "to tell her I was coming, but it kept going to voicemail. This gig was a last-minute thing. I guess somebody flaked out on them. A total fluke, that we were both gonna be *here* at the same time. I'm supposed to play at some bar called the Mug Shot. Do you know it?"

"Sure. It's not far," Nadine says. "I'm sure Lark can show you . . . that is, if you're up to it. I know the owners, and I feel sure they'd understand if you . . . "

"No, I want to play," Suzy says. "It's like therapy for me."

"Is there anything else we can do for you?" Nadine asks her.

"There is one thing. I don't actually . . . have a place to stay. I came here to the hotel 'cause I knew this was where Didi would be. Figured I'd crash with her."

In the Captain's Cottage? With Keyheart? Yikes. Hard to believe that Keyheart would have gone along with that plan, I think.

"Stay at my house," I say. "We have an extra room. It's kinda far from town, but I can give you a ride. Or you can use my bike."

"Are you serious?"

"Sure. It's no problem, as long as you're okay with a bunch of kids. I have a sister and three brothers."

"Do you want to check with Thomas first?" Nadine says.

"Nah. He'll be fine," I say. "Thomas is used to me springing little surprises on him. He'll hardly notice one more person at the table for breakfast."

"As long as you're sure. I'm . . . yeah, that would be awesome," Suzy says.

"You wouldn't find a hotel room anyway," notes Nadine.

"With Swallowtales, everything's booked—no pun intended."

"Do you want me to take you out there now?" I ask Suzy. "Or do you need to stay here for a while? Either way's okay with me."

"I could really use a coffee," she says. "If we could stop someplace, that would be cool. But yeah, I'd love to crash for a while. It sounds like it might be a busy night at the Mug Shot. The ferry was packed. I guess everybody's trying to get one more trip in before the end of summer."

"They're all day-trippers," Nadine says, handing Suzy one of her cards. "You would *not* want to be on the last ferry off the island tonight. It will be a wild one. Call me if you need anything. That goes for both of you."

After a stop at the coffee shop for an extra-large latte for Suzy and an iced tea for me, I drive us back to the hotel in order to show her the Captain's Cottage. I was a little surprised that she wanted to see it, but if I've learned anything in life, it's that everybody deals with the big stuff in their own way.

"This is it," I say when we approach it on foot after parking the golf cart.

Even though Officer Pawlowski insists that no crime has been committed, the front door is crossed with plastic crime scene tape.

"I guess that's to keep the cleaning people out for now," I say. "We can go around the side. There's a nice deck that sticks out over the lake."

"Hmmm. I see what you mean. That's amazing," Suzy says when the front of the cottage and the lake come into view. A man in a kayak paddles silently past, following the shoreline for a while before turning south toward Inchworm Island, a half mile or so away. "It's so peaceful here. Didi told me it was nice, but I always thought, you know, Lake *Erie*. How nice could it be?"

We walk back to the front of the cottage, where Suzy stands on tiptoes and tries to peek through the porthole window in the door. "I can't really see anything," she says, backing away from it. Then she shakes her head and kicks angrily at the dirt. "I just don't get it. Why didn't she call 911? Or use her EpiPen?"

"I think she tried. The phone, I mean. It was in her hand when . . . when she died."

"Oh. No. *Wait*. I just remembered something. When Didi was packing on Friday night, she flipped out a little because she couldn't find her EpiPen. She was *positive* it had been in her bag when she went to work, but it was gone. She said she'd be okay because Keyheart always has one with her, and they'd be together anyway."

"I guess that makes sense," I say. "And Keyheart *does* have one. She showed it to everyone. But . . ."

"What?"

"It's just that I *saw* Didi's room. Super organized. Everything *exactly* where it was supposed to be."

"Tell me about it," Suzy says. "She's the neatest, cleanest, most organized person I've ever met. We're, like, *polar* opposites. She won't even look in the door of my bedroom in our apartment. It makes her crazy." She pauses before adding, sadly, *"Made."*

"But somehow this super organized person lost her EpiPen *and* her phone in a stretch of about twelve hours."

"She lost her phone? Wait a minute. You said it was still in her hand."

"That was the landline. She lost *her* phone . . . well, technically, *she* didn't lose it. Keyheart did. She borrowed it from Didi on the ferry and somehow it ended up in the lake."

"Ho-ly crap. What did Didi do?"

"She was *not* happy. Keyheart did promise to buy her a new one, though, as soon as they got back to New York."

We're still standing there, three feet away from the front door, when it swings open. Officer Pawlowski glares first at me, then at Suzy, and finally, at the cardboard box in his hands.

"You *again*. What are you doing?" he demands. "You're not supposed to be here."

"I'm showing . . . this is Didi's roommate. She just got here."

Pawlowski pulls the door shut and checks that it is locked.

"Look, I'm sorry about your friend, but you can't be here," he says to Suzy.

"What's in the box?" I ask.

"None of your . . . it's personal effects of the deceased," he says, tilting it toward his body to make it harder for me to see inside. "Some books. A notebook. I still have to pack up the clothes."

"Where are you taking it?"

"Back to the station. I have to hold it until someone from her family picks it up."

I point at Suzy. "This is her roommate. Can't she take it? I mean, if she wants to."

"Uh, yeah, I could take it," Suzy says.

Pawlowski looks skeptically at Suzy's pink hair. "Can't do it unless I get the okay from the dead girl's family, but it would be doing me a favor. We don't exactly have a lot of storage. Tell ya what. I'll call 'em and let you know. I've got your number. And your name is . . . "

"Suzy. Suzy Cue. That's C - U - E. It's my stage name, actually, but Didi's parents know me. Oh, and I guess I'm staying at *her* house, if you need to find me."

"Okay. Suzy Cue. It's easy to remember, anyway."

"That's kind of the idea," says Suzy.

"Hey, as long as you're here, you can do me a favor," Pawlowski says with a smirk in my direction. He unlocks the door and reaches inside, removing a small trash bag, which he hands to me. "You *do* know what to do with trash, don't you? I'm just saying, you don't *seem* especially obtuse, but you never know."

Well played, Officer Pawlowski.

"*That* was kind of random," Suzy says. "What's his problem?"

"Kind of a long story. And actually, I'm glad he gave me this," I say, pointing to the trash bag that (I hope) holds the cellophane and wrapping paper from the box of chocolates that Keyheart insisted I open. "I thought I was gonna have to sneak in somehow to take it."

"Wow. Happy with a bag of trash. You must be *really* easy to shop for."

Suzy doesn't have to be onstage at the Mug Shot until nine fifteen, so she gets to experience firsthand the chaos of a Sunday afternoon and evening at the Roost with the Emmerys and the Heron-Finches.

Thomas is a bit startled when I arrive home with Suzy and inform him that she'll be staying with us for a few days, but once I explain who she is, he welcomes her. He opens the windows in the spare room to air it out and puts clean sheets on the bed even though the ones on it hadn't been touched since the day in June that we arrived.

"This is perfect," she says, admiring the view of the lake

below. It's a thousand times nicer than any hotel I could afford to stay in. Thank you *so* much."

"Everybody out," Thomas orders, spinning Pip, Jack, and Nate by the tops of their heads and pushing them toward the door, where Blake stands, trying hard not to look *too* interested in the exotic, pink-haired Suzy. "Give Suzy a little room and some peace and quiet for a while. You can talk to her at dinner—you are staying for dinner, right?"

"I-I sure. You really don't have to—"

Thomas waves off her objection. "Look at this motley crew. What's one more?"

"Let me know if you need anything," I tell her when the others are gone. "And, uh, I am really sorry about Didi."

"Thanks. I think it's still sinking in. I can't believe she's . . . gone. Like *that*. Life is so . . . weird. And unfair."

"That's exactly what I was thinking. I mean, I know there's lots of things about life that aren't fair, but . . . anyway, I wish I could see you play. I don't think I can pass for twenty-one, though. They'd never let me in."

"Tell you what. I'll play for you guys after dinner. I've got my guitar. I don't suppose you've got an amp around here?"

"That is *so* weird. We *just* got one, like a week ago, and a guitar. I don't know if it's any good. Thomas saw this ad in the paper. Somebody was moving and selling all kinds of stuff, super cheap. He's hoping one of us will learn to play."

"So nobody plays?"

"Not yet. Blake's talked about taking lessons, but he hasn't started. Actually, I think Jack—he's the youngest—would be good. He has a good voice, too."

"He should definitely take some lessons. Next time I come we can play a duet. Anyway, do you think it'll be okay if I play a little?"

"Are you kidding? Did you see the way they looked at you . . . and your guitar case. You're like a real rock star. They would *kill* to see you play.

"Ha! I'm not exactly a star, but I'll do my best."

CHAPTER

8

WHEN IT'S TIME TO SIT down for dinner, Pip and Jack rush to claim the coveted chairs right next to Suzy. Thomas sets a gigantic bowl of spaghetti and meatballs in the middle of the table, followed by two long loaves of garlic bread, and a coffee table-sized platter of sliced tomatoes and fresh mozzarella topped with basil leaves snipped from the small garden outside the kitchen door.

Suzy's eyes grow wider and wider as the food keeps coming. "Omigosh. That is a *lot* of food."

"Growing boys. And girls," Thomas says, setting down a bowl of freshly grated parmesan. "Do you have brothers and sisters?"

"I'm an only child. So was Didi. Probably why we got along, even though we were really different. But this—all this food, a big family, everybody together for dinner—this is nice. Makes me wish—"

"It's not always so great," I say.

"Seriously," adds Blake.

"Don't pay attention to these two," Thomas says. "I'm sure you remember what it was like to be a teenager."

"Just keepin' it real," Blake says.

"And, by the way, I'm not a teenager yet," I remind Thomas. "You have a whole year till that's true."

"Gee, I can hardly wait," he says with an eye roll that any teen would be proud of. "So, Suzy, tell us about yourself, your music career. Is it something you've always been interested in? I've been trying to get *somebody* here to take up an instrument. Maybe you can inspire one of them to do something with the guitar I bought."

"I hear you're the singer in the family," Suzy says to Jack, who turns bright red. "I'll give you your first guitar lesson after dinner."

"What do you think about that, Jack?" Thomas asks.

"Cooool," answers Jack.

"I was twelve or thirteen when I started playing," Suzy begins. "It was my first year at Carton. Seemed like everybody there was going to be an actor, a singer, or an artist."

Thomas's ears perk up at the mention of Carton Academy. "Oh, you went to Carton? Interesting. Lark is considering that as an option. Maybe we can talk about it later?"

"Sure. Happy to. That's where I met Didi. I had a great time there. Well, after the first few weeks, you know, when I got used to being away from home," Suzy says. "Anyway, like I was saying, I started playing, and writing songs, and by the time I got to college, I was in a few really bad bands. And then suddenly I'm an adult, living in New York and working about sixty hours a week. But about a year ago, I was playing some of my own stuff at an open mic night on the Lower East Side, and some guy offered to help me get some gigs . . . I know, I know, it sounds like the oldest line in the book, right? *Hey, baby, I can make you a star.* But I swear, he's *totally* legit. I have a regular gig in the city on Friday nights and I'm working on some demo tracks, so one of these days there'll be an album."

"Is there a story with your name?" I ask.

"Ah. Yes. My real name is Susie-with-an-s Cutler. Right after I started playing, I was staying at my grandparents' house and the only thing on TV were reruns of that show *Happy Days.* It's from the seventies, but it's about kids in the fifties. There was this character named Leather Tuscadero—she played bass in a rock 'n' roll, and I thought she was the coolest thing *ever.*"

"It was actually Suzi Quatro, right?" Thomas says. "I remember her. She was the real thing. Had some big hits."

"Absolutely," Suzy says. "She was huge. A legend. And she's *still* playing. So I dropped a few letters from Cutler and became Suzy Cue, C - U - E, in her honor."

"Atsocool," Nate says through a mouth crammed full of

spaghetti. "Imachange mynametoo."

"To what, Nate the Great? Too *late*," Pip says, earning a high five from me.

In a matter of minutes, the bowls and platters are empty and plates have been wiped clean with the last of the garlic bread.

Suzy shakes her head in disbelief at the scene before her. "I can't believe how much I ate. I'm gonna burst. That was, seriously, the best meal *ever*."

"You need to get out more," Thomas says, laughing.

"I have a little surprise for everyone," Suzy says. "I mean, if it's okay. I was going to play a few songs for you, out on the patio. Like the old days. Playing for my supper."

Pip, Jack, and Nate drag poor Suzy by the arms out of the kitchen as Thomas and I look on, horrified but helpless. Blake, meanwhile, continues to play it cool.

Despite the pressure from her audience, Suzy insists on waiting for Thomas, who has been tackling the disaster in the kitchen singlehandedly.

"*Finally*," says Jack when Thomas joins us.

I have to hand it to Thomas. The guy works all week, cooks about ninety percent of the meals, and does more than his share of cleaning up, but he never complains. If I were him, I'd be *strangling* Jack about now. Instead, he musses Jacks hair and smiles.

Here's the GHT about Suzy: she is *really* good. Like, amazing. I don't know much about music, but I know when somebody sounds too good to be playing on our patio, or even at a bar on Swallowtail Island. This girl deserves a big stage, a big audience.

She plays her own guitar, a mint-green beauty, for the first couple of songs, and then switches to the black one Thomas bought at the garage sale. It takes her a minute to tune it, but when her fingers start plucking and strumming, it's like magic, and soon all three boys and Pip are claiming the guitar as their own and demanding that Thomas pay for lessons.

After half an hour of playing, she hands the black guitar to Blake and starts to zip hers into its case.

"Nooo! One more song," Pip cries.

"No, she has to get going," I say.

"'Fraid so," Suzy agrees. "I've got two hours of singing and playing ahead of me. But I'll play for you tomorrow. And I'll give a lesson to whoever wants one."

"I'll give you a ride into town," I say. "What about after?"

"I feel bad making you . . . it's gonna be late," she says. "Probably after midnight."

"No worries," Thomas says. "I'll be awake. I'll come get you. There's not a lot of options for getting out here, this far from town, at night. Thanks for the concert. That was a treat. I think you've converted some kids into musicians."

After I drop off Suzy at the Mug Shot and drive back to the Roost, I bring the bag of trash from Keyheart's cottage inside and set it on the floor next to my bed. Pogo lifts her head from my pillow, and sniffs, but apparently decides that whatever it is isn't worth getting up for.

Blake sticks his head in the door. "Hey. That was pretty cool. Suzy, I mean."

"Yeah. It was."

"What's that?" he asks, pointing at the trash bag.

"Garbage. From Keyheart's and Didi's living room."

"Why is it in *your* room?"

"I'm looking for evidence." Just in case there's something really disgusting inside, I open the bag slowly and risk a sniff.

I can't smell anything besides the plastic bag itself, so I reach in and pull out some folded-up green paper and cellophane. Reading the label confirms that it came from a box with *dark* chocolate truffles. "Yup. These are definitely the ones that I opened. Keyheart brought them with her from New York. And *this* is the cellophane wrapper from that same box. I remember folding it exactly like this."

"I don't get it. What does that . . . "

"Keke uses blue paper for the boxes with nuts and green for no nuts, so there were no nuts in this box when it left Keke's. Which means somebody must have put them in after. The box and the wrapping *looked* normal, but somebody could have messed with it." I unfold the heavy, kelly-green paper and spread it out on the floor, using my hands to flatten it as much as possible. "I was trying to be careful when I opened it—"

"So you could save the paper—"

"Of course. Mom would have killed me if I ever opened a present like this. But Keyheart was like, just *open* it! That's why it's ripped."

A gold sticker printed with the Keke's logo was used instead of tape in the process of wrapping, and it is undisturbed.

Or so it *seems*.

I take a closer look. "Wait a second. Take a look at this sticker."

Blake kneels and leans over the paper. "What? I don't see any—*ohhh*. Yeah."

There's a line through the center of the sticker where it has been sliced in half. I bend it gently on the cut line and slowly pull it apart. Underneath is a small loop of tape holding it in place.

"Somebody cut this!" I say. "It's perfectly straight, and exactly where the two layers of paper overlap. And then used a piece of tape so you can't tell."

"But there was cellophane on top of that," Blake says. "What about that?"

I do my best to flatten it on the floor next to the wrapping paper, trying not to tear it. "I was having trouble opening it and Didi gave me a knife. Look, here's the straight cut that I made. But look at this." I hold it up to the light so Blake and I can both look through it.

"That's Scotch tape," he says, pointing to what looks like a seam in the cellophane. "I'll bet that was on the bottom of the box where you couldn't see it. It's almost impossible to see, unless the light is just right. Dog my cat. You're right. Somebody messed with that box."

"Did you just say *dog my cat*?"

"Um, yeah. I guess I did. I don't know where it came from."

"Mom used to say that. Remember? To tell you the truth, I never really understood it. Anyway, yeah. This is *proof* that somebody tampered with the box in order to try to kill Keyheart. I'm gonna show this to the cops first thing tomorrow."

d d done done.

Sadly, I'm not there to witness it for myself, but the crowd at the Mug Shot is bigger than expected for a Sunday night, and Suzy doesn't finish up until almost midnight. By that time, I am sound asleep with Pogo's head resting on my legs, so Thomas picks her up without me.

My alarm goes off at six thirty, and on my way downstairs, I peek into the spare room where Suzy is sleeping and then head for the kitchen in search of breakfast. Not surprisingly, Pip is already in her usual chair, finishing a bowl of cereal before going out to the barn to feed Tinker *her* breakfast of hay and oats.

"Why are you up so early?" she says.

"Gotta lot to do."

Without pausing for breath or waiting for my answers, she reels off a string of questions and observations: "When do you think Suzy will wake up? I wonder what she wants for breakfast. Do you think she'll play some more for us today? That was so cool. I'm gonna learn to play like her."

"You may have to fight the boys for the guitar," I say, pouring myself a glass of orange juice. "Anyway, leave Suzy alone. It must have been pretty late when she got back here, so let her sleep. And make sure the boys keep quiet too. Remember, she had kind of a crazy day yesterday. She came to Swallowtail thinking she was gonna be on a little vacation, hanging out with her roommate and doing tourist stuff."

"Ohhh. I completely forgot about that," Pip says. "I promise, we'll be quiet."

"I'll be back for lunch. I think. There's a special lunch today for everybody at the book thingy—the faculty and the students, that is. Pages don't have to go. Tell Suzy that she can use my bike to go into town, but I can give her a ride if she wants to wait."

"Got it. Lunch. Bike. Wait." The screen door slams shut behind her as she runs toward the barn.

A few seconds later, there's a knock at that same door and I jump, spinning around so fast that I spill half my juice. It's Officer Pawlowski, in full uniform and holding the same box I'd seen him with outside the cottage. Didi's small rolling carry-on bag is on the porch beside him.

"Good morning," he says. "Took a chance that somebody'd be up. Brought the deceased girl's property. Her roommate—Suzy, uh, Cue? She's here, right? Need her to sign this and get it back to me. Anytime today's fine." He tucks a sheet of paper into the handle of the suitcase.

"She's still sleeping. Come on in," I say. "I'm glad you're here. Saves me a trip. I need to talk to you."

"Oh, boy. Lucky me," he says, setting down the box on a chair and collapsing the carry-on's handle. "What is it now? You want me to bring in the FBI to run a DNA test on that chocolate box? Or should I just go ahead and arrest the lady in the chocolate shop?"

"No! Keke didn't do anything," I insist. "She's not the one with the motive."

"Motive to do *what*?" he asks, utterly bewildered. "There was no motive. There was no *crime*. It was a tragic accident, pure and simple. You have to accept that."

I shake my head, determined to be heard. "Yeah, no. That's not gonna happen. I have proof that it wasn't an accident. Somebody was trying to kill Ms. Keyheart, but something went wrong and they killed Didi by mistake."

"That's—that's *crazy*. Who? *They?* Listen to yourself: It was murder. No, it was a mistake. You're not even making sense. Promise me you're not spreading that story around town."

"Only because I don't want to tip off the killer. Or *killers*. I think it was more than one."

"You're impossible. Please, *please*, stay out of this."

"You don't want to see my evidence?"

Before he can answer, Thomas comes downstairs and into the kitchen. "I thought I heard voices. What's going on? Officer Pawlowski. Good to see you. Coffee?"

"That would be great," Pawlowski says. "I was just dropping off some things for Ms. Cue."

"That's me," Suzy says, standing in the doorway. "Miscue."

"And right on . . . *cue*," Thomas says with a sheepish grin. "Sorry. Couldn't resist. I'll start the coffee."

"I can't believe I'm up already," she says. "Pogo jumped up in bed with me. She's such a sweetie. The sun was coming in the windows and I could hear the waves. I just *had* to get up. It's too beautiful to stay in bed."

"Sorry about Pogo waking you up, but I'm glad you're here," I say. "I was just about to explain to Officer Pawlowski why he needs to open an investigation into Didi's murder—"

"What!" cries Suzy.

"Murder!" Thomas says, spilling water all over the coffee maker. "I thought she—"

"And the *attempted* murder of Ann Keyheart. She was the intended victim." I pull a Ziploc bag holding the wrapping paper and cellophane from my backpack. "*This* was in the trash from Keyheart's cottage."

"You were *supposed* to throw that out," Pawlowski says. "Serves me right for not doing it myself."

I shrug. "Sorry. Can't help myself. And besides, I was right. Somebody tampered with that box of chocolates from Keke's. *I'm* the one who opened it. Keyheart handed it to me. There didn't *seem* to be anything weird about it. But when I took a closer look last night, I saw plenty. Look at this paper. See how this sticker has been cut in half? *Perfectly.* There's a piece of tape under it now because somebody REwrapped it and it had to look like the sticker was still in place. But that was the easy part. Before they even got to the paper, they had to figure out how to get this cellophane off—and back on again—without looking any different. It's tricky, because the cellophane is shrink-wrapped in place. I saw a video about it once; they use a thing like a hair dryer. But if you look really close right *here*, you can see a piece of Scotch tape that somebody used to tape it back together. They must have cut the cellophane with a razor blade in order to get it off. It would have been on the bottom, so it was incredibly unlikely that anybody would see it."

"Let me get this straight," Pawlowski says. "You're saying that somebody opened this box of chocolates . . . and did what?"

"Well, *obviously*, they replaced the chocolates that were nut-free with ones full of nuts. And then they rewrapped the box with the paper and cellophane so it looked exactly like a new box. To somebody as allergic as Keyheart or Didi, that innocent-looking box of chocolates was a murder weapon. I don't know *why* yet, but whoever did it didn't replace them all, because I saw Keyheart *and* Didi eat one. And I had one that tasted like soap."

"Or *maybe* not every piece in the blue boxes has nuts," says Suzy, totally getting it. "Maybe the blue box just means that there might be nuts, right?"

"Yeah, that's a good point," I say. "The police should look into that."

"The police are *not* going to look into it," Pawlowski says. "A couple of pieces of tape don't prove anything. There's a million possible explanations.

"Have a seat, Officer," I say as Thomas hands him a mug of steaming coffee. "Let me tell you a story."

He sits, as do Thomas and Suzy, and they spend the next ten minutes utterly captivated by the sordid tales of Ann Keyheart and her former friends and colleagues, Wendy Eppinger, Howard Allam, and Jordie Holloway.

When I finish, Thomas refills everyone's coffee and says, "Yikes. I think I need a shower after that."

"No wonder Didi was going crazy working for her. She's psycho," adds Suzy. "I'm really sorry about Didi, but *man*. If one of them did try to kill Keyheart, it's almost, like, justifiable homicide. She totally had it coming."

"Well?" I say to Pawlowski. "You have to admit, it makes sense."

"I'll admit that those folks all had good reason to dislike Ms. Keyheart. But these are writers you're talking about. I don't know what goes on in their books, but in real life, people like that don't commit murder. Tell you what. I'll—" He pauses before finishing through gritted teeth. "I will . . . look into it. I'll talk to Keyheart, see if she's noticed anything unusual. But you have to promise not to mention this . . . *theory* of yours to anyone else. Deal?"

"Fine. But what about the suspects? You gonna talk to them?

At least two of them bought chocolates at Keke's. What if they try again? To kill Keyheart, I mean."

Pawlowski swallows the last of his coffee, sets the mug down, and rises from the table. "Thank you for the coffee, Mr. Emmery. You folks have a nice day. Gonna be a hot one."

I'm not sure I believe that Officer Pawlowski is going to "look into it" but I'm willing to give him twenty-four hours. Wait. On second thought, that seems too long. He has *twelve* hours to take some action, or I'll have no choice. I've already solved one major crime on Swallowtail Island, and nothing is going to stop me from solving *this* one.

Suzy confides that all she really wants is a quiet day to herself. "I've got a lot to think about. I'm just gonna find a quiet spot, maybe a beach, to chill and start to, you know, *process* all this. I mean, Didi's *gone*. It's surreal."

I suggest a few options where she'll be guaranteed some privacy and then drop her off at the coffee shop. From there, I head over to the hotel to make sure Keyheart is still alive and able to find her classroom again.

"She *lives*," says Keyheart, opening her door. "Oh. I suppose that's not exactly in good taste, is it? Oh, well. I figured you'd abandoned me."

"W-What? I'm sorry. Did you need something?" I absolutely hate to disappoint anyone, even annoying people like her.

"No, it's just that one minute you were here, buzzing around like a busy little bee, and then . . . poof! Gone."

"I-I didn't know . . . I thought you were . . . you should have—"

"Relax. Geez, Lulu, I'm yanking your chain. I don't need a thing. I've got it all under control. Two classes, just like yesterday. I've already had breakfast. Room service. Seriously, is there anything better? Have a croissant. They're not the worst ones I've had."

"No, thanks," I say. "Um . . . don't know if you know, but Didi's roommate is here. She came yesterday."

"Oh, yeah? The one with the pink hair and the guitar? Suzy something. Heaven help us if the future is in *her* hands. What's she want, anyway?"

"I don't think she *wants* anything. She's playing at a bar on the island. I guess the police talked to Didi's parents, and they said it was okay for the police to give Didi's stuff to her."

"Fine by me," Keyheart says. "Don't know what I would have done with it. I doubt that the roommate is really broken up. Gets the place to herself, assuming she can afford it. Which she probably can't. *Musicians.* Pfft. Worse than writers, if that's possible."

"I don't know—she seems pretty upset. They knew each

other a long time. They went to boarding school together." I
pause to consider whether my next question breaks my vow to
myself and Pawlowski, but decide it doesn't. "Hey . . . I was
just wondering . . . you know how you said that you're allergic
to nuts, too?"

"Uh-huh."

"Did you ever think that—"

"Somebody switched those chocolates on purpose, trying
to kill me? I'd have to be an idiot *not* to think that. So, I guess
you've heard the stories. What are they saying? I'll bet you're
not even allowed to use some of the words they're calling me."

I manage to stammer a few words in an attempt to deny that
I've heard anything negative about her, but she motions for me
to stop.

"Puh-leeeze. I wasn't born yesterday. I hear them. They're
not exactly whispering. Especially that little weasel Howard
Allam. He tells everyone he meets about how I ruined his life.
But you know what? They can say what they want. I. Don't.
Care. I'll let you in on a little secret. Tomorrow night, my
editor—I should say my *new* editor, Jean Morse—is going to
make an announcement about my new book. We're still working out the details, but it's gonna be *ha-yuuuge*. Who knows,
I may even read a little excerpt, just to rub their noses in it a
bit. It is going to blow them all away. Just you wait. It's the best
thing I've ever written. Maybe the best thing *anybody's* written

in the past twenty years. *Way* better than *The Somewhere Girls*. This book is going to put me right back on top, where I belong. No more Swallowtales for me. I'll be on the couch chatting with Jimmy Fallon and that chubby English guy, the one who's always singing in his car."

"But I thought . . . Didi said you haven't been writing."

"Despite what she thought, Didi didn't know *everything*."

I may have promised Officer Pawlowski that I wouldn't tell anyone else about my theory, but I never said that I'd stop investigating on my own. It didn't take much effort on my part to find out where the Three Amigos were staying. As one of the bigger names on the Swallowtales faculty, Wendy Eppinger is on the top floor of the hotel in a "deluxe" corner room with an unobstructed view of the lake. Jordie Holloway, on the other hand, is stuck in a small room in the back, overlooking the parking lot. According to Nadine, he complained loudly and often and asked for an upgrade, but she finally had to tell him that he was, frankly, lucky he didn't have to share a room with a stranger. After all, he was the last to sign on to the event. The writer Howard Allam landed the second-best cottage, the Harborview. It's more rustic than the Captain's, where Keyheart and Didi started out, but in the words of the hotel brochure, "it has charm galore and spectacular views of the harbor."

When I peek out from behind some shrubbery only a few yards away from the Harborview Cottage, I see Howard Allam and Wendy Eppinger on the front deck, leaning against the railing and staring out at the lake. There's a box of Keke's Cocoas on the railing between them—a blue box, the kind with nuts. Definitely not the box that would have been in his gift basket, because according to Keke, those were all of the no-nut variety.

"It is a great view," Eppinger says. "When Brad and I were still together, he came with me one summer and we stayed in one of these cottages. I like the hotel, though. It's easier."

Allam stares out at the ferry *Niagara*, heading south for Port Clinton with a big crowd on deck, but says nothing. He reaches into the box of chocolates and throws them, one by one, into the lake. It's a box of nine, but he makes only five throws. Then he drops the empty box into the firepit, where the remains of a fire continue to smolder, sending up a thin trail of smoke.

"I just can't bear to look at those anymore," he says. "They remind me of *her*."

Allam runs his hands through his hair and rubs his face so violently that I cringe a little. His shoulders shake—clearly, he's crying—and he blurts out, "This isn't how it was supposed

BETRAYAL BY THE BOOK

to go. I still can't believe that she's *gone*. And all because of *my* bruised ego. One bad review. That's all it was, but I just couldn't let it go. I let that *witch* drag me down into the mud, and now look at me. I will never get over this."

"I'm sure it feels that way now," Eppinger says. "Give it some time. You made a mistake, and yes, there might be some changes in your life, but at the end of the day, you still have a bright career ahead of you. You can be the voice of a generation. You can't let one mistake define you."

"No. There's nothing I can do to bring her back, but I can confess everything, come clean. If I don't, I'll regret it for the rest of my life."

Eppinger takes him by the shoulders and shakes him gently. "Howard, listen to me. Do *not* do that. And for Pete's sake, don't *write* about it, either. It will only make things worse. For *everyone*. In a few days, we'll leave this Godforsaken island and go back to civilization. You'll go back to work on your book and I'll continue to search for . . . for whatever it is I'm looking for. I'm not even sure I know anymore. In the meantime, pull yourself together. A lot of people paid good money just to be in the *presence* of Howard Allam, one of the most promising young writers in America. You can't disappoint them. Come on. We need to go. We can talk about this later, after you've calmed down."

They go inside the cottage and exit through the back door

147

a few seconds later, on their way back to the hotel. As soon as they're out of sight, I climb up onto the deck. One corner of the box is black from the fire, but the rest is still in perfect condition. Trying not to touch it any more than I have to, I take it from the firepit and slip it into my backpack. It's evidence, and I know that it would be better if I left it where it is, but when the time comes, I'm going to argue that it would have been destroyed if I hadn't taken it when I did.

CHAPTER

9

BASED ON WHAT I JUST saw and heard, I'm more convinced than ever that Didi's death was the result of a murder gone bad. It's obvious that Wendy Eppinger and Howard Allam are involved, but something tells me that Jordie Holloway played a part, too. Did he really drive from New York, as he claims, to talk to Didi in person about her book? The more I think about that, the less likely it seems. According to Blake, whom I run into in the hotel parking lot, Holloway has been a last-minute addition to the Swallowtales faculty and has agreed to hold a handful of one-on-one conferences with writers who have finished their masterpieces and are looking for an agent.

"He was totally dreading it," Blake says. "He says it's like trying to find Rembrandt in a stadium full of house painters."

"But isn't that his *job*?" I say, leading Blake inside the hotel.

"I need something to—oh, crap. They saw me."

"Who? What? Oh. *Them*."

Gabby is in an upholstered chair in one of the lobby's "conversation areas," and in the chair next to her is Owen Cheever. Gabby knows that we've seen her and waves us over.

"I really don't want to go over there," I say through gritted teeth.

"Kinda awkward now if we don't," Blake says.

"More awkward if we do. What's he *doing* here anyway? Come on. Let's get it over with. Think of an excuse so we can't stay."

"We were just talking about you!" Gabby says.

"No, we weren't. Don't listen to her," says Owen, blushing a little. "I just walked in the door ten seconds ago. I'm supposed to pick up some friend of my dad's, to give him a ride to the office."

"Are you guys just going to stand there?" Gabby asks. "Have a seat."

"Uh, no . . . I can't," I say, rummaging around my brain for a good lie. "Have to . . . have to pick some things up in town for Ms. Keyheart."

Gabby snorts, "She has you doing her errands now?"

"I don't mind. It's really no big deal."

"Hey, I hear that her P.A.'s roommate is playing at the Mug Shot. And she's staying at your house."

Well. That didn't take long to get around the island. "Uh-huh."

"*And?*" Gabby says. "Tell me about her! What did she say when she found out about . . ."

"*Didi,*" I say. "I dunno. She's nice."

"She's a really good singer," adds Blake. "And guitar player."

"*You* went to the Mug Shot?" Owen asks. I can't tell if he's impressed or shocked, or both.

"No, no, no," I say. "She played for us at the house."

"You should bring her to the yacht club tomorrow," Owen says. "You *are* coming, aren't you?"

"She has to," Gabby says. "It's one of the big events. All the authors read something they're working on. I can't *wait* to hear Keyheart. Everybody says she's had writer's block for years and hasn't written a word."

"I didn't realize it was at the yacht club," Blake says. "I guess you're a member, huh?"

Another snort escapes Gabby's mouth. "Owen's family *founded* the club back in the twenties. His dad is the commodore."

Owen rolls his eyes and dismisses her with a wave. "It's no big deal. It's not exactly the New York Yacht Club." He makes eye contact with me and adds, in a hopeful tone, "So . . . we'll see you there? I mean, you and Blake?"

"Yeah, I guess so," I say.

"And bring the singer," he says. "I mean, a bunch of people listening to other people read out loud? A little music might be good."

Keyheart has been invited to a dinner party on Put-in-Bay, so I have the night off. After dinner, Pip and the boys talk poor Suzy into another mini concert out on the patio, followed by a guitar lesson, in which she successfully teaches both Jack and Nate how to play a C major chord and leaves them to battle over possession of the guitar.

"How did it go today?" I ask Suzy when we have a minute alone.

She leans back in her chair, nodding. "I'm getting there. I'm past the shock and well into the pain and guilt phase. Like all the ways I could have been a better roommate. A better friend. There's definitely some therapy in my future."

"I've got some experience with that," I say. "It helps. Sometimes. Sometimes it just takes . . . time."

"*You've* been in therapy? Like, after your mom . . . you don't have to talk about it if you don't want to."

"No, it's okay. It is sort of connected to that, I guess. I have some . . . issues. Sometimes I just kinda lose it. A couple of weeks ago, I punched a kid. In a soccer game. On the *beach*. One minute we're having fun, the next he says something I don't like. I shoulda just walked away, but I didn't. And it wasn't even the first time."

"I wouldn't have pegged you as somebody with a temper. You seem so chill."

"Thomas says I'm like a duck on a pond. Cool and calm on top, but under the surface, I'm paddling like a maniac."

"Sounds a little like Didi," Suzy says. "She could be a little manic. Hey, before I head into town, I was going to check out the stuff that the cop brought. You want to give me a hand?"

Yes!

Up in the guest room, Suzy lifts the suitcase onto the bed and unzips it.

"This feels strange. Like I'm snooping through her things. Didi would have hated this. She was super private. More than anything else, she wanted her own place. I think she hated having a roommate. I mean, we got along fine, we didn't fight or anything like that, but you could just tell. And now . . ." She wipes her eyes and sits on the edge of the bed.

"I'm sorry . . . do you want me to . . ." I take a step toward the door.

"No, no. Stay. I'm fine. I just don't know what to do with it all." The first thing she takes from the suitcase is a worn hardcover book, its dust jacket held together with yellowed tape. "Ah, her Oxford anthology. *Romantic Poetry and Prose.* This was her bible. She read from it every night. Sometimes she'd read a poem to me and then talk about it. I used to tease her about being in love with John Keats." Suzy sets it down on the bed and reaches for the next item.

Smiling, she unfolds a gray Carton Academy sweatshirt

and hands it to me. "Here. Take this at least. She would want you to have it."

"I-I can't. Why don't you keep it?"

"Nah. I've got one. Don't need another. If you're seriously thinking about going to school there, you should have it." She takes the remaining clothes, all still perfectly folded, from the bag and makes a pile. "I guess I'll just take the rest back with me and let her parents decide what to do with it. Along with her furniture, her pots and pans. Pictures. Books."

"What's this?" I ask, lifting a lone thick wool sock. "There's something in here. It's heavy."

"I dunno. What's in it?"

I reach deep inside and feel around at the bottom of the sock, which reaches all the way to the elbow of my good arm. "It feels like . . . " I pull my arm free and stare open-mouthed at the object in my hand. It is a small bird, made of silver with some of the feathers done in brilliant reddish-brown enamel that looks like melted glass.

"Ohhh. Yeah," Suzy says. "I forgot about that. She takes it everywhere she goes. I know, it's kind of strange, but it's her most prized possession. She just told me the story of how she . . . no, I'm not supposed to . . . anyway, she said she couldn't write unless it was on the table next to her. Along with . . . what's the matter? Why are you looking at it like that?"

"I have to show you something," I say, and run to my room, returning with a hardcover copy of Charles Dickens's *The Pickwick Papers* in hand. "My mom found this in a junk shop here on the island about thirty years ago. It looks like an ordinary book, but when you open it up . . . *this* is inside." I remove the swallow from its secret hiding place and hand it to Suzy.

She holds it by its tiny silver body, admiring its pointed, fighter jet wings and the brilliant blue-green enamel on the back, and then picks up Didi's bird with its similar silver body with her other hand. "They're beautiful. So different, but it's like they came from the exact same set, or were made by the same person. The engraving's identical."

"I think you're right. Mine is a tree swallow," I say. "And that one is a nightingale. In real life, nothing special to look at, but they're famous for their song. People have been writing about them for centuries. They don't live in North America. Mostly Europe and Africa. What's crazy is . . . these two birds *belong* together. They have something to do with this women's club in England, the Procne & Philomela Club, but I don't know what, because it no longer exists."

"Procne and Philomela? Like the myth?"

"I-I guess." I'm embarrassed to admit that I don't know this.

When I got the letter from Mr. Crackenthorp, I meant to look it up, but it kept slipping my mind.

"They're two sisters in Greek mythology. I took a class in college: Feminism in Mythology and Religion. I know, right? Anyway, I don't remember the whole story, but the gist of it is that something really terrible happens, yada yada, and they get turned into birds." She holds the two birds in the palms of her hands. "A swallow. And a nightingale."

"Omigosh. I feel so *stupid* that I didn't know that," I say. "They must have been important to the club. Like mascots. Does . . . *did* Didi have the book, too?"

"You mean, a book like *that*? Now that I think of it, she *did* say something about a book that was like a nest. I don't think she has it, though. I've certainly never seen it. She always kept the bird on her desk, right next to her laptop—hey, where *is* her laptop?" She takes the lid off the cardboard box and looks inside. "It's not here."

"Maybe the police still have it," I say. "Seems weird that he didn't bring it with everything else. I know it was in her room. I even have *proof.* After I called 911, I took some pictures while I was waiting, and it's *definitely* there, on her desk."

"Yeah, you're probably right. Or maybe her parents don't want me to have it. It *is* almost new. Well, we'll figure it out. Sorry, what were we talking about? The book."

"Right. Somewhere, there's a copy of *Little Dorrit*, another Dickens novel, carved out like this one. You see, the thing is . . . I've been *looking* for this exact bird. Having it show up like this is an *insane* coincidence."

I show her the letter from Archibald Crackenthorp, the story about me from the *Swallowtail Citizen*, and finally, the letter to the editor from Roseann Flaherty, the lady who remembered seeing the nightingale inside a carved-out book back in the seventies.

She reads all three quickly and then picks up the nightingale again. "You're right. This *is* crazy. More than you . . . "

"There's something else," I say. "On Saturday, right after they got here, Didi asked me to drive her out to the point on the other side of the island, over by the beach. She wanted to go to Big Egg Island. I didn't even know you could get out to it, but she knew about this sandbar . . . I guess she used to spend summers here."

"With her grandmother," Suzy says.

"She went to summer camp while she was here, and that's how she . . . she knew my *mom*."

"*What?* How?"

"Mom used to take kids from camp on these birdwatching trips, and Didi went on a bunch of them, including the one to Big Egg. Mom showed them something really cool—a bird carved into the top of a big rock there. Nobody knows if it was carved by someone, or if it's just an indentation that happens to look like a flying swallow, but somehow it led to this really deep conversation with Mom talking about how everyone wants to leave a mark on the world. Long story short, Didi said it was the day she knew she was going to be a writer. That's why she wanted to go back."

"So it was your mom who inspired her. That is . . . and then you two . . . get thrown together at a book thingy." Suzy purses her lips as if to whistle, but no sound escapes.

"I know, right? I would love to know where she got *that*," I say, pointing at Didi's silver nightingale. And did she, like, know that Mom had *this* one? She was even *here* once, she said. She remembered me. I was just a baby."

Suzy squeezes her eyes shut for several seconds, thinking hard about *something*. "I know where she got it. And how. And when. But I promised not to . . . Aaagh! I'm gonna explode unless I tell you. She would want me to. I'm sure of it. I need to find her—" She reaches into the box and pulls out a thick leather-bound journal stamped with Didi's initials. She unties the heavy ribbon that's wrapped around it and slowly lifts the cover. Inside is a small envelope that she hands me. "Take a look at this."

"What's is it?" I ask, examining the envelope, yellow with age, and brittle-feeling in my hand. It is addressed to Mrs. Joanna Murray, 22 Buckeye Street, Swallowtail Island, Ohio, in a child's slightly shaky

handwriting. Above the return address is Didi's name. The envelope is still sealed shut. There's no postmark and the stamp has not been canceled. "I don't get it. Why didn't she . . ."

"It's kind of a long story."

"I've got no place to go. If you're sure you have time."

"Yeah, I'm good for a while." Suzy leans back against the headboard. "A couple of months ago, somehow both of us ended up being home on a Friday night, so we ordered Chinese, and after a bottle of wine, she started talking. She swore she'd never told *anyone*, not even her therapist. She was so ashamed, which was crazy. I mean, she was just a kid when it all happened. When she was seven or eight, her grandmother showed her this bird for the first time. The way Didi described it, the house had a library in a kind of a tower room and the whole thing was this super-special bonding moment for the two of them. Her grandmother told her that the bird had been left behind by the previous owner when she bought the house in 1976, and said that as far as she was concerned, it belonged to the house. Or the house belonged to it."

"*That's* interesting," I say.

"Seriously. But Didi swore there was something to it. The moment her grandmother shared it with her, and Didi held it in her own hands, she felt this . . . she said it was a *connection* to her grandmother, and the house. Like they were all on exactly the same wavelength is how Didi put it. Something she'd never felt with her mom, who isn't exactly the warm, maternal type, if you know what I mean. Taking care of a kid just didn't fit into her social life. And her dad is some kind of bigshot in the sailing world. He's always off at some big regatta in Europe or New Zealand or someplace. So, for Didi, summers with her grandmother meant something really special. She couldn't wait for the school year to end so she could head out here to see her grandma and hold the bird in her hands. And then . . ." Suzy pauses, shaking her head slowly.

"Uh-oh," I say.

"Yeah. She was twelve years old and had been at her grandma's all summer. As she's packing up to go back to the city, she snuck into the library and swiped the bird. She cried about it the whole way home, terrified that her grandmother would find out that she'd stolen it and wouldn't love her anymore."

"Oh. That's horrible. Poor Didi. Her grandmother probably would have given it to her."

"Wait. It gets worse. Didi was trying to work up the courage to tell her grandmother what she did, and to promise to return it. She was afraid to call, so she wrote a letter. *That* letter. It was in the envelope, on her desk with a stamp and everything when she got the news: her grandmother was dead. She died in her sleep. Didi was devastated. And, in the way that only a twelve-year-old's brain can twist things around—no offense—she blamed herself. Not just for her grandmother dying, for *every-thing* that went wrong afterward. And a *lot* went wrong, and all of it right after she stole the bird. Her mother disappeared in Europe for a few months, leaving Didi in New York with her nanny. Said she was 'looking for herself' but more likely, she was looking for a way to avoid taking care of Didi, and to spend the money she'd inherited on clothes. The whole time her mother was gone, her father never once came home. Their dog got hit by a car. There was a fire in their apartment. First she gained a bunch of weight. Then she developed an eating disorder. When I first met her at Carton a couple of years later, she was a *mess*. She went through three or four roommates her first year. She chased one of them out with a broom because she misquoted Shakespeare. Honestly? I didn't think there was much hope for her."

"But she got better, right?" I say. "Saturday, she seemed . . . *happy*."

"Yeah, totally. Especially after she got serious about writing. She'd been in therapy for years, but she said that writing was better than spending an hour a week with a therapist. She started writing seriously during her last two years at Carton—you know, poetry, short stories, stuff for the literary magazine. Then college and grad school, more of the same. I've never met anyone so dedicated. *Every* night after work, she sat down and started writing at exactly eight o'clock and kept at it until midnight. And I mean *every* night. Other than the laptop, there were two things on the table, always in the same position: the letter that she never mailed and *that* bird."

"She told me that she wrote every day, that she had just

finished a book," I say. "She was so excited about it."

"Yeah, she was psyched. She worked on that thing, writing and rewriting, over and over, for years. Never let me—or anybody else, as far as I know—read a word of it. Said I'd have to wait till it was published like everyone else. That's the thing, though. She was *sure* it would get published. Positive."

"Supposedly, Keyheart promised to talk to her editor about it," I say, "but Didi wasn't sure if she actually did. It sounded like Didi knew she couldn't count on Keyheart, so she also sent it to an agent who really liked it. What's gonna happen with *that* now?"

"Her book? That's a *great* question. She didn't have brothers or sisters, and I doubt that she has a will, so it belongs to her parents, I guess. It could still get published. It's happened before. But man, that *sucks*. It's all she wanted. The finish line was in sight, and then . . . " Suzy turns her attention to the box with the rest of Didi's things, and starts going through it. She smiles as she holds up the pendant that Didi wore—the interlocking *D*s on a silver chain.

"The chain broke when she . . . when she fell," I say. "She was holding *that* in her hand when I found her."

"She wore it everywhere," Suzy says. "Since we moved in together, I don't think I ever saw her without it. She never said anything, but it must have had some sentimental value. It's not even real silver. It feels kinda cheap. Unlike her *watch*, which is the real thing." She sets the pendant on top of the pile of clothes and reaches back into the box.

"I don't remember her wearing a watch," I say.

"I'm not surprised. Most of the time, it sat on the table next to her bed. Ah! Here it is." Suzy dangles the watch in front of me, a brand that I recognize from billboards along I-95 between New York and Connecticut. "College graduation gift from her parents—not that they had anything to do with picking it out, I'm sure. I'm amazed they even remembered. Didi never wore it. She didn't like wearing something that expensive that she didn't earn for herself."

"Maybe her parents will want you to have it," I say. "For helping out and all."

"As much as I love it, I couldn't take it," Suzy admits. "It wouldn't feel right, ya know what I mean? It would be one thing if she gave it to me, but knowing that she had to die for me to have a nice watch . . . I could never wear it. I guess she and I weren't so different."

"You know what I think?" I say.

"What?"

"I think you were a better friend to Didi than you give yourself credit for. And vice versa."

Suzy smiles, but it's a sad, thoughtful smile, and her eyes turn watery again. "I think you might be right."

"And you know how you said that she would want me to

have this sweatshirt? She'd want you to have that watch, I'd bet anything."

"Yeah, well, we'll see. In the meantime, it's going to her parents. I think I *will* keep the pendant, though." She opens the clasp of the chain around her neck and threads it through the loop on Didi's silver *DD*, and smiles as she tucks it under her shirt collar. "Our little secret, okay?"

I nod and pull a make-believe zipper across my lips.

"What about this?" Suzy says, holding out the silver nightingale in her hand. "It's weird, I know, but it *belongs* on Swallowtail Island. This is where it came from. I think it's *home*."

The clock next to my bed reads two thirty when the wind shifts and one of the French doors to the balcony off our bedroom slams shut. Pogo hops down from the bed to investigate as I glance over at Pip, still fast asleep.

"It's okay, girl," I tell Pogo. But she stays at the door, sniffing and insisting that perhaps I should investigate, so I climb out of bed, too. It's one of those perfect nights, the kind that makes me angry that I have to sleep. There's a half moon hanging low and yellow, its reflection painted with smooth, even strokes on the ruffled surface of the lake. Just to the north, the lighted buoy at Ada's Shoal flashes its warning once every second, and farther off in the distance are the lights of a freighter heading west for the Detroit River Light.

Pogo leans against me as I stare out across the water, and my mind starts to wander. Before long, I'm thinking about the never-mailed letter to her grandmother that Didi carried with her for so many years. But as I picture the envelope with twelve-year-old Didi's handwriting, something about the address stands out: 22 Buckeye Street. That's the same house where Barrie Francis, the girl who took the nightingale to school for show-and-tell, lived. Didi's grandmother must have bought the house from the Francis family when they moved away in 1976, and stayed there until she died about ten years ago.

"Swallowtail Island is a strange place," I say.

Pogo's tail thumps against my leg; clearly, she agrees with me.

CHAPTER
10

IT'S TUESDAY, DAY THREE OF Swallowtales—the halfway point. There are some special guest speakers in the morning and Keyheart's morning class has been moved to late afternoon, so I'm officially off-duty until four. The event at the yacht club doesn't start until seven thirty, which means that it's going to be a late night babysitting Keyheart and making sure she gets back to the hotel without falling (or being pushed) into the lake.

Also on my agenda for the day: a follow-up snooping session on Howard Allam and Wendy Eppinger. His words keep running through my head: *This isn't how it was supposed to go. I still can't believe that she's* gone. *And all because of* my *bruised ego. One bad review. That's all it was, but I just couldn't let it go.*

I mean, he has to be talking about Didi, and how Keyheart's review of his book drove him to try to kill her, right? He's obviously feeling really guilty about it—so guilty that it's obvious that Wendy Eppinger is concerned that he's going to confess his crime. And who knows how involved *she* is. One thing for sure, she has her own reasons to hate Keyheart. The only reasonable conclusion is that one of them—or both—switched the chocolates.

Getting close to Howard Allam may require me to hang around with Gabby Bensikova, though, which adds a degree of aggravation. I don't care how talented she is; she's a pain in the butt.

Thomas enters the kitchen for a refill of his coffee and sees me just as I'm thinking about Gabby. "What's *that* face all about? You look like you did that time you tried espresso."

"What? Oh. Nothing. Just something I have to do later. But not for a while. I have the morning off."

"This is *excellent* news," Thomas says. "In that case, you can do me a huge favor."

"Oh, yeah?"

"Yup. Pip's taking Tinker over to Nadine's today for a riding lesson with a friend of Nadine's, but I didn't know what to do with Nate and Jack. If *you* take them all over there for the day, though, I'm sure you can find some way to keep them entertained and out of trouble. And this way, I can get some work done. Two of the paintings I'm working on are ready to go back in their frames, and I would love to be able to get them back on the museum wall."

Thomas is an art restorer, and has been working all summer long on some artwork at the Cheever Museum.

"Sure," I say, grinning as Pip, Jack, and Nate cheer enthusiastically.

Thomas looks suspiciously at me. "That's it? No argument?"

I shrug. "No big deal. I have some things I need to talk to Nadine about anyway."

"Sounds serious. Everything all right? How is your, er, Ms. Keyheart? Still making friends and influencing people?"

"Ha. Yeah, you could say that."

A few minutes later, the boys and I are on bikes right behind Pip and Tinker as we make the turn out of the yard when we spot Suzy coming down the lane. She is in shorts, T-shirt, and a New York Mets cap with her pink ponytail pulled through the back, and strolls up to us flashing a bright smile. "It is a *perfect* day," she says. "I love this place."

"I thought you were still in bed," I say. "Your door was shut."

"I've been up for *hours*," she says. "It's too beautiful to sleep. First I said hello to Pip's pony, and then I went for a long walk, past the museum, all the way out to this little tip of land. On the way back, I ended up talking to this old woman—Dinah somebody—for a long time. Boy, she sure likes *you*. When I told her I was staying with you guys, she lit up like a Christmas tree. Told me how lucky I am."

"Dinah Purdy," I say. "She's awesome, isn't she? Nadine's writing a book about her. She's had an amazing life. You won't believe the people she's met."

"I love that she lives way out there all by herself. I wanna be that independent when I'm old," Suzy says. "And I agree, by the way, about how lucky I am. Can I just thank you again for inviting me to stay here? You've changed my life. Seriously. I'm gonna take my guitar down by the lake and just chill today. Finish the song I started writing last night. Kind of inspired by Didi. Where're you all off to?"

"Nadine's. Come by if you want. Thomas can draw you a map."

"Maybe I will," she says dreamily.

"She is so cool," Nate says, watching her walk toward the house.

"*Somebody* is crushing hard on Suzy," I say.

"How old d'you think she is?" Nate asks.

"Too old for you, that's for sure. Don't worry, when school starts, you'll meet lots of girls your age. You're gonna be the new kid. They're gonna *love* you. You, too, Jack."

"Ewww," Jack says. "Girls are weird."

"What about Pip and me?"

"That's different. You're not regular girls. You're my sisters."

"I see. Thanks for clearing that up."

"You're still weird," says Nate.

Pip's face lights up when she gets her first glimpse of the fenced-in paddock adjacent to Nadine's enormous horse barn. Two other horses with riders about Pip's age and size are trotting in slow circles, while a guy in jeans and a Hiram College sweatshirt watches and gives instructions. When he sees Pip, he climbs over the fence and greets her and Tinker.

"Hi there! I'm Eric. Nadine's nephew. I remember this pretty little girl," he says, petting Tinker's nose. "Hello, Tinker. And you must be Pip. Go ahead in. We're just getting everybody warmed up."

"Have fun, Pip," I say. "See you later."

Nadine waves from her porch and the boys and I join her.

"I wasn't expecting everybody," she says. "What a nice surprise. You met Eric? Hey, do you boys want to see something really cool? Follow me."

She leads us to the smaller, older barn on her property. The roof sags noticeably, there are some gaps in the siding, and it is well beyond needing a coat of paint. On the day I started working for her back in June, she showed me what's inside: the wreck of her grandfather's speedboat. The smashed-up hull collected dust in the barn for seventy-five years, but ever since we proved that the crash was no accident—it was a murder, planned and carried out by Gilbert Cheever, the brother of Captain Edward Cheever—a number of people have shown some interest in buying and restoring the boat to its original, varnished mahogany beauty.

When I saw it in June, it was bottom side up with the damage clearly visible. It has been turned over, though, revealing the deck and two cockpits. It doesn't take much imagination to see how beautiful it must have been when it was new.

"Awesome!" Nate exclaims.

"I tried to clean it up a little," Nadine says. "Les Findlay brought some guys out from the boatyard and they flipped it and put it up on blocks. One of them really wants to buy it, but I'm still debating whether to sell it or not. If I can talk Les into doing the work, I might just keep it. It would be fun, don't you think, tooling around the islands in this?"

"How fast does it go?" Jack asks.

"About fifty miles an hour," Nadine says. *"Fast."*

"Can we get in it?" Nate asks.

"Be my guest," Nadine says. "Take her for a spin. Just be careful of rusty nails and that sort of thing."

Nate and Jack climb in immediately and sit on the torn leather seats. Nate grips the steering wheel in one hand and waves at us with the other. "Catch ya later! Vroooommm!"

"Hold on, Jack!" I shout over Nate's impression of a motor.

"Come back here for lunch," adds Nadine with a wave.

"Well, that was easy," I say. "I wasn't sure what to do with them today, but they'll be entertained for hours. You're sure it's okay? 'Cause if there's anything breakable, Nate will find a way to break it."

"Eh. No worries. It's been sitting for seventy-five years. Let them have some fun. So. Pip's all set, the boys are all set. Let's you and me have some tea and gingersnaps and chat a bit. I'm dying to know the latest with Ann Keyheart."

"I've got a *lot* to tell you," I say. "And not just about her. I've decided that Swallowtail Island is in the Twilight Zone. There's just too many weird coincidences."

We sit in the shade on her porch where I tell her everything that's happened since the last time I saw her at the hotel when Suzy arrived, finishing up with the discovery of the second silver bird from Crackenthorp Books in Didi's things, and my middle-of-the-night revelation about the house on Buckeye Street.

Nadine lets out a whistle when I finish. "Wow. You're right. Very Twilight Zone-y. But one thing I've learned in all my travels and doing the research for my books, is that most coincidences are not as unlikely as you'd think. I have an old college friend who's a math professor, and she uses this example to teach people about coincidences. It's called the birthday problem. There's three hundred and sixty-six possible birthdays, right? Well, here's the thing. If you put twenty-three random people in a room, there's a *fifty* percent chance that two of them will have the same birthday."

"Wa-ait," I say. "Twenty-three? That can't be right."

"Remember, it's not saying two will *have* the same birthday, just that there's a fifty-fifty chance of it. But it only takes *sixty* people to get it up to ninety-nine percent. Crazy, isn't it? I can tell you're skeptical, but google 'birthday problem' and you'll see."

"Yeah, I'm gonna have to. That doesn't sound right."

"So, what do we know about the two birds?" Nadine asks. "According to Crackenthorp's letter, his father sent them to Captain Cheever in nineteen forty-one."

"The *swallow* never left the island, as far as we know. It ended up at a junk shop, where Mom found it in nineteen eighty-nine or 'ninety. The nightingale was here until about twenty ten when Didi, um, got it from her grandmother."

"The next question is, how did it get from Captain Cheever to Didi's grandmother in nineteen seventy-six? Who owned it from forty-one till seventy-six?"

"Barrie Francis must have left it in the house," I answer. "They left in a hurry. They were moving to South America. Maybe she couldn't take it. Or just forgot it."

"Where did *she* get it? There's still thirty-five years to account for."

Before I can attempt to answer, Nate and Jack come tearing across the yard at a full sprint, with Nate shouting, "We found something!"

He drops a badly stained and cracked leather envelope on the table. Most of the flap has been chewed away by mice, and all the stitching has rotted away, but still visible in the corner are the initials *AMP*, deeply embossed in the leather.

"It was all the way under the seat," Jack says. "I dropped a gummy bear and was looking for it, and there it was."

"We didn't open it, I swear," Nate says. "But you can feel something inside."

"This was my grandfather's," Nadine says. "Those are his initials. Albert Michael Pritchard. You're serious? This was under the seat all those years? And no one ever looked. Amazing."

Nate shrugs. "Me and Jack are always finding cool stuff."

"Yeah! We found a really cool old motor—" Jack starts, but Nate quickly shushes him and points at the envelope.

"You gonna open it?" he asks.

"Definitely," Nadine says. She lifts what is left of the flap, gently folds it back, and peeks inside. "I feel a little like Indiana Jones."

"Who's that?" Nate asks.

"Who's that! Are you serious? Nate, Nate, Nate. We have some work to do," she says as she carefully removes a heavy manila folder with several sheets of paper inside, followed by a black fountain pen, two unopened—and undisturbed by mice—packs of Beemans gum, a small campaign button that reads I Want Roosevelt Again and finally, a tarnished silver keychain with a single key attached.

"Cool," says Nate.

Inside the folder, the papers are wrinkled and stuck together, and the ink has faded or disappeared, so Nadine struggles to pull them apart enough to make sense of the contents. First she shakes her head, and then she rubs her chin. Finally, she sets the papers on the table and intertwines her fingers on top of her head.

"This is unreal," she says. "You are *not* going to believe it. I've read it and I'm not sure I do."

"What is it?" I ask. "Something about Captain Cheever's will?" Nadine's grandfather was a lawyer and had drafted a new will for the captain shortly before his death.

"No, nothing like that. It's the papers for a house he and my grandmother were buying. Everything's signed. The deed is here. That's the key. They bought it right before he went to

Canada, right before he died in the boat crash. He never lived in it. I don't know if she did. It's not the house she was living in when I was growing up."

"Is it—the house—here on the island?" I ask.

Nadine nods solemnly. "That's just it. That's the crazy part. The address. It's Twenty-two Buckeye Street."

I feel my mouth drop open. "No. Way."

"I take back everything I said about coincidences," Nadine says.

"No, wait. This makes *total* sense," I say. "Think about it. What if, back in the forties, Captain Cheever gave the book with the nightingale to your grandfather. That would explain how it ended up in the house. And maybe it just, you know, *stayed* with the house all these years."

"It's *possible*, I suppose," says Nadine.

Ten minutes later, a call to the registry of deeds confirms that Nadine's grandmother Maria Pritchard owned the house for more than twenty years, selling it in 1967 to the Francis family, who sold it to Didi's grandmother in 1976.

"Who owns it now?" I ask. "Wait, let me guess. Reggie Cheever?"

Nadine's eyes are suddenly as big as dinner plates. "How did you . . . you already knew that, didn't you?"

"No, I swear," I say. "I just figured, you know, with all these coincidences, who else? Besides, it seems like they own everything."

"That's not far from the truth. It's a small island and the Cheevers *have* been here for a long time. They own a number of houses. They buy them cheap and rent them out for the summers. I'm sure they bought the house in an estate sale. From what you've said about Didi's parents, they don't sound like the Swallowtail type. And it's hard to imagine they had any sentimental attachment. They may have sold it 'as is'—furniture and everything—just to be rid of it."

"I would *love* to look around in that house," I say.

"What do you think you'll find?" Nadine asks. "You already know where both birds are."

"Yeah, but not the second book. *Little Dorrit* might still be there."

"Maybe there's a doggie door," Nate says. "I could crawl in. Or a basement window. We need a plan, like last time, when I got to jump out the window and then you did and broke your arm. That was cool."

"No. No, no, no," Nadine orders. "No jumping or crawling or sneaking of any kind. You need to keep on the down-low as far as Reggie Cheever is concerned. Don't give him any more reasons to come after you. Promise?"

"Scout's honor," I say.

"Hmmm," Nadine says, eyeing me skeptically and then turning to Nate and Jack. "You two are my witnesses. No shenanigans."

"What's a shenanigan?" Jack asks.

"I'll explain it later," says Nate. "Nadine, can I ask you a question?"

"Sure. Anything."

Nate, biting his lip, shoots a nervous glance in my direction and then whispers to Nadine, "Ummm, in private? About something in the barn."

"What are you up to?" I say as he and Nadine start across the yard toward the barn where the old speedboat is stored.

"Nothing."

"Mmm-hmmm." I turn and stare at Jack. "What's going on, Jack? Tell me."

"I don't know anything!" he cries, and then runs after Nate and Nadine.

When they exit the barn a few minutes later, they're all smiling.

"This is just *wrong*," I say.

"Remember," Nadine says to Nate, "nothing happens till I talk to your dad, all right?"

"I promise," Nate says.

"Come on, you guys. You *know* you can't keep a secret from me. Especially *Jack*."

Jack hides behind Nate, afraid to look me in the eyes.

"Don't let her scare you, Jack," says Nate. "She's always keeping stuff from us. Now it's her turn."

CHAPTER
11

THE INVITATION TO THE EVENT at the yacht club specifies *dressy dress*, which Thomas interprets as a button-down and tie for Blake, and a dress for me. I'm tempted to wear the same apple-green number that Nadine bought me for the museum gala in July, but it seems too soon, especially since some of the same people will be there. Unfortunately, I only have one other choice, which is exactly the same shade of blue as Blake's shirt.

"You look like twins," Pip says when Thomas insists on taking a picture of Blake and me in the front yard. "It's so cute. Just like the museum party, when you and *O-wennn* were all matchy-matchy."

"Ewww. I forgot about that," Nate says. He and Pip still view me as a traitor for being friendly with Owen Cheever, and on the few occasions they stoop to mention his name, it always comes out as *O-wennn*. They definitely preferred the version of me that punched him in the nose for calling Blake names during what had been a friendly game of soccer on the beach.

"We were *not* matchy-matchy," I say. "I can't help it if he *happened* to wear a tie that was the same color as my dress. It's not like we planned it."

"Is he gonna be there tonight?" Nate asks.

"Yeah," Pip says. "Maybe you should call him and ask what he's wearing."

"All right, all right," says Thomas. "That's enough. Lark, you look great. You, too, Blake. That shirt could use a little ironing, but . . . never mind. Go. Have fun."

As we're settling into the seat of the golf cart, Nate goes to Blake's side and whispers something to him.

"Twenty dollars!" Blake cries. "For what?"

Nate shoots a look at me and then turns back to Blake. "Shhh! It's for the . . . you know. I . . . it needs something. A couple of things. I'll pay you back."

"Yeah, right. When?" says Blake.

"Next week. I promise. C'mon."

"What's going on?" I ask.

Blake and Nate together: "Nothing."

"Fine. Keep your secrets. *I* don't care." The GHT? I do care. A lot. "Come on, Blake. Give him the money so we can get out of here."

Blake reaches into his pants pocket and pulls out two ten-dollar bills. He hands them over to Nate, who takes them and runs back into the house. "Dad! I have to go into town. And then to Nadine's. I'm taking my bike! See you later!"

Blake steps on the accelerator and we rumble down the drive and make the turn for town.

"So, seriously, what was that all about?" I ask. "What is the big secret?"

"I'm not allowed to tell," he answers. "He wants it to be a surprise."

"A surprise for . . . what?"

"Who knows. This is Nate we're talking about, remember."

"Right. I see what you mean," I say before changing the subject. "He *is* gonna be there tonight, you know. Owen, I mean."

"Yeah, I know. I was with you when you talked to him. Remember?"

"Oh. Yeah. His father will probably be there too."

"It doesn't matter," Blake says. "He's not gonna do anything at his own yacht club, in front of a million people."

"I know, I know. Just stay away from him."

"Are you *worried* about me?"

"No, but I don't trust him. Even Owen doesn't really like him. When we were talking about boarding school, he said he wanted to go, to get away from his dad."

"Wow. Really? His own father. I can't believe he's *that* bad."

"You didn't see him out on the water that day," I say. "I've never seen anybody so mad."

"Well, you *did* sink his boat."

"*I* didn't sink it. He did that all by himself."

"Maybe *you* should stay away from him, just to be safe," Blake advises as he parks the cart on the street in front of the yacht club. "I would tell you to stick close to Keyheart, but she scares me a little."

"Join the club," I say. "*Everybody's* afraid of her."

The inside of the yacht club is pretty much what you'd expect: lots of ship models and paintings of sailboats covering most of the dark wood paneling, and the smell of cigars and something else that I can't quite put my finger on.

"It's *money*," Blake says.

There's a crowd around the bar, and another in the much larger Commodore's Room, where a podium is set up for the readings. Blake spots Jordie Holloway at the end of the bar and gives me a quick wave goodbye as he squeezes between two rather large women in gaudy floral print dresses. If Keyheart is here, she'll be within spitting distance of the bar, so I rise onto my toes and scan the room. I hear her husky voice calling out to the bartender for a refill, and follow the sound until I spot her holding her glass above her head. The ever-present superfan, Irwin, is at her side. With a sigh, I follow Blake's path, smiling at the same two flowery women as I slip past them, and then tap Keyheart on the shoulder.

She spins around in a crush of people and ends up practically pressed against me. In slow motion, she tilts her head back to look up at my face. She doesn't seem to recognize me at first, but after a couple of seconds says, "Oh. It's you. Linda Lou. Where have you *been* all day?"

"I-I thought you said to . . . I didn't know . . . "

Keyheart lets out a loud cackle. "You should see your face! I . . . I . . . I didn't *know*. I thought you said to take the day off. Ha! Relax! I'm yanking your chain."

"Oh. That's good. I mean, that you were, that you didn't need anything."

She takes a swig of her drink, frowning when she realizes the glass is still empty. "Geez. Would it kill them to pour a decent drink? Bartender! Oy! Another, but this time try putting some booze in it. I thought sailors knew how to drink."

A flurry of activity at the other end of the bar makes her turn around, and when she does, she spots Suzy, chatting with Blake and Jordie Holloway.

"Is that who I think it is?" she asks, motioning toward Suzy. "How did *she* get in?"

"She, uh, Nadine gave her Didi's ticket," I say. "It seemed like a nice thing to do."

"Oh. Right. Saint Didi." She makes the sign of the cross and I take a step back, waiting for lightning to strike her on the spot.

Meanwhile, the bartender sets her drink on the bar. She looks at it, and then up at him. "Really? That's the best you can do? I thought we had a real connection."

He grabs a bottle and pours another half inch into her glass, glaring at her all the while.

"That's more like it," she says, spinning around.

"You're welcome," the bartender mutters at the back of her head.

A few feet away, I recognize the back of another familiar head: Owen Cheever's. His blond hair is not pulled up into its usual boy-bun and hangs down nearly to his shoulders. I lean to the left to see who he's talking to, and quickly straighten back up when I realize that it's Gabby Bensikova. She's hanging on to his arm with both hands and laughing at something he's said. Her pretty head tilts back just so, showing off that long, elegant dancer's neck, and just like that, I find myself aggravated enough that I have to remind myself to unclench my jaw.

But wait.

What do I care if she flirts with Owen? I don't like him, not like that. I mean, I don't, right? The GHT is that I don't know *what* I'm feeling, and that is *not* a good thing. If I'm not in complete control of my feelings, that means somebody else is, which is totally unacceptable in my world.

A moment later, I want to crawl under the rug when he turns around and catches me mid-stare. I avert my eyes as quickly as I can, but not before watching him yank his arm back from Gabby's two-handed grip or her eager smile and wave in my direction.

I'm spared any further embarrassment when Nadine's voice rings out over the PA system, asking everyone to gather in the Commodore's Room for the start of the main event, the reading of new works by the Swallowtales faculty and guest authors.

"You must be really excited," I say to Keyheart. "Are you nervous? I mean, because it's your new book and all? Is this the first time you've read from it?"

"This is it," she says. "I've kept it secret long enough. Time for people to see what I've been doing the past five years."

"Good luck," I say as she toddles off toward the line of chairs set up behind the podium for the authors.

When she's gone, I meet up with Blake and Suzy, and we choose a spot at the back of the room to stand and watch. Owen slides into the space next to me, but a second later, Gabby squeezes in between us.

"Who's the cute guy?" Suzy whispers in my ear, motioning in Owen's direction.

"Remember the story I told you about me punching a boy?" I whisper back.

"*That's* him?" she says loudly enough that both Owen and Gabby turn their heads.

"Shhh!" I say, wishing I was invisible.

Suzy's moves her face right next to mine and without moving her lips, she murmurs, "He likes you." After I shoot her a look, she adds, "Okay, okay. I'm just making sure you know, in case you, well, you know."

Keyheart, who has insisted on being the final reader of the night, is seated in the last chair to the right of the podium, where I have a clear view of her. For the most part, she is well-behaved through the readings, although she yawns and makes a point of checking her watch when she thinks someone has gone on too long.

Howard Allam, next to last, is in the seat next to Keyheart, and he looks absolutely *miserable*. There is nothing subtle about his body language. He is literally sitting on the edge of his chair, with his body turned and legs crossed away from Keyheart.

When Nadine introduces him, he rises and walks slowly to the podium, tightly gripping a handful of loose pages and looking as if he'd rather be almost anywhere else.

"Thank you," he says quietly as the audience applauds enthusiastically. Then, for what feels like a long time, he stands there shuffling the papers, staring at them with a bewildered expression.

Wendy Eppinger, standing against the wall on the left side of the room, shakes her head in disbelief, while Keyheart looks on with a smirk.

"Well, *this* is awkward," Suzy whispers.

"Seriously," I say.

"He's just nervous," Gabby says. "He told me that he's not very comfortable in front of a crowd. Plus, you know, a lot of writers are *super* insecure when it comes to sharing new stuff for the first time."

Finally, Allam looks up at the gathered crowd. "I'm sorry, everyone. I'm—I'm not quite myself tonight. I don't know . . . I have to confess . . . I've made a mess of things. My life is chock full of truffles, er, I mean, it's chocolate troubles." He stops and gathers himself. "My life is chock full of *troubles* at the moment. I've made some terrible, *horrible* mistakes—mistakes that have hurt people. I just want to say I'm sorry. So sorry."

Whoa. Once again, my mind goes back instantly to his conversation with Wendy Eppinger on the deck of his cottage, and the image of him throwing Keke's Cocoas into the lake because they reminded him of *her*.

Wendy Eppinger starts toward the front of the room, probably to drag him away from the microphone before he says anything more, but stops when he seems to pull himself together.

He tilts his head back, takes three long, deep breaths, and with one big final exhale, starts to read from his novel in progress.

When he finishes, he gets thirty seconds of well-deserved applause, which seems to bring him out of whatever funk he has been in.

"He is *so* talented," Gabby says. "I can't *wait* to read the whole thing."

"What was that whole chocolate truffle thing about?" Blake whispers to me. "For a second, I thought he was having a stroke or something. It was *weird*."

"It's even weirder than you think," I say as Howard Allam returns to his seat. "I'll tell you about it later."

Nadine introduces Ann Keyheart as the "bestselling author of more than a dozen books, including the modern classic *The Somewhere Girls.*" When she mentions that particular book, the crowd applauds and I find myself suddenly looking forward to hearing something new from the writer who wrote the book that I've spent so many hours reading and rereading.

"Well, this ought to be entertaining, at least," Suzy says as

Keyheart steps up to the microphone, all humility and smiles, and looking like butter wouldn't melt in her mouth.

"Thank you, thank you. You're too kind," Keyheart begins. "I would like to dedicate tonight's reading to my assistant and dear, dear friend, Didi Ferrer, who sadly passed away earlier this week. Didi was"—she pauses to wipe away a tear, and then continues—"Didi was the best assistant I ever had. She put up with me and took care of me and I will miss her tremendously. Didi, my friend, this is for you." She looks up at the ceiling and dramatically blows a kiss upward.

Suzy's eyes meet mine and we both stifle a laugh.

"Unbelievable," Suzy says, shaking her head. "The woman has no shame."

Up at the podium, Keyheart places a hand over her heart. "Goodness. I'm actually a little nervous. I'm reading from my new book, and I haven't shared this with anyone. It's called *A Drowsy Numbness,* and the narrator is a young woman named Dorie. This episode is a flashback to when she was twelve."

She takes a breath and in the moments before she starts to read, the room is eerily silent.

And then it gets weird. Like, *really* weird.

In the flashback scene that Keyheart reads, the young Dorie is visiting her grandmother at her home on Carleton Island at the eastern end of Lake Ontario. But other than that minor change in the setting, the story is very, very familiar; it is Didi's story, from the summer that she stole the silver nightingale from its secret hiding place inside a book. In the days that follow, she struggles with the guilt, finally writing a letter to her grandmother, confessing her crime. In the final lines that Keyheart reads, though, Dorie reveals that she never gets to mail the letter, because she learns that her grandmother has died.

Keyheart closes her folder and looks up, and after a collective *ohhh nooo*, a hundred hand-to-the-heart gestures, and many heads slowly shaking in sympathy for poor Dorie, the audience explodes in a lengthy ovation.

Meanwhile, Suzy and I stand frozen in place, staring at each other with mouths open wide in utter disbelief and horror. Jordie Holloway, a few rows in front of us, storms out of the room, muttering, "She did it again," to Blake as he goes by.

When he turns to watch Holloway leave, Blake sees our faces. "What's going on? Why do you two look like that?"

"Because she *stole* Didi's story," Suzy hisses.

"B-But wait a second. Didi was supposed to be here too," I say. "Obviously, *she* would have recognized her own story. Is it possible she . . ."

I stop myself because I know the answer: Not a chance.

"She *swore* to me that I was the only person she ever told," says Suzy. "And I believe her. She never lied. And the letter to her grandmother? No way she told Keyheart about that."

Nadine joins the still-beaming Keyheart at the podium. "Wow. That was . . . *unexpected*. I think we can all agree that this has been a special evening. Something tells me that this is one of those Woodstock moments. One day soon, we'll—all of us who are lucky enough to be here tonight, that is—will be telling people that we were *here* for the very first reading from Ann Keyheart's new book. Ann, will you stay and answer a few questions from the audience? I'm sure everyone would love to hear what you have to say."

"You can say *that* again," Suzy says. "I have a few questions for her."

The first question, from a girl I recognize from Keyheart's class, is the usual "where did you get the idea for the story," and Keyheart replies with a rambling, nonsensical answer in which she mentions a story she had heard "somewhere, I don't remember where, but a long time ago," and had only recently figured out how to turn it into a complete novel.

"What's the deal with the title?" asks a burly guy with a shaved head and a long black beard. "How'd you come up with that?"

"Oh, good," Nadine says. "I was hoping someone would ask that. As a writer, I struggle to find titles for my own books. Tell us how you landed on *A Drowsy Numbness*. It certainly is interesting."

"Oh, thank you so much," Keyheart gushes. "It's a line from that Walt Whitman poem, 'Ode to a Nightingale.' I just thought it was a good fit, you know? There's a kind of melancholy to it, and, of course, there's a nightingale in the story."

Blake pokes me in the ribs with his elbow. "That's wrong."

"What?"

"'Ode to a Nightingale' isn't Whitman. Not even close. It's Keats. *Everyone* knows that."

"You're sure?" I ask. "I don't know much about poetry."

"I'm *positive*. I love that poem," Blake answers. "We read it in class last year. It's the first line: *My heart aches, and a drowsy numbness pains my sense, as though of hemlock I had drunk.*"

"Wow. First, I'm really impressed," Suzy says. "And you're right. It's Keats. Didi loved that poem. She knew it by heart, too."

"Something's wrong," I say. "It doesn't add up. First, Didi tells me that Keyheart hasn't written anything in over a year. But somehow Keyheart shows up on the island with a book that she is super confident is going to be a bestseller."

"And then she gets up there and tells *Didi's* story," Suzy says.

"And now *this*, with the poem," I say. "How could Keyheart possibly *not* know who wrote the poem that she used for the title? Unless . . . "

The noise and bustle of the crowd fades into silence in my head as I stare at a knot in the paneling above the glowing red exit sign at the far end of the room.

"Uh-oh," Blake says, backing away from me. "I've seen that look before. Thomas calls it your thousand-yard stare. What are you thinking?"

"Keyheart didn't steal Didi's story," I say.

"What are you *talking* about? You heard it!" Suzy cries.

"Wait, let me finish. She didn't just steal *that* story. I think she stole Didi's entire *book* and is going to pass it off as her own."

"Whoa," Suzy says quietly. "That is . . . oh, man. We can't let her—"

"We've got to figure out a way to *prove* that Didi wrote it," I say.

"Her laptop!" says Suzy. "We have to find that thing."

"If *anyone* can find it, she can," Blake says, pointing at me. "It'll probably involve a broken bone or two and an insane chase scene with bikes, horses, and speedboats, but trust me, she'll find it."

I work hard to avoid Keyheart for the rest of the night because, knowing what I *think* I know, just the thought of listening to her blow her own trumpet leaves a bitter taste in my mouth. Lucky for me, there is a line of hotel golf carts waiting outside the yacht club for all the Swallowtales big shots who don't want to make the walk. After Suzy leaves for her show at the Mug Shot, Blake and I hang out on the docks for a while with some of the other pages, most of whom are still talking excitedly about Keyheart's new book.

"You are so lucky," says Rachel Oliver, whom I know a little from soccer camp earlier in the summer. "Do you think she'll let you read the whole thing? I can't believe I'm gonna have to wait almost a *year*."

Gabby Bensikova, still hanging on to Owen Cheever, joins the group. "I have to admit, it was a lot better than I expected. Her other books—*ugh*. So *trite*. This one actually seems to be on a totally different level. It's almost like it was written by somebody else."

I have to cover my mouth to keep from spitting ginger ale all over Owen, who is right next to me.

"You okay?" he says as I wipe my mouth.

"Yeah, fine. I . . . guess I choked a little."

He points at the can in my hand and smiles. "Yeah, well, that stuff can kill you."

"I think I'll be all right. I have a rule. One can a week."

"Do you have a rule for *everything*?"

"*Almost* everything," I say before turning the conversation to him. "So, you and Gabby, huh?"

The docks are well lighted, so it's easy to see him blushing. "What? Me and Gabby? No. We're just friends. Our families are . . . she comes every summer. I've known her since we were little kids."

"Uh-huh," I say. "If you say so."

"I do. Say so. Really."

"It's okay," I say. "She's cute. And rich. *And* she's a ballet dancer." He starts to protest again, but I cut him off before he can get a word out. "Hey, can I ask you a question?"

"As long as it's not about Gabby," he says.

"No, it's about a house on Buckeye Street. I think your family owns it. Number twenty-two. You know it?"

"Buckeye Street? Is that the one with the tower?"

"Uh-huh."

"Do you want to buy it or something, now that *you're* rich."

"Ha. No. I just need to see the inside. I mean, as long as nobody's living there."

"What do you want to see?"

"It's kinda hard to explain. Okay, maybe I don't *need* to. I want to. Look, you must hate me—I know your dad does—but I *promise*, I *swear* to you that this doesn't have anything to do with the whole Captain Cheever land thing. There's a ninety-nine percent chance that what I'm looking for isn't there, but I have to know for sure. And I happen to know that nobody's living there right now."

Owen shrugs. "Sure. No big deal. I can show you. I know where Mom keeps the key. She's in charge of all the rental properties. And for the record, I don't hate you. My dad . . . well, that's another story. Probably best if he doesn't know. You wanna go tomorrow? How 'bout eleven o'clock?"

"Are you serious? Yes! That would be awesome. I'll meet you there," I say.

"Hey, uh, my turn. Can I ask *you* a question?" Owen says, leading me a few yards away from Gabby and the others.

"Um . . . sure." Uh-oh. My mind whirls with so many possibilities that I feel dizzy, so I repeat his line: "As long as it's not about Gabby."

"What? Why would it . . . Oh, I get it. Because I said . . . No. Hey, look, I know we kind of . . . and it was totally my fault, I know," he stammers, struggling to maintain eye contact. "I was a jerk. No. Worse than a jerk. And I understand completely if you don't want to . . . but hopefully you're starting to see that I'm not . . . "

"Owen!" I say. "What are you *talking* about?"

He closes his eyes, takes a deep breath, and then reopens them. "Okay. Right. Yes. What I was trying to say was, they're showing this movie on Saturday and I was wondering if, um, you would, you know, like to go? With me." He exhales slowly, relieved that he was able to finally get the words out.

"You mean, like, a *date*?"

"A movie. That's all. You don't have to call it anything else."

"Where?" As far as I know, there's not a movie theater on the island.

"The campground. They show them outside on a big screen. You sit on the ground. It's fun."

At least he's starting to sound like the Owen I sort of know. "I-I . . . Thomas might not let me go."

"There'll be a million people there. You'll be safe. So, if he's okay with it, will you go?"

"What's the movie?"

Owen laughs. "You're *killing* me. It's a classic. *Close Encounters of the Third Kind.*"

I turn my nose up. "Never heard of it. Is it *good*?"

"It's Steven *Spielberg*, for crying out loud. It's *awesome*. I've seen it a bunch of times. You're gonna *love* it."

"What is she going to love?" asks Gabby, slipping away from the group and sidling up to Owen.

"What? Oh, uh, nothing. School, here on the island," Owen says. "Instead of Connecticut."

"Yeah, it's gonna be different, that's for sure," I say. "Well, I'd better find Blake and head home. Busy day tomorrow. Keyheart in the morning, and then I'm meeting . . . *someone* at eleven."

"Toodles," says Gabby.

"See ya 'round," Owen says with a hint of a satisfied smile.

Blake, too, can't stop grinning as we walk to the golf cart and start for home.

"Okay, what's going on?" I say as we make the turn onto Lake Road. "Why are you so happy?"

"You know that girl, Rachel, from soccer camp? She asked me to go to this movie with her on Saturday. It's at—"

"The campground. I know. Owen just asked me. Don't say a *word*. And you don't have to look so surprised."

"I'm just surprised he asked *you*. I thought he was with Gabby. She was hanging all over him."

"He says they're just friends. So, I take it you're going. Do you *like* Rachel?"

"I dunno. Why do you say it like that? Is there something I don't know about her?"

"No, she seems fine. She's nice, I guess. And pretty. Maybe *too* pretty. She might be out of your league," I tease.

"She asked me!" Blake says. "If anything I'm out of *hers*."

"Yeah, you keep tellin' yourself that," I say. "Oh, *crap*."

"What's wrong?"

"Pip. And Nate. When they find out I'm going to a movie with Owen Cheever, they're never going to talk to me again. They *hate* him."

"Don't tell them."

"Easier said than done," I say. "I can't lie to Pip. If she asks me, I'm gonna have to tell her."

"Maybe she won't ask."

"Have you *met* Pip? There's a better chance that Tinker will win the Kentucky Derby next year."

CHAPTER

12

"WELL?" PIP ASKS AS I set my bowl of cereal on the kitchen table.

"Well what?" I reply, knowing full well what she's asking.

"Was O-wennn there?"

"What? Oh. Yeah, I guess."

"Did you talk to him?"

I take a big bite of cereal and chew slowly before answering. "A little. There was a bunch of kids around."

"Humph."

"Where is everybody anyway?" I ask, eager to change the subject. "Nate and Jack aren't in their room. They're *never* up this early."

"Nate said something about going to Nadine's. He took some of Thomas's tools."

"What is he up to? Are you sure he hasn't told you *anything*?"

Pip shakes her head. "I swear!"

"Well, I'm gonna figure it out. He and Jack found something in the old barn at Nadine's yesterday, where the old speedboat is. It's some big secret. Blake knows, but he won't tell me." I check my watch and slurp up the last of the milk in my bowl. "I've got to get going."

On my way to the sink to rinse my bowl, I pick up a receipt from the floor. "Western Auto. That's the hardware store, right? Who bought a spark plug and motor oil?"

"What's a spark plug?" Pip asks.

"It's a thing for a motor. You know what? I'll bet it's for a lawn mower. Nate's gonna mow people's lawns for money. He *is* kind of mechanical. Remember how he fixed our bikes? And the washing machine?"

"Yeah, but why is a *lawn mower* such a big secret?"

"He's a ten-year-old boy," I say. "Who knows what goes on in that tiny brain of his."

Keyheart is *still* in a good mood when I find her having breakfast in the hotel dining room. She's even nice to the waitress who brings whole wheat toast instead of the asked-for rye. The poor girl cringes, waiting for the explosion, but Keyheart tells her that it's no big deal, whole wheat will be just fine. I can't blame the waitress for expecting the worst. Earlier in the week, Keyheart had started foaming at the mouth when a different girl brought her *skim* instead of *whole* milk for her coffee, sending her back to the kitchen in tears.

When this waitress finally slinks away, Keyheart makes a show of placing her knife and fork on the table. Then she crosses her arms and looks straight at me. "Well?"

"W-What? Do you want me to get you some rye toast?"

"No, I don't want rye toast, you mutant. The *book*? You're supposedly such a big fan, I wanna know what you think. If you play your cards right, I'll have my people send you an advance copy. So c'mon. Let's hear it."

"I-I thought it was good," I say. I want nothing to do with pumping up her ego; she seems to be doing just fine on her own. "It seems like an interesting story. The writing was really nice."

Keyheart glares at me, and I get ready to run in case she reaches for the knife. "*Good?* An *interesting* story? *Nice* writing? Are you friggin' kidding me? Oh, why am I even asking you? What do you know? You're a kid, a hick. From *Ohio*, for Pete's sake. You wouldn't know a great book if it reached up and bit you on the butt."

"Connecticut," I say under my breath.

"What? Speak up."

"I said, technically, I'm a hick from Connecticut, not Ohio."

Keyheart's eyes narrow and she shakes her head. "My, my.

You are a cheeky little brat, aren't you?"

Before I can tell her that yes, as a matter of fact, I am a cheeky (not-so-little) brat, I am distracted by Jordie Holloway, barreling through the dining room, and pushing aside tables and chairs like a runaway tank. Unlike Keyheart, the intervening ten hours since he rushed out of the yacht club have done nothing to calm him down.

When he's twenty feet away and closing fast, he shouts, "Keyheart! You *fungus*. You miserable, unspeakable . . . *gargoyle*. This time you've gone too far. I am going to cut you into little pieces. And when I find that dried mushroom you call a heart, I'm gonna feed it to the seagulls."

"Why, hello, Jordie. Good morning to you, too," Keyheart says.

"Don't. Talk. To. Me," he says. "You stole that girl's book, and I am gonna prove it. You didn't even wait till the body was cold. That little charade last night didn't fool me. You couldn't write that well, with that much passion and honesty, if there was a *gun* to your head."

For the first time ever, I'm glad to see Officer Pawlowski, who approaches our table from behind me.

"What's this all about?" he says.

"You heard him, Officer. He threatened me. Twice. If you missed anything, there's my witness," Keyheart says, pointing at me.

"Shoulda known *you'd* be right in the middle of this,"

Pawlowski says. "Come on, Mr. Holloway. Show a little respect. The lady's had a difficult few days. Let her finish her breakfast. Geez-o-Pete! Can't you people just *try* to get along till you get back to New York? Then you can do whatever you want."

Holloway continues to hover threateningly over Keyheart until Officer Pawlowski takes him by the shoulders, spins him around, and marches him back toward the lobby.

Meanwhile, Keyheart crams a piece of whole wheat toast into her mouth, chews it a couple of times, and then spits it out. "Gak! What is this? I ordered rye!"

I don't stick around for the rest of the show, because I have a pretty good idea how it's going to go, and besides, I want to talk to Pawlowski before he leaves. The lobby is full of Swallowtale-ers waiting for class to start and whispering about Keyheart's run-in with her former agent. Jordie Holloway is nowhere in sight, but I catch up with Pawlowski as he's climbing aboard his official police golf cart.

He actually smiles at me as he puts the key in the ignition. "Ah. My old friend. Do me a favor. Try to keep your boss, what's her name, Keyheart, and this Jordie fellow away from each other. Two more days. And call me if he harasses her."

"He's right, you know. She did steal that book."

"I don't care."

"But what if—"

"No buts, no what-ifs," he says. "All I want is to see the

backsides of *both* of them on the ferry as it pulls away from the dock. Them two have been nothing but a headache for me. Fighting over that dead girl's daggone computer."

"That's exactly what I wanted to talk to you about. Why wasn't it with the rest of her stuff? Where is it now?"

"Locked up at the station," he says. "Day after the girl dies, this Holloway character comes in, tells me he's her agent and wants to hold on to her computer for safekeeping. Says she's written a book and he's the only one who knows about it, the only one who can be trusted to keep it safe. I tell him that's great, but I'm not handing the computer over to him without something official from the girl's next of kin. So, off he goes to call them, I suppose."

"Did he get hold of them?"

"Oh, yeah. The mother leaves me a bunch of frantic messages. I know she just lost her daughter and all, but between you and I, lady's got a few screws loose. Total loony tunes. But she tells me that she heard from Holloway, saying he's her agent and is gonna publish her book, yada yada. She's not sure what to do so she calls Keyheart, who tells them that Holloway's a fraud and he's not even the girl's agent, so they shouldn't give him anything."

"So, did they tell you to give the laptop to Keyheart?" I ask. "*Please* say no."

"Sure. No. The mother doesn't trust *her* much, either. I guess the girl told her some stories about what a nutcase this

Keyheart is. Anyway, she told me to keep it locked up until she gets here. She's traveling someplace overseas and is having trouble getting a flight back. Something about a volcano."

"Look, I know we've had our differences," I say, "but I have an idea. We—you and me—can *prove* that Keyheart stole Didi's book. I—*we* just need to look at her files. If she wrote a book, it'll still be there."

"After that disaster with you and the Cheevers, you expect me to trust you? Don't forget, I was on that boat, too. The one that you sank."

"I *really* wish people would stop saying that! *I* didn't sink anything. It's not my fault that he doesn't know how to drive a boat."

"Irregardless, I'm not letting you touch that computer."

"You don't have to. Just let me be in the room when you do it. Come on, this is important. A girl, a really *nice*, *smart* girl, is dead. She really *did* write a book, so don't we owe it to her to make sure that it at least has a chance of being published with her own name on it, not somebody else's?"

Pawlowski scratches his chin for a few seconds before he answers: "All right, fine. I have a guy I trust. Come by the station later. Three o'clock. Just to be clear, you are not going to touch *anything*."

I nod vigorously. "Scout's honor. Three o'clock. Omigosh. Thank you. You're my hero."

"Let's not get carried away," he says, driving off.

Owen is waiting for me outside 22 Buckeye Street on his bike, which is a first. He's usually driving a golf cart with the Cheever Construction logo on the front. If he's trying to prove to me that he's just a normal kid, I'm still not convinced.

"Right on time," he says. "I've got the key."

"Cool. Thanks for doing this, especially since I didn't exactly tell you why I want to see inside."

"It's no big deal. It's not like there's anything valuable in there. They rent it out to total strangers, after all."

We park the bikes behind the shrubs in the backyard and Owen tries keys until he finds the one that unlocks the back door. The house has been closed up tight for a while, so inside it is a little too warm and musty smelling.

"Okay. We're in. Now what?" Owen asks.

"There's a room with a lot of books, right?"

"Library. Second floor. A *lot* of old books. Follow me." He leads the way up the worn wooden stairs and then to a room at the end of the hallway, the front of the house.

The library is in the tower that forms the right front corner of the house, so it's circular, probably ten or twelve feet in diameter. Not exactly huge, but the ceiling must be a good twelve feet above me, and bookshelves cover every inch of wall except for four narrow, stained-glass windows.

"Pretty cool, huh?" Owen says. "See how those windows all have that one circle of clear glass in the middle? Supposedly, on certain days of the year, the sun shines through them, like that Stonehenge thing."

"Really? That *is* cool. Maybe some other time we can . . . Oh, wow. You weren't kidding. There *are* a lot of old books. I'm looking for one called *Little Dorrit*, by Charles Dickens. It'll be pretty thick. I'll start down here and work my way up."

"*Little Dorrit*. Never heard of it. I'll start at the top." He moves a sturdy wooden ladder into place and climbs it while I run my fingers across the spines of everything on the bottom shelves. Many of the books are old and worn, with the titles barely visible, so it's slow going.

We work in silence for a few minutes, finishing the first two stacks. As Owen moves the ladder to start the third, he asks, "What's so special about this book anyway? Is it worth a bunch of money?"

"Not if it's the one I think it is. If I'm right, it's gonna have a big hole in the middle."

"Ohhh. And there's something valuable hidden inside."

I shake my head. "Nope. Already have the thing that was inside and it's not really valuable. At least I don't think so."

"I'm confused. So, if the book isn't valuable and you already have what was hidden in it, and *that's* not valuable, why do you want this book so bad?"

"I don't know, to tell you the God's Honest Truth. It's connected to my mom, but it's a long, complicated story."

"You can save it to tell me on Saturday night," Owen says, adding, "At the *movie*," when I look blankly at him.

"*Right*. The movie."

"Have you looked up anything about it?"

"Uh, no. What's it—"

"Hey! There it is! Little. Dorritt." He points to a shelf that is just beyond his reach. "I have to move the—"

Downstairs, the unmistakable sound of the front door opening is followed by voices. "*Shoot*. That's my mom," Owen says as he climbs down the ladder. "She must be showing the house to somebody. We have to get out of here. I haven't told them about . . . you and . . . it's kind of complic—come on, we can sneak down and go out the back."

"B-But what about the book? It's right there!"

"I'll get it for you. I promise. But first, we gotta get outta here." He starts to reach for my arm to pull me, but thinks better of it and instead waves me on.

We tiptoe down the stairs, freezing momentarily when his mother's voice suddenly sounds as if it is getting closer. Thankfully, somebody asks her a question and we listen as her footsteps on the hardwood floors fade into the distance. Seizing the opportunity, we race down the rest of the way and out the back door.

"That was close," Owen says. "Wait over there, behind those bushes. I'll go in the front door and get the book." He runs around to the front of the house, returning five minutes later with *Little Dorritt* in hand.

"You got it!" I say. "What did your mom say?"

"Nothing. She didn't even notice. I told her I was riding by and saw her cart, and then I waited until they headed into the kitchen."

He hands me the book, and with my fingers metaphorically crossed, I turn to the inside cover and nod knowingly at the familiar stamp on the inside:

CRACKENTHORP BOOKS
59 DOVER STREET
MAYFAIR, LONDON

Then I flip to the middle, where, as expected, holes have been cut into the pages to create a "nest" for Didi's nightingale.

"*Yes!*" Owen says. "That's it, right? It has to be."

"Yeah, this is the one. What, um, do you . . . I mean, can I—"

"Take it. It's an old book with a big hole in the middle."

"You sure? I don't need to keep it. I'll bring it back on Saturday. 'Cause, I don't want to get you in trouble or anything. And I swear, as far as I know, it's not valuable."

"You don't have to return it. My parents have been talking about getting rid of all those books anyway. Mom thinks they smell bad. You're doing her a favor. Seriously. Keep it."

I hand the book back to him. "Look at it first. Make sure there's no money or anything stashed inside."

He rolls his eyes—at me!—but does what I ask. He examines the front and back cover, quickly flips through the pages, and then holds it upside down and shakes it several times. Satisfied that no secret treasure lurks inside, he hands it back to me—and that's when I see something he has missed, sticking out a tiny fraction of an inch beyond the edge of the pages of the book. I turn pages until I reach a single sheet of stationery, pale blue with a border of yellow daisies, stuck firmly into the crevice made by the pages. Written in the unmistakable cursive of an artistic young girl is this message, which I read aloud:

June 20, 1976

To the future owners of 22 Buckeye Street,

My name is Barrie Francis and I'm 11 years old. This book and the nightingale (I call her Dorie) who live inside, belong to me. We are moving away and my mom says I can't take <u>any</u> of my books with me, which really isn't fair. I <u>promised</u> Dorie that I will come back for her one day, but the problem is, I don't know <u>when</u>, so I am asking you for a favor. If you are reading this note, I guess you found her, but <u>please, please, please, please, please</u> keep her safe for me. She likes to stay on the bookshelves, nice and high, away from cats and other dangerous things, and where she has a good view of the world.

Thank you for helping me and Dorie. I miss her already and can't wait to see her again.

Yours truly,
Barrie Francis

"Wow. Five *pleases*," Owen says. He thinks for a second and adds, "Wait. Does this mean she came back, or not? Is that why it's empty? But why didn't she take the book, too?"

"It wasn't her that took it," I say. "I'll tell you *that* story on Saturday, too. It's a really good one. But right now I'm *dying* to know whatever happened to Barrie Francis."

"Sounds like a job for Google," says Owen.

I leave Barrie's note exactly where I found it and close the book. "Thanks. This is awesome. I should probably get back to the hotel."

"See ya Saturday. Hey! Why don't we go for pizza first? We could even bring it to the movie if you don't want to . . . "

I hear myself saying, "Okay. Fine. Yeah," before I even fully grasp what I've just agreed to.

"You want me to pick you up at your house, or—"

"No! Wait. I don't know. Let me think about it." The thought of those disappointed faces on Pip and Nate is too much to bear. "It's a little complicated."

"Okay, no problem. Just don't forget."

"Something tells me that you won't let me," I say.

Blake is with Jordie Holloway in the lobby just after twelve thirty, so I invite myself to join them for a walk into town. Our first stop is Cassie & Drew's Place for sandwiches and sodas, which we take to a picnic table by the water to eat. There's not a breath of wind, and except for the wake of a sailboat motoring toward the yacht club, the harbor is like glass.

Holloway, still fuming about Keyheart, doesn't talk much, and I can't help but wonder if it's because of my association with her. I decide that it's time to lay my cards on the table, so I chug the rest of my soda.

"You're right," I say as I lean back casually against the table-top and watch a pair of swallows darting overhead.

"I am?" Blake says. "I mean, yeah, of course I'm right. Uh, what are we talking about?"

"Not *you*," I say. "Mr. Holloway."

Blake gives me a look that clearly says: *Are you sure you want to go there?*

Holloway, on the other hand, never takes his eyes off his chicken salad with lettuce and tomato on ciabatta, but his bushy eyebrows twitch menacingly, and his chewing slows.

Several *long* seconds later, he swallows and looks up at me. "Okay, I'll bite. What am I right about?"

"Keyheart's book."

"What about it?"

"She stole it. Her assistant, Didi Ferrer, wrote it."

He sets his sandwich on its wax paper wrapper. "Yeah. Obviously. But what makes *you* so sure?"

"Because I *talked* to Didi. On Saturday, the day she got here. First of all, she told me that Keyheart hasn't written a word in over a year. And then she told me that *she* wrote a book and sent the first part to you. She didn't say your name, but it wasn't hard to figure out. She said it was Keyheart's old agent—you. And her roommate is here, a girl named Suzy. She was at the reading, too, and she couldn't believe it when Keyheart read the part where the girl steals the bird from her grandmother. See, the thing is, that story is from Didi's *real life*. And Suzy is the *only* person she ever told the story to. There's no way Keyheart could know all those details."

By the time I finish my speech, Holloway is sitting up straight. "Pfft. A *monkey* could see that Keyheart didn't write it. She's never written anything deeper than a mud puddle. *That* book, on the other hand, is like—" He points at Lake Erie, but then shakes his head. "No, deeper than that. The ocean. If the rest of it is *anything* like the first three chapters, it's the Marianas Trench of first novels. But unless you can *prove* it, that gnome Keyheart is gonna get away with it."

"I'm trying, believe me. You still have what she sent you, right? That's a start."

Holloway frowns. "Sure, I've got it, but it's not gonna matter. It's only three chapters, and Keyheart'll say that Didi stole the book from *her*. I'm trying to get into her computer, even if it's just to look, but the local cop is on some kind of power trip.

And now Keyheart has made Didi's parents paranoid about me. She convinced them that I'm trying to steal the book for myself. She even had the . . . the *nerve* to insinuate that I had something to do with Didi's death, that I somehow switched boxes of chocolate or some crazy thing."

I don't have the heart to tell him that until very recently, I'd had exactly the same suspicion.

Holloway buries his face in his hands. "This is a nightmare. Out of the blue, I get a gift, like manna from heaven. Normally, my assistant takes the first read of stuff like this, chapters from a complete unknown, but this girl . . . even her query letter was compelling. I'm not exaggerating when I tell you that it's the best opening I've read in years. I was *desperate* to talk to her, to read the rest of it, and get her on board as soon as possible. I have a feeling that this is gonna be a book that publishers *fight* over. The kind that wins prizes *and* sells a million copies. I've never been so sure about a book—about *anything*—in my life. She'd said something in her letter about Swallowtales, so I took a chance. I couldn't get a flight, so I rented a car and drove all the way out here. And then I find out that she died in some kind of freak accident."

"Well, I might have some good news. At three o'clock, Officer Pawlowski is gonna let me be there when his guy opens up Didi's laptop. The book just *has* to be there, and then we can . . . "

"I wish I could share your confidence," Holloway says. "But I've been to battle with Keyheart before. She doesn't fight fair, and she doesn't lose. Anyway, it's all over for me. Even if you find the book and prove that Didi wrote it, her parents are never gonna trust me to agent it. I'm gonna be standing in line to buy a copy for $27.95 like everybody else."

Blake and I share a look that ends with me standing in front of Holloway, palms up and Blake looking on nervously. He knows what's coming.

"This isn't just about you, Mr. Holloway," I begin. "I'm sorry you're not gonna get to make a bunch of money and all from the book, but you seem to be forgetting something. Geez! Didi *died*. She put her whole heart and soul into this book. And, you know, the ironic thing is, from what Suzy says, writing this book probably *saved* Didi's life. But now she doesn't get to enjoy a moment of its success. If it's *half* as good as you say, people *need* to read it. That's what Didi would want. That's what all writers want, for crying out loud. We *owe* it to her to get it published with *her* name on the cover, not Keyheart's. *Something* good has to come out of this."

As I speak, Holloway leans back farther and farther from me and my swinging arms, especially the one encased in hard, heavy plaster; clearly, I have scared the bejeezus out of him.

"Okay, okay," he says. "You're right, you're right. I'm just so . . . I'll help you however I can."

"Good to hear," I say.

Holloway's phone chimes at the moment he stands. After reading the text, he shakes his head, one corner of his mouth turning up in a wry smile. "You won't believe this. It's an email from Keyheart's lawyer—a cease and desist letter. She's gonna sue me if I say another word about her not writing the book. I'm not surprised. She sues *everybody*."

CHAPTER
13

OFFICER PAWLOWSKI COMES through as promised. He's a little surprised when I show up with my entourage of Blake, Suzy, and Nadine, but he shrugs and invites us all into his office. Inside, Didi's laptop is on a folding card table that's pushed against one wall.

"Kyle. You're up," Pawlowski says to a wannabe hipster in cargo shorts, plaid linen shirt, and a straw fedora that's perched on his head in a way that I'm sure *he* thinks is cool.

"Yo," Kyle says without taking his eyes from his phone. "Be with ya in a minute, boss."

"Now," orders Pawlowski. Under his breath, he mutters, "Daggone summer intern. September can't get here soon enough."

Kyle still takes his time coming into the office, but his

attitude changes the second he gets a good look at Suzy.

"Oh. Heyyy," he says to her, turning on what he *thinks* is charm. "I saw you at the Mug Shot. You're good. What's up?"

She elbows me as soon as he's past her, and then rolls her eyes. "*Somebody's* dreaming today. Like he has a chance."

Pawlowski motions with his finger for me to come closer to Kyle, who has opened the laptop and turned it on. "Tell him what we're looking for."

"It's a manuscript for a book," I say. "So some kind of a Word document, a couple of hundred pages, probably."

"What's it called?" Kyle asks, clicking on icons on Didi's desktop.

"There ought to be a file called 'the GRAMNO,'" Suzy says. "It was a little joke we had. Whenever I asked her what she was working on, she always answered, the Great American Novel. I said she needed to shorten the title, so she took the first couple of letters from each word, the GRAMNO."

"Nothing like that on the desktop," Kyle says. "Let me check a few other places. You're sure she didn't use a cloud service, you know, like Google Docs?"

"Positive," Suzy answers. "I tried to talk her into it, but she was paranoid about stuff like that. She may have said something once about backing up on a thumb drive, I'm not sure. That *sounds* like something she'd say."

"Any chance she has an external drive?" Blake asks. "You know what I mean? It's about yea big, and it plugs into—"

Suzy shakes her head. "No, nothing like that. I'm sure."

"Try a search for the title," I suggest. "*A Drowsy Numbness.*"

Kyle nods and tries, but still nada.

"How about her email?" Nadine says. "Maybe she sent it to herself. Lots of writers do that. We aren't always great with new technology, so when something works, we stick with it."

"I'll give it a shot." Kyle opens the browser to Didi's email, but she's logged out. "Password?"

Suzy scrunches her lips and shakes her head. "No idea."

"Try 'nightingale,'" I say.

Kyle looks to Suzy for confirmation. She shrugs and says, "Try it."

"Nope," says Kyle after typing it in. "The password needs a number in it."

Blake slides in next to Kyle. "*Ode to a Nightingale.* All one word, but use the *number* two instead of the word."

Kyle keys it in and then turns to Blake with a huge smile on his face. "High five, dude," he says. "We're in."

"Annddd?" Suzy insists.

Kyle clicks here and there on the page before stopping to rub his chin. "Huh. This is crazy. This account has been *wiped.* The only emails here are from after Saturday afternoon, around five o'clock. Those are in her inbox. Everything else, and I mean *every* folder, is empty. Sent mail, spam, folders she set up, drafts, the trash, there's not a single email in any of them. Was she the kind of person who—"

"*Nobody* is that kind of person," Nadine says. "I'm pretty good at keeping things cleared out, but I still have hundreds of emails stashed away in folders, just in case . . . of what, I don't know. But they're there if I need them."

Suzy is nodding in agreement with Nadine. "She was a P.A. When she was working, she *lived* on email, hers and Keyheart's. Millions of them. Every day. So let me get this straight: no email *and* her book is missing? That is just *wrong*."

"Think about the time line," I say. "Didi and Keyheart got to the island on Saturday at eleven o'clock. Didi and I left the hotel patio a little after two fifteen and she was with me until I dropped her off at the yacht club a few minutes after four. When I picked up Keyheart at the cottage at six thirty, Didi definitely wasn't back yet. So there was plenty of time for *somebody*—somebody like *Keyheart*—to steal the book and clean out her email."

"Why was she at the yacht club?" Pawlowski asks.

"She was supposed to go sailing with the Cheevers," I answer. "There wasn't any wind, so I doubt if they even left the dock, but I saw the Cheevers at the Swallowtales reception at the hotel, a little after seven thirty."

"In any event, Keyheart was alone in the cottage for four hours, plus or minus," Nadine says. "With Didi's laptop."

"More than enough time to do it," Suzy says. "Unbelievable. It had to be her. She stole Didi's book and is going to publish it as her own. You have to arrest her."

"Whoa, whoa, whoa," says Pawlowski. "I'm not arresting anybody. Geez-o-Pete. On Monday, you're telling me that she was the victim of some crazy murder plot. Now you say somebody stole her book. I can't keep up. As far as I can see, there's no proof this girl even *had* a book to steal. Find me a book, prove to me that she wrote it, and then we'll talk."

"I'm afraid he's right," Nadine says. "Keep looking for the book. There has to be a copy somewhere. I have to scoot back to the hotel. Promise that you'll let me know if you find anything."

"*When* we find something, you'll be the first to know," I say. When Nadine is gone, I lean in next to Kyle. "So, is there any way to, you know . . . in the movies, they can trace who—"

"I know where you're going with this," he says. "That's for when somebody hacks their way in from another computer, which is *really* unlikely. *If* somebody stole something, they did it in person. Fact is, it was probably really easy. Anything on the desktop is a click away from attaching it to an email or copying to a thumb drive, and she was probably already logged in to her email, so they didn't have to worry about a password. If you give me enough time, I can probably tell you *when* it happened, but that's about it. Sorry."

Pawlowski closes the laptop and sends Kyle back to his cubicle in the main room. "I don't know what to think," he says. "I got all these New Yorkers, writers and agents and parents, fighting over a book that you tell me the dead girl wrote, but now it disappeared, or maybe somebody stole it from her email, or who knows. Well, here's what I'm gonna do. I'm gonna lock that computer up in the safe until a judge or somebody a lot more important than me tells me I can take it out."

Across the street from the police station is Our Lady of Victory Catholic Church. It's a simple, gray-shingled building with a tidy front yard and perfectly trimmed hedges that line the side-walk and the brick path to the front door. Making the turn onto that path at the very moment I exit the police station is Howard Allam. I freeze when I see him, and hold out my arms to stop Suzy and Blake.

"What?" Blake says, turning to see where I'm looking.

"Shhh!"

When Allam reaches the church door, he puts his hand on the knob and starts to pull it open, but stops. As he turns to see if anyone is watching him, I duck behind a rhododendron bush, out of Allam's sight, yanking my two companions' arms along the way.

"Hey, that's the awkward guy from last night," says Suzy.

Allam, meanwhile, steps inside the church, and the door bangs shut behind him.

"Follow me," I say. "Hurry!"

We race across the street and up the path to the church door and peek inside. "Hey, he's going into the confessional," Suzy says.

I'm not Catholic, but I can guess what that means: Howard Allam feels really guilty about *something*.

"You think this has something to do with what he was saying last night?" Blake asks. "What happens in there anyway? What if he confesses to a murder?"

"Basically, you tell the priest your sins and then he tells you what you have to do to be forgiven. Like say ten Our Fathers and ten Hail Marys," answers Suzy. "But the important thing is, the priest can't tell *anybody*, no matter how bad it is. I grew up Catholic, even went to a Catholic elementary school—that's how I know this stuff."

"What do you think he's saying?" Blake asks me.

"I think he switched the chocolates," I say, and then describe the scene I witnessed on the deck at his cottage that ended with Allam throwing nut-filled chocolates into the lake.

"So what he said last night when he was on the stage, was *totally* a Freudian slip," Suzy says. "Chock full came out as *chocolate*, and troubles came out as *truffles*. That is one *seriously* guilty conscience."

"Let's get out of here," I say.

"Now what?" Blake says when we're out of hearing range of the church. "I'm no expert, but I don't think a guy going to confession and *acting* guilty is enough to send him to jail. We need some real evidence, you know, like fingerprints. Or video of him going into Keyheart's room and switching out the chocolates."

"Unfortunately, there's no security cameras down by the lake where the cottages are," I say. "I already checked. Supposedly, they're going to be installed next week. Which doesn't help us at all. So, it looks like we have some work to do. Maybe going to confession makes him feel better, but it doesn't change anything. If he killed Didi, he's gonna pay."

I know that I'm far from the first to say this, but here goes: Life is funny. The answers we spend the most time looking for are the ones that *should* be the easiest to find, because they're right under our noses. Those answers also have the unfortunate habit of coming into focus at the worst possible time. Let me explain.

When we leave the church, Blake and I go home, where twenty-five straw bales have just been delivered outside the barn. Pip, Nate, and Jack are trying to move them inside because the sky has turned gray, there's rumbling to the west, and the maple leaves are overturned. But they can barely budge the fifty-pound bales.

"We have to hurry," says Pip, practically frantic. "Tinker can't sleep on wet straw!"

"The horror!" Blake says. "Excuse me, but isn't Tinker part

Chincoteague pony? Aren't they *wild*? Where do you think *they* sleep?"

"Don't joke about Tinker," I say. "Pip has a *long* memory. You'll pay for it later."

A few minutes later, the bales are all safely inside the barn, ready to be hoisted up to the loft above the stalls. There's a pulley with rope hanging from a beam, so the plan is to have the little kids push the bales into position and tie the rope around them. Then Blake and I use our three good arms to yank on the rope with all our might to lift the bales up and through the trapdoor in the loft floor. With the straw safely in the loft, we pull the kids up one by one. They *say* that it's so they can help us stack the bales, but the truth is that they love the ride, especially when Blake and I pretend to let go of the rope and let them drop a few feet, stopping their fall inches from the floor.

As we're stacking the last bale in the loft, we all practically jump out of our skin when lightning strikes *very* close by—so close that the air crackles and sizzles and the barn shakes down to its foundation. Jack's eyes are big as dinner plates, so I put an arm around him.

"It's okay, bud," I say as the first drops of rain ping against the metal roof. Ten seconds later, it's coming down by the bucketful, filling the hayloft with deafening noise.

"Looks like we're here for a while," Pip says. "Remember that time we got caught in the rain in New York?"

"I can't believe *you* remember it," I say. "That was a long time ago."

"It was before Mom and your dad got together," I explain to Nate and Jack. "Mom took us to the city to see *The Lion King* on Broadway. After the show, we decided to walk to the Metropolitan Museum, because Mom wanted to show us her favorite paintings.

"That's right!" Pip cries. "And we got caught in a thunderstorm and got *soaked*. We went into the Plaza Hotel, and remember? I looked *everywhere* for Eloise."

"And Mom bought us those charms," I say. "That was a fun day. We never made it to the museum."

"What's a *charm*?" Jack asks.

"It's a little thing that hangs on a necklace. Or a bracelet. People collect them to remind them of someplace they've been. Or someone. Mom saw these tiny painted goldfinches in this jewelry store. I think they used to be earrings, but the guy turned them into charms, one for Pip and one for me. I'll show you when we go inside. I don't wear it 'cause I'm afraid I'll lose it."

"Oh, I get it. Finches, like your dad's name," says Jack.

"Yep. And the funny thing is, you know how different

flocks of birds have different names? Like a murder of crows, or a parliament of owls? Guess what a bunch of finches is? A *charm*. Isn't that cool?"

The rain slows momentarily, and Thomas seizes the opportunity to run from the house to the barn, where he sticks his head up through the hole in the floor.

"Ah. There you are. I got home and nobody was there except Pogo. Oh, I see the straw came. Thanks for getting it inside before the rain," he says.

"What's for dinner?" asks always-hungry Nate.

Thomas looks at me and winks before saying, "I was thinking that it's a perfect night for tuna noodle casserole."

Mom was many things, but she was *not* a great cook, and this particular casserole (which she started making way back in college) just might be the worst recipe ever.

His suggestion is instantly met with a chorus of hostility: "No! Eww! Yuck! I *hate* that!"

"What about you, Lark?" he says.

"Sounds good to me," I say. "I *love* tuna noodle casserole."

The chorus resumes: "Lark! No! It's *terrible*! How can you *like* that disgusting stuff?"

"Geez. I had no *idea*," Thomas says. "I thought everybody loved it."

"You are such a liar, Dad," says Blake. "We tell you *every* time you make it. We *hate* it. *All* of us. Including Lark. She must want something. That's why she's sucking up."

Thomas raises his hands in surrender. "All right, all right. I give up. No more tuna noodle casserole. Maybe we should have a ceremonial burning of the index card with the recipe, what do you think?"

Now it's my turn to protest. "No! You can't. I know it's really bad and all, but it's such a classic *Mom* dish. We have to keep the recipe, even if we never make it again."

"You're right," says Thomas. "I have a better idea. In the meantime, I guess it's tacos. Again." He disappears down the hole with a loud sigh.

CHAPTER
14

AFTER THOMAS'S TACOS (not as good as mine, but *way* better than tuna noodle casserole), I take a quick spin into town. Nate tags along because I've promised him that he can drive the golf cart, at least when we're not in town where anyone can see us. Technically, I don't have to go, but I want to make sure that Keyheart shows up on time and in the right place for a panel discussion about rewriting and revising that's called This Just Isn't Working.

"Do you think the hardware store is still open?" Nate asks when we're about halfway to town.

"I doubt it. It's almost eight o'clock. Why?"

"Oh . . . nothing. I just wondered."

"Something for the lawn mower?" I guess.

Nate looks confused. "Lawn mower? We don't have a lawn mower."

"Uh-huh. If you say so."

"I don't know what you're talking about," he says.

"Two words: Spark. Plug."

"How'd you know about that?"

"I have my ways."

"It was Jack, wasn't it?"

"It wasn't Jack. So, what else do you need for the lawn mower that we don't have?"

"You're weird."

"Did you really think you could keep a secret from me?" I say. "As *if*."

He mutters something under his breath as he turns left onto Buckeye Street with its pristine houses and perfect lawns.

"I'll bet you can make good money," I say. "Look at all these lawns. Somebody's got to mow them. Guarantee you the summer people aren't doing it themselves. Even Thomas pays somebody to do it. I guess that's your first job. Some of these yards are pretty big, though. Is it the kind you ride? Or push?"

"Oh, it's definitely the kind you ride," he says with a silly grin.

When we get to the hotel, Nate and I stay close to the door at the back of the room where the discussion is being held, ready for a quick exit. Six comfy chairs from the lobby are arranged in a semicircle on the stage for the discussion. Katherine Bensikova, Gabby's mom, comes out first and introduces herself as the moderator. Then she invites the panel, which includes Howard Allam and Wendy Eppinger, to join her.

A few minutes later, Eppinger is in the middle of explaining how she tells an author that something in their book really isn't working, when Howard Allam's phone rings loudly. Apologizing, he takes the phone from his jacket pocket. When he glances at the screen, his eyes grow wide and he whispers something to the writer in the chair next to his.

"I'm so, so sorry," he tells his fellow panel members. "I have a, uh, a family emergency and I have to go. Thank you, everyone, for understanding." And with that, he exits the stage and rushes up through the aisle, brushing past Nate and me, and out the door.

I figure it's one of two things. Either the guilt has finally gotten to him and he's going to the police station to confess to the crime, or he realizes that he's going to be found out and is making a run for it.

Of *course* I follow him, all the way to the ferry dock, where passengers are coming down the gangplank of the eight fifteen boat. Then I spot Allam, running toward a woman, shouting her name: "Tricia! Tricia!"

I didn't stick around for the whole thing, but the long and the short of is that I was a hundred percent wrong about

Howard Allam. That scene on the deck of his cottage, with him throwing the chocolates, and then the whole going-to-church-to-confess thing? Absolutely *nothing* to do with Keyheart or Didi. From the bits of the conversation I overheard, I was able to piece together that Allam's wife left him a few months back after she found some text messages on his phone that he had sent to another woman. After lots of phone calls, flowers, and boxes of—you guessed it, Keke's Cocoas—Tricia had apparently reconsidered and was going to give him a second chance.

The phrase *back to the drawing board* springs to mind as Nate and I head for home. On the way back to the Roost, a million questions swirl madly in my brain. The most important one: if Howard Allam didn't switch the chocolates, who did?

It's a little after ten o'clock when I find Pip lying on my bed, wide awake. Next to her is her treasure box—an actual cigar box that she found in the attic that now contains her prized possessions. She looks up at me, those beautiful pale blue eyes full of tears, and her nose a darker shade of pink than usual. She sniffs, wipes her eyes with the sleeve of her pajama top, and shakes her head sadly.

I lie down next to her and stroke her hair. "Hey, hey, hey, what's going on? What's wrong, kiddo?"

She holds out her hand, opening it to reveal her goldfinch

charm. "I-I took it out after you left, but then—" Sobbing, she buries her face in a pillow for a few seconds, but soon recovers enough to continue: "I was squeezing it and looking at it and *trying* to remember everything from that day, but . . . but I can't see Mommy in my mind anymore. She's *disappearing*. I had to get out a *picture* to really remember what she looks like!" She buries her face against me, her whole body shaking with every sob.

I squeeze her tightly, wishing with every cell in my body that I could make it better, that I could tell her that it's only a temporary condition. I can't, though, because the GHT is that I've been through it once already with Dad (Pip was only three when he died, so she basically has no memory of him) and now the exact same thing is happening with Mom. It's not that I don't remember how she looks, but when I see her in my mind now, it's more like I'm looking at a *picture* of her, not our actual *Mom*, if that makes sense.

And so I hold her for a long time before saying anything.

Finally, she lifts her reddened eyes up to mine, and I say, "Remember, right after we got here this summer, when I said that every time I walk into this house, I half expect to see Mom? Well, I still do. And you know why? Because she's here, Pip. She's everywhere we go. I don't mean like a ghost or anything cheesy like that, but . . . it's just something I know. I *feel* it. Your perfect little head is crammed full with a million memories of her, and they're not going anywhere. And on top of that, we have pictures, and videos, and all the things she gave us, like these charms, and all her books, and this beautiful house, and her terrible tuna noodle casserole, and Thomas and the boys, and Nadine, and Tinker, and Pogo, and crazy Bedlam, who still says 'sweet dreams' in Mom's voice every night. And best of all, we have each other. Every time I see you, I see a little piece of Mom. You know, maybe it *will* get a little bit harder to remember exactly what she looked like with your eyes closed, but I *promise*, you're never gonna forget her. So, stop worrying, okay?"

It's her turn to squeeze me, and then she whispers, "I love you so much. You are the best big sister ever."

"Ha! I don't know about *that*," I say. "Somewhere out there, there must be a better sister than me."

Pip shakes her head. "Nope. No way. But . . . can I say something?"

"Of course."

"It's about Bedlam. It creeps me out a little when he does that. You know, talking in Mom's voice."

"Yeah, I know what you mean. I still get the shivers every time he says it. But it's kinda like what I was saying, about feeling like Mom's here with us, so I don't want him to stop."

"D'you think he'll always do it?"

"I don't know. I suppose as long as we're here to say good night to him, he will."

"Well, I guess that's nice."

"So . . . are you all right?"

"Mm-hmm. Thank you."

"You're welcome. It's all part of the service," I say. "Hey, you know what? I think we should start wearing our goldfinch charms. Every day, like we used to."

"B-But . . . what if I lose it?"

"*Life* is one big *what if*. It's like trying to protect a one-goal lead in a soccer game with thirty minutes to go. It never works out. You have to take chances."

Pip looks uncertain. "I dunno. It's not just a lucky charm. It's *so* much more."

And . . . there it is, the answer I've been searching for: *It's not just a lucky charm. It's so much more.*

Suddenly, inside my head, lights are flashing, alarm bells are ringing, and sirens are screaming. "Omigosh!" I shout as I leap to my feet, waking Pogo and scaring poor Pip half to death. Even Bedlam squawks, hopping back and forth on his perch.

Pip looks frantically around the room for whatever spooked me. "What's the matter? You look like you just saw a ghost."

"I did, kind of," I say. "Pip, you're a genius. It's *not* just a lucky charm. There's something else, and I think I know what it is."

"What *what* is?" Pip says, examining her goldfinch charm with a baffled expression.

"I'll explain later. Is Suzy back yet? I've *got* to talk to her.

Right. Now. Shoot! She's still in town. I have to go. If Thomas asks, I forgot something at the Islander and had to go back."

Pip lifts her head, listening. "Wait! That's the back door."

I race down the stairs with Pip right on my heels, knocking Blake into the table when I burst into the kitchen.

"Where's Suzy?" I shout at him.

"Nice to see you, too," Blake says.

"I'm right here," says Suzy, standing on the porch with her guitar case in hand. "What's going on?"

"Yeah. Geez, Lark," Blake says. "Out of control much? And why does Pip look like she's been crying? What did you say to her?"

There's a part of me—a really small part, it's true—that could hug him for being so protective of Pip, but another part that wants to punch him for even *thinking* that I've done something to hurt her.

"Aaghh. I didn't do anything. I'll explain later," I say, brushing past him and opening the door for Suzy. "Boy am I glad to see you. I figured something out. Thanks to Pip—and Mom's tuna noodle casserole—I know where Didi's book is."

"Can I sit down?" Suzy asks. "It's been a long day."

I basically push her down into a chair. "Blake! Take her guitar."

"Okay, I'm sitting," she says.

"Didi's necklace," I say. "Are you wearing it? Can I see it?"

"Sure. Here." Suzy reaches under the collar of her T-shirt,

slips the chain and pendant over her head, and hands it to me.

I hold it up to the light for a second and then tug firmly on the two *D*s, pulling them apart.

Pip gasps, thinking that I broke it, but Suzy, Blake, and I all smile, because we see the secret of Didi's lucky charm: it's a USB flash drive!

"Whoa! That is amazing," says Suzy. "How did I *not* know that thing was a . . . and how did you figure it out?"

"It was something Pip said about being afraid to lose her goldfinch charm. She said that it's *more* than just a lucky charm. And that reminded me of something from Saturday, when Didi and I walked over to the yacht club. She put this in her pocket because she didn't want to lose *her* lucky charm out on the water. She said something like, it holds all the answers, even if you don't know the questions. At the time, I thought it was strange, but I didn't say anything, and then, well . . . but then I remembered that you said something about a thumb drive. I put two and two together."

"I'm gonna get your laptop," Blake says. "We've gotta see what's on it."

"You're not like any kid I've ever known," says Suzy. "And believe me, there were a bunch of smart kids at Carton."

"You would have figured it out," I say.

"Nope. Maybe, *eventually*, I would have accidentally pulled that thing apart and wondered why it took me so long," Suzy says. "No. You're the real deal. *And* you're tall. I think I hate you."

"I'm just . . . stubborn, that's all" I say. "Ask Thomas. I hate to lose. And the tall thing? I didn't have much to do with it. Genes."

Blake thumps down the stairs seconds later with my laptop. I plug in the flash drive and wait. "Look! There's a folder called GRAMNO—Great American Novel. This is it," I say, clicking on the icon in the folder labeled *A Drowsy Numbness*. "This is actually it. Oh, man, I can't wait to show this to the police. Maybe now he'll believe us, and do something."

"Look at that," Suzy says. "Two hundred and fifty-five pages. Seventy-two thousand words."

I scroll quickly through the first few chapters until Suzy stops me. "Wait. Back up a little. This is the part that Keyheart read the other night. Little bit farther . . . yeah, there! That's where she started."

All four heads crowd around the screen and read silently. I continue scrolling until we reach the end of the chapter, which is where Keyheart stopped, too.

"That's *exactly* what Keyheart read," Blake says. "This is proof that she stole it!"

"Well, sort of," I say.

"What are you talking about?" he says. "It's so obvious."

"Remember what you said earlier about Howard Allam. Him *acting* guilty isn't enough. And by the way, he . . . never mind, I'll tell you later. What I'm saying is, just because Didi has a copy of the book on a flash drive doesn't *prove* that she wrote it," I explain. "She was Keyheart's assistant, after all. I can hear it now. Keyheart'll say that Didi stole the book from *her*."

"So, what do we do?" Suzy asks. "How do we prove it?"

"I'm working on it," I say. "It's too late to do anything tonight anyway, and we have to think . . . *really* think about this. We can*not* let Keyheart outsmart us. If it's all right with you, I'm gonna read this—all of it—tonight. I guess I can make a copy if you want to, too."

"That's all right," Suzy says. "I don't have my tablet with me, and I'm way too tired to read it on my phone. Hey, you think it's okay if I stay another night? I don't want to overstay my welcome."

"Yeah, definitely," I say. "Stay as long as you want."

"Shouldn't you check with Thomas?" she asks.

I wave off her concern. "Nah. No worries. Right, Blake?"

"What? Oh. Yeah. Dad doesn't care."

"Thank you *so* much. I owe you big-time."

"One last thing," I say to Blake and Pip: *Nobody* knows we have this, so, not a peep to anybody, okay? The element of surprise might just come in handy."

I check the clock next to my bed when I start reading; it's five minutes after eleven.

At 3:43, I read the last paragraph and close my eyes, but only for a few seconds.

I open them and read the last chapter again, and then close my laptop and stare up at the ceiling. It is four o'clock on the dot. In all my twelve years, I've never been so tired, or so alive, as I am in that moment. It is, without a doubt, the best book I have ever read, and I think there's a good chance that it's the best book, period. As in, *ever.*

A Drowsy Numbness is not merely a good book, or even a great one. I honestly believe that it is a book that will change people's lives. How do I know this? Well, it changed mine. You're going to have to trust me, because attempting to explain *why* it's so wonderful would be a bit like Thomas going on (and on, and on) about what makes the painter John Singer Sargent so great. You just have to see it, or in this case, read it, for yourself.

Despite the late hour, I feel as if ten thousand volts of electricity are running through me. It's absolutely pointless for me to attempt to sleep, so I tiptoe down the stairs to the kitchen, where I spread peanut butter half an inch thick on some Ritz crackers and pour myself a big glass of milk. For a long time, I sit at the table and continue to let Didi's words soak in.

"I have to do something," I say out loud as the living room clock chimes four thirty. "I need to think. *Really* think."

Although my soccer career has been marked by a couple of

key moments in which I clearly *didn't* think, the fact is that I do my best thinking when I'm kicking a soccer ball. I pull on my soccer cleats and go into the backyard, where Thomas has recently erected a regulation-sized goal, complete with a net that he made from some plastic fencing used to keep birds and deer away from fruit trees. My favorite thing about it, though, is the target net, a sheet of black plastic that hangs down the full width of the goal, with six evenly spaced circles cut out of it. The plan is to improve my accuracy by aiming for a specific hole, and to be able to hit it consistently.

The moon is not quite full, and so bright that there's no need for the floodlight at the corner of the house. However, after a few practice kicks, the light comes on and Thomas steps out onto the porch, a puzzled expression on his face.

"Lark? What are you doing?"

"Oh, hi, Thomas. I needed to think. Sorry, did I wake you up?"

"You needed to . . . come inside. Go to bed."

I dribble the ball to a spot about fifteen yards out from the target net. "Tell you what. You pick the target, and I get one shot from right here. If it goes in without touching the plastic, I can stay. If I miss, I go in."

Thomas sighs and shakes his head. "Okay. Fine. Upper left corner. *One* chance."

"That's all I need," I say, taking three steps back from the ball. I stare at my target, a hole that is exactly eighteen inches in diameter, and with only a brief glance down at the ball as I run toward it, strike it cleanly with the inside of my right foot. The ball sails toward the goal. For a second, it looks like it's going to land in the plastic to the right of the hole, but as it gets closer, the ball curls just enough to the left to slip through the target hole.

I pump my fist. "Yes!"

"It touched the plastic on the way through," Thomas says.

"What! No way!"

He nods. "I heard it."

When I open my mouth to protest, he holds up a hand. "It's okay. Close enough. You can stay. I'm too tired to argue with you. Just promise you won't leave the yard."

"Wait. What? Close enough? Geez, Thomas, why don't you just drive a stake through my heart right now? I'm going again." I retrieve the ball from the net and take it out to roughly the same spot.

"Lark, I said you can stay."

"Yeah, but you also said it was *close enough.* I *hate* that. Close enough means that the goalie got a finger on it and it went over the top of the goal. Not good enough."

I line up the shot and kick the ball even harder. It looks perfect, but at the last moment, the ball curls a bit too much and scrapes the plastic on the way through.

"Shoot!" I kick the ground with my cleats. "One more time."

Thomas slaps his palm to his forehead. "La-aark. It's all good."

"No! It has to be a clean goal, or it doesn't count. Last one, I promise."

The third time is not the charm, however. My cleat catches on the grass in front of the ball and it sails over the goal by a good two feet.

Thomas shrugs at me, palms up. "I don't think you can expect perfection at . . . let's see, four forty-three in the morning. I'm going back to bed. Stay in the yard. 'Night, Lark." The screen door slams shut behind him.

I drop to the ground and sit on the damp grass for a long time, collecting myself and refocusing my energy on the real issue: What am I going to do about Ann Keyheart and the fact that she stole Didi's wonderful, amazing book? Time is running out. It's already Thursday, the final day of Swallowtales. Keyheart is scheduled to be on the first boat off the island Friday morning, which means I have about twenty-four hours to prove to the world that she's a big phony, and that she had nothing to do with the writing of *A Drowsy Numbness*.

Climbing to my feet, I glance at the target net. "Middle right," I say, and then kick the ball. As it flies straight through the center of my intended target, my mind drifts back to the first time I set eyes on Didi and Keyheart, on the deck of the *Niagara*. There's Didi, weighed down with Keyheart's bags and grumbling about her boss disappearing just when it is time to gather their luggage. And here comes Keyheart herself, hard to miss in that lime-green outfit and a straw hat with a wide

BETRAYAL BY THE BOOK

brim and matching green hatband. The first sound I hear from Keyheart's mouth is a shriek when her hat is carried off by the wind and then deposited in Swallowtail Harbor.

But watching that hat sail away a second time triggers a momentary flash of memory, one that is perfectly formed in my brain. Before I went to the ferry dock that morning, I drove out to the point beyond the hotel to watch the ferry go past. With everything else that has happened in the past week, I had completely forgotten about the woman standing at the stern of the ferry—the one I assumed to be a local, tossing what I *thought* was an empty can of CoffLEI overboard. I was wrong on both counts.

"Upper left," I say quietly. One, two, three steps, and . . . my foot makes contact with the ball and I see the woman at the stern once more. Even though she is in the shadows and it's hard to make out what she looks like, the hat gives her away: a big sun hat with a lime-green hatband. A hat that, a few minutes later, will be on its way to the bottom of the harbor. There's no doubt in my mind. The woman at the back of the boat is Keyheart, and that wasn't a can of CoffLEI—it was Didi's phone.

The ball flies through the center of the hole in the upper left corner of the target. "That's more like it," I say.

One thing for certain: Didi's phone going over the side was no accident. Keyheart definitely tossed it, and I'm starting to understand why.

I roll the ball a few yards farther from the goal for my next attempt. "Center, top." Another perfect kick. And then another in the upper right hole. Something is happening. Something amazing. Something . . . *mysterious,* as if some outside force is *guiding* the ball through the target while giving me the ability to focus my brain in an entirely new way. I peek over my shoulder, half expecting to see Obi-Wan Kenobi looking on, nodding sagely. And then, two more shots, both exactly on target.

With every perfectly placed shot, I complete another section of the puzzle. Besides the phone, there's the cellophane wrapper that somebody tampered with. A box of nut-free chocolates that somehow contained nuts. A missing EpiPen. An empty email inbox. An entire book gone missing from a laptop.

Six shots, six goals, six clues. And, as they say on TV, a whole new theory of the case.

CHAPTER
15

BY SEVEN FIFTEEN ON THURSDAY morning, I'm already outside the Captain's Cottage with a measuring tape that I borrowed from Thomas. (I would have arrived even earlier, but Thomas insisted that I sit and have breakfast with him and Pip.) From the front door of the Captain's Cottage to the exact spot where I stopped in my tracks when I heard Keyheart's scream is seventy-eight yards and two feet, a little shorter than the soccer pitch at my old school. I think back to that night and retrace my steps, starting a timer the moment I leave the door. Walking at my normal pace, without any stops, it takes between forty and forty-five seconds. But that night, I know that I stopped once for at least fifteen seconds to check my phone and send a text to Thomas to let him know that I was on my way home. So it's basically one minute from the moment I left Keyheart until the scream when she finds Didi. A *lot* can happen in a minute.

On to the second question. This one requires the cooperation of Officer Pawlowski, so I stop by the coffee shop and, thanks to some input from a barista with a fantastic memory, pick up a large coffee prepared just the way my favorite Swallowtail Island cop likes it.

Pawlowski literally *growls* when I hand it to him inside the police station. "I thought I made it clear that you are to stay away from here. From me. What's this?"

"It's coffee. Half-and-half, three sugars, and an extra shot of espresso. A peace offering."

He peeks under the lid and gives it a good long sniff.

"I didn't poison it, if that's what you're thinking," I say. "Here, I'll take a drink from it to prove it." I reach for the cup, but he swats away my hand.

"I trust you. Mostly. So, whaddya want? I know you didn't bring me a three-dollar coffee out of the goodness of your heart."

"Ouch," I say. "You're so cynical. Actually, I like that. But you know, now that I *think* of it, there *is* one tiny little favor you could do for me."

"*Nooo*," he says in a mocking tone. "*You?* This is *most* unexpected." He takes a big swig of coffee, clearly very proud of himself.

"Yeah, yeah. I know. I'm not exactly subtle. But this is really important. Like, I'm-about-to-solve-another-murder important."

"Tell me you're not back to that. It was an *accident.*"

"You know, at about four o'clock this morning, I was starting to think you're right," I say. "But then I had a—"

Pawlowski's eyebrows disappear under his cap and his eyes get big. "So help me, if you say *vision*, I am going to throw you out of here myself."

"I was going to tell you I had a *revelation*," I say. "Anyway, now I'm positive it *wasn't* an accident. I just need to see Didi's laptop again. I have to check something. You can do it all. I won't touch it, I promise."

"Look, kid, I appreciate the coffee and this whole Nancy Drew thing you've got going, but give it up. You should know better than most that life ain't fair."

"Two minutes," I say. "That's all. And then, if I'm wrong, I'll never say another word about it. I swear."

Pawlowski pinches the bridge of his nose, grimacing and then giving in with a loud sigh. "Fine. Let's get it over with." He waves me into his office.

"Thank y—"

He raises a hand to cut me off. "I'm only doing it 'cause if I don't, I'll never get rid of you. You're like a booger on the end of my finger."

"I can live with that," I say. "Pretty sure I've been called worse by Reggie Cheever."

"Oh, definitely," he says. "Lots worse."

He takes the laptop from the safe and presses the power

button. When it is fully booted up, he looks at me for instructions.

"Down at the bottom, the one that looks like a gear. System Preferences." A dashboard appears, showing rows of icons. I point to the one that is a picture of a light bulb. "That's it. Energy saver. Click on that."

There are two sliding scales, one labeled Computer Sleep, the other Display Sleep. The movable "slider" is in the same spot on both scales: ten minutes.

I take a picture of the screen and check to make sure it's clear. "Okay. Thanks. You can turn it off."

"What? That's it? That's all you wanted?"

"Got everything I need," I say. "Like I said, two minutes."

Pawlowski squints at me, clearly confused. "And that means you're dropping it, right?"

"Well . . ."

"*Right?*"

"I'll keep my word," I say, and then run as fast as I can from the room.

With the evidence-gathering portion of my grand plan complete, it's time to get all the actors in place for the final scene. First stop, Swallowtail Meadows, the old folks' home in town, to visit Simon Stanford. The *Swallowtail Citizen* gave me all the credit for solving Albert Pritchard's murder, but the GHT is that I couldn't have done it without Simon's help. He's ninety-three, but you'd never believe it. He's a snappy dresser who wears khakis (pressed with a crease sharp enough to draw blood), an oxford cloth button-down shirt, and a tie every day. He can easily pass for seventy, which seems about right for the role I have in mind for him.

"Miss Heron-Finch!" he says from a chair on the Swallowtail Meadows porch. "This is a delightful surprise. Come up, come up, have a cup of tea."

"You're looking dapper as ever," I say. "I love the bow tie. The blue matches your eyes."

"Still the charmer, I see. I'd better stay on my toes around you. To what do I owe the pleasure of your company?"

"I have a job for you. An acting job. If you're interested, that is."

"Oh, you know me too well. I'm always interested in a chance to show off. Tell me all about it."

When we finish our tea, Simon and I take a ride to Dinah's house out at Rabbit Ear Point. Dinah and Nadine are waiting for us, along with Suzy, Blake, and the other players waiting for the curtain to rise on what Dinah calls "an inspired piece of experimental theater."

"Think of this as kind of a dress rehearsal," I say, "but without the real star of the show."

"I hope you're all able to improvise a bit," Nadine says. "Considering who we're dealing with, there's an element of *uncertainty*, to say the least."

"That's putting it kindly," says Suzy.

Nadine hands me a marker and points to the large sheet of craft paper that she has taped to the wall in Dinah's tiny living room. "All right, *Madame Directeur Artistique*, the floor is yours."

I create a time line on the paper and spend about ten minutes going over the details—over everything that we can control, that is. "As for all the stuff that's *not* under our control, keep your fingers crossed," I say in conclusion.

Nadine chews on the arm of her reading glasses and shakes her head. "By George, I think you've done it. *Again*."

"Ingenious, even," Dinah says. "I do hope you'll save me a seat."

"Oh, you're in the front row," Nadine assures her. "Along with all the headaches of being on the Swallowtales board, there *are* some perks."

Technically, I'm still Keyheart's page until Saturday at noon, or whenever she steps aboard the ferry for Port Clinton, so after leaving Dinah's house, I stop at the hotel. Keyheart has a class—her last—until twelve-thirty, and I'm waiting outside the classroom door when it opens. She's talking with an eager-to-please student, a thirtyish woman with a perfectly round face and a pantsuit that looks like it might have come from Keyheart's own closet.

They stop in the doorway, where Keyheart spots me and smirks.

"So, basically, you hate my story," the woman says.

"Hate is a strong word," Keyheart replies. "But if I were you, I'd toss it in the nearest trash can and start over. I'm not you, so if you think it's worth salvaging, then by all means keep going."

Unfortunately, the woman doesn't accept defeat easily. "What, exactly, is so bad about it?"

I cringe in expectation of the truth bomb that's about to blow this poor woman's confidence to smithereens.

"Look . . . Katie . . . it is Katie, right?"

"Um, it's Phoebe, actually."

"Of course. Phoebe. The biggest problem with your story is that it lacks *honesty*."

In my attempt to stifle a laugh that is halfway out of my mouth, I end up choking and have to turn away before I finally manage to splutter, "Sorry."

Keyheart scowls at me, shakes her head, and continues: "The thing is, I don't believe a word your narrator says. A story has to come from *here*"—Keyheart points to her heart—"not *here*," she adds, pointing to her head. "Yours is all head and no heart."

My own head is about to explode. Gabby and Didi are right. The woman is a monster.

As poor Phoebe slinks down the hall, Keyheart turns and faces me. "So. You survived. Almost a whole week. I gotta hand it to you. You don't scare easily. I like that. You lasted longer than some of my assistants." She scoffs, adding, "Snowflakes."

"So, that was your last class, right?" I say. "Can I help you with anything?"

She checks her watch. "In about twenty minutes, you can give me a ride. Meet me in the lobby."

"Sure. Twenty minutes. You going into town for lunch?"

"No, but that reminds me. Can you order a club sandwich for me, to go. On rye toast. With extra mayonnaise. And a bottle of seltzer. Lime. Think you can handle that?"

"Yes, ma'am."

"Well, get on it. I'm on the one-thirty boat out of here and I'm taking it with me."

"Wait. What? What do you mean?"

"I'm done. That was my last class, and now I'm leaving. On the *boat*. We're on an *island*, remember?" She looks at me like I'm an idiot for not understanding.

"But you can't leave now! What about all the farewell stuff? The party. The dinner. The awards. You *have* to come."

"Puh-lease. I'd rather have toothpicks shoved under my nails."

Think, Lark, think. How do you get her to stay?

I edge closer to her than I'm really comfortable being. "Nadine would *kill* me for telling you this, but they have something . . . special planned for you tonight. It's kind of a big deal. I don't want to say too much, but you *really* don't want to miss it."

Keyheart backs up a step and looks me up and down. "Something special, huh? Like what?"

"All I can say is that it's *really* nice," I say, making stuff up as I go along. "You know Dinah Purdy, the civil rights lady? It's a special award named for her. It's for, uh, outstanding writing in the field of, uh, *writing*. You're gonna be the *first* winner. Like I said, I don't know everything, but I overheard Nadine and the other board members talking about it yesterday. They were super impressed with what you read the other night."

"Unlike *you*. Humph. I don't know. I already told the hotel that I'm leaving," she says, which tells me that she's at least *thinking* about it. But then something happens that pushes her off the fence. Her phone dings with an incoming text and she digs it out of her bag to read it. Her eyes widen and she says, "Good grief. Jordie Holloway. What does *he* . . . well, *that's* interesting. He wants to meet with me. This afternoon. Says he has something I *need* to see. After that little outburst of his in the restaurant, I should probably wear a bulletproof vest."

"So, you're gonna stay?"

She reads the text again and nods. "I suppose."

"Oh, thank goodness," I say. "I don't know what they would have done if I let you get away before the ceremony. I'll go down to the lobby and tell them that you changed your mind. You can take the first boat off the island in the morning. I'll get you to the ferry dock on time, I promise."

"I guess one more night on this Godforsaken island won't kill me," she says. "My flight out of Cleveland is tomorrow anyway. I was going to spend the night in a *real* five-star hotel, not this dump."

Whew. I take a deep breath and feel my heart slow down to a normal pace. "Just don't tell anyone that I told you about the award, though, okay? It's supposed to be a big surprise."

"Don't worry. No one will suspect a thing," she says. "I'm *very* good at pretending to be surprised."

Jordie Holloway is already on his second drink when Keyheart shows up at the Mug Shot for their meeting. He's been waiting for twenty minutes in a corner booth opposite the bar when she finally sits.

"Scotch. Double," she says to the bartender on her way to the booth.

"She's here," says Suzy, giving me the play-by-play over her phone. Over the past few days, she's gotten to know the staff at the Mug Shot well enough that they're letting her spy on Keyheart from the kitchen, where the monitors for the security cameras are mounted. Before Holloway arrived, she "bugged" the corner booth, using her wireless microphone so she can listen in on the conversation and dial me in remotely. The mic is hidden on the back of a framed picture of Leroy Kelley, a Cleveland Browns football player from the sixties, that's hanging on the wall next to the booth. A helpful Mug Shot employee made sure that all the other booths needed cleaning in order to guarantee that Holloway and Keyheart would sit in that particular one. Meanwhile, I'm a couple of doors away, on the porch of the coffee shop, sipping on a ginger ale across from Blake.

So far, everything is going according to my plan.

"Okay, you should be able to hear them now on the other phone," Suzy says. "Don't forget to hit the record button."

I'm using my phone to talk to her, and Blake's to snoop on the conversation in the booth. "Got it." I hold Blake's phone to my ear just as Holloway greets Keyheart.

"I thought maybe you changed your mind," he says.

Into my phone, I tell Suzy, "Wow. It's good. Really clear. It sounds like they're in the room with me."

"I'm here," Keyheart says. "Even though I'm sure it's a waste of my time."

"I wouldn't be too sure of that," says Holloway. "I think you will want to hear what I have to say."

"So, say it. Let's get this over with."

The bartender sets her drink down on the table. "Double scotch. Anything else?"

"We're good," Holloway tells him. "Put that on my tab. Thanks."

"It must be serious," Keyheart says. "You're buying me drinks. You haven't done that since—"

"Since you pushed me under the wheels of the Keyheart Express?"

Keyheart laughs. "Cheers! Here's to keeping that train running."

"No matter who gets in the way, right?" Holloway says. "All's fair in love, war, and publishing."

"Well, this little *jaunt* down memory lane has been fun, but let's get to it. Why am I here, Jordie?"

"Fair enough. Okay. Here's the thing, Ann. Real simple. I can *prove* that you didn't write *A Drowsy Numbness*. Your assistant did."

"This again? Aren't you getting tired of playing the same old tune? You think *I* was rough on you? My lawyers are going to put your sorry excuse for a *derriere* through a wood chipper."

"Are you done threatening me? Because I'd like to continue. I have a little story to share."

"Fine. Be my guest. I love fairy tales."

"Then I'm afraid you're going to be disappointed. This is strictly nonfiction. I met someone very interesting last night right here on the island. A retired college professor. He's on his way here right now. He has something you really *must* see."

"How *exciting*," says Keyheart. "Cardigans. Corduroy. Elbow patches. I'm all a-tingle."

"He's not just any professor," Holloway continues. "He teaches creative writing at Columbia, Didi Ferrer's alma mater. Dr. LaRue Struna. Lovely man. He retired last year, and moved into a house on Swallowtail Island, of all places. Seems there's a family connection. He grew up in Cleveland and spent summers here."

"*Fascinating*," says Keyheart. "Tell me, is this story going to end in my lifetime?"

The door swings open behind Jordie, and an old man in a striped seersucker suit and a bow tie walks in.

"I think your guy just came in," Suzy says. "Light blue suit, bow tie?"

"That's him," I say.

"He is *adorable*. Where did you find him?" Suzy asks.

"His real name is Simon Stanford. He helped me out with that other thing I told you about. He was the kid on the dock who saw *everything*."

"Well, he's perfect. *I* believe he's an English professor. Okay, he sees Holloway. Heading over there."

"Professor Struna," Jordie says. "Thank you so much for coming. This is my friend, Ann Keyheart."

"A pleasure to meet you," Simon says.

"Ann also . . . *has an interest* in the story you showed me last night. Did you bring it with you?"

"I have it right here," answers Simon. "After we talked last night, I did some thinking. Perhaps you should take it, give it to her family. They should have it."

"Well, only if you're sure," Holloway says. "But yes, of course, I'd be honored."

"That's settled, then," says Simon. "I'll leave you to read it and talk about it. It really is quite extraordinary. Didi was talented, of course, but she was so much more. I don't know that I ever met a writer with a better baloney detector. Of course, Hemingway didn't use the word *baloney*, if you know what I mean. And she was truly a lovely young lady. I understand that she worked for you?"

"That's right. She was my assistant," Keyheart says.

"It's a shame, what happened. So much more tragic when it's a young person. Especially one with such promise. I can't help but wonder what books she might have written if she'd had the chance. The world is a poorer place without her. Well, I must be on my way. I'm helping a friend resuscitate a rare orchid. *Au revoir.*"

"Okay, he's out the door," says Suzy. "Holloway's holding the story and Keyheart hasn't taken her eyes off it."

"Lovely man," Holloway says, but Keyheart stays silent.

Finally, she bangs her empty glass on the table. "Well? I met your professor. Yeah, yeah. I get it. Didi was wonderful.

Didi was talented. Didi was the second coming of Ernest Hemingway. Am I gonna get to read this story or what?"

"*Patience*, Ann," Holloway says. "Before I let you read it, allow me to point out a few things. The title, for instance. *A Drowsy Numbness*. Sound familiar? You can read Professor Struna's comments at the end, along with the grade: *A*-plus. But the most fascinating thing about this story is this, up here in the heading. Look at the date. May 20, four *years* ago. Three years before Didi Ferrer even knew who you were. Or you her. And yet, when I read this story last night, I was *astonished* by the similarity to *your* new book. There are sentences, entire passages, even, that are *identical*. Now, you can go on pretending that you wrote *A Drowsy Numbness*, and chalk all this up to an extraordinary coincidence, or we can put a stop to this nonsense and get real. Oh, and by the way, Walt Whitman didn't write 'Ode to a Nightingale.' It was John Keats. Sort of an important detail, don't you think?"

There's a long stretch of silence, and I wonder if I've lost the connection to Suzy.

"What's going on?" I ask Suzy. "Is she reading the story?"

"She kinda skimmed it. Looking at the last page right now."

"Good, isn't it?" Holloway says. "You have to love Professor Struna's comment about the *pathos*, don't you? I don't think anybody ever said that about *your* writing. He's good. He ought to be—"

"What's this all about?" Keyheart hisses. "Revenge? Is this

your way of getting back at me for dumping you? Seriously? Get over it. So I didn't write the book. Big deal."

Yes! My heart skips a beat as Keyheart's own words echo in my ears:

"*I didn't write the book.*"

"*I didn't write the book.*"

"*I didn't write the book.*"

"Did you hear that?" Suzy says. "Boy, I hope you're still recording."

"Oh, yeah. I got it," I say.

"Actually, it *is* a big deal," Holloway says.

"Oh, come on," says Keyheart. "It's not like I'm the first author to engage in a little bit of aggressive . . . *borrowing*. Everybody does it. So, is that what you want? To embarrass me?"

There's another long pause, followed by Keyheart screeching, "Why are you *smiling*? Stop it!"

"I'm sorry, I can't help myself. *Embarrass* you? No, Ann. You misunderstand. I have no intention of exposing you as a thief. On the contrary. I'm planning to tell everyone that you're a *genius*. You see, what I *want* is a piece of the *Drowsy* pie. We're getting the band back together, so to speak. I'm going to be your agent. Keyheart and Holloway, together again. Like Lennon and McCartney. Or Simon and Garfunkel. But this time, under the circumstances, twenty-five percent instead of the usual fifteen, don't you think?"

"Twenty-five percent! That's ridiculous. Twenty."

"This is not a negotiation," Holloway says. "I could have asked for fifty. It's twenty-five. Take it or leave it."

"What about your new friend, the professor? What if he comes forward?"

"*This* is the only copy of the story. The guy is a million years old. He still uses a typewriter, and a Rolodex, for crying out loud. He actually has a landline—and his phone has a *rotary* dial, I kid you not. Don't worry about him."

"What about *you*? What if you suddenly develop a conscience?"

"Thanks to you, Didi's parents don't trust me, so even if they had a copy of the book—which, again, thanks to you, they *don't*, and they're not *going* to—they'd find another agent. Don't forget, I've read enough to *know* how good it is. It's gonna sell a bazillion copies. Translations. Film rights. Why would I do anything to jeopardize all that? This book—*your* book—is my retirement plan."

"Oh, he's good," I say.

"He's holding out his hand for her to shake," Suzy says. "She's thinking about it . . . yes! She shook it. She made the deal."

Yesss! I high-five Blake so hard that he almost falls off his chair.

"Now what?" he asks.

"A short intermission. Then, tonight, Act Two."

CHAPTER

16

SWALLOWTALES'S FINAL EVENT gets underway at five thirty when Blake and I arrive with all the other pages, drivers, and other assorted volunteers and helpers for the official thank-you from Nadine and the rest of the Swallowtales executive committee. After the group photos, we each receive a Swallowtales fleece and a signed book by one of the guest authors. Gabby, nominated by the writer Howard Allam, wins the Best Page award, and when she prances up the aisle to receive the plaque, I have to laugh when I see that the signed book she's carrying is Keyheart's *The Somewhere Girls*.

Meanwhile, everyone else gathers on the patio for the cocktail hour. I get a big surprise when Thomas arrives with Pip and Jack in tow. Pip is adorable as usual in her red blazer and riding pants, and Jack in khakis and a white button-down looks like a miniature version of Thomas as he practices dribbling a soccer ball on his toe.

"I didn't know you guys were coming," I say as Pip throws her arms around me.

"It's all Nadine's doing," Thomas says. "She showed up with tickets and said that we just *had* to come. And you know I can't pass up a free meal. Even if I have to put on a tie."

"I'm more amazed that you got Jack to dress up again. That's twice this summer. A new record," I say.

Jack picks up the soccer ball and tugs at his collar, acting as if he's choking, but stops when Nadine and Dinah approach.

"You boys all look so handsome," Dinah says. "And Pip, I do love that blazer. You look as if you belong in one of those period dramas on PBS. Did you come on Tinker?"

Pip twirls in place to show off her outfit, and then sticks out her bottom lip in her best Pip fashion. "Thomas wouldn't let me. We got a ride from Mr. Findlay. Except for Nate."

"That's right. I'm the bad guy," Thomas says.

"Where *is* Nate?" I ask.

"He should be here in a few minutes," Thomas answers. "He was going to ride with Suzy. I guess she rented a golf cart. It wasn't exactly clear, to be honest, but he promised that he'd come."

"That was quick thinking to get you-know-who to stick around," Nadine whispers in my ear. "The Dinah Purdy Award for Outstanding Writing in the Field of Writing. That's *inspired*."

"Honest, it was the first thing that came into my head."

"Is she here yet?" Nadine asks.

"She's over there, in the middle of that big group next to the bar," I say.

"What are you two up to now?" Thomas says to Nadine and me. "What is this surprise that you promised?"

"You'll just have wait and see, like everybody else," Nadine answers. "After tonight, everybody is going to know who Lark Heron-Finch is."

"She hasn't exactly been flying under the radar since we got to the island," Thomas replies.

"Hey! There's Suzy and Nate!" cries Jack. He hands the soccer ball to Thomas and waves his arms over his head until she sees him.

"Hey there, handsome," she says, high-fiving Jack. "Looking *sharp*. I do love a man in a tie. Pip! Are you the cutest thing ever? And omigosh, *Lark*. Love that dress. I'd borrow it from you, but it'd come down to my ankles."

"These guys are going to miss you, Suzy," Thomas says. "I do hope you'll come back and visit. There's always room for one more at the Roost."

"You definitely have *not* seen the last of me," she says. "I like this place. It's not what I expected. And it's a lot different from New York. But there's something about it. . . . I feel like I understand Didi better now. And I really, really wish she was here for me to tell her that in person."

"I know you're hurting right now," Thomas begins, "but I'll tell you what I told Lark and Pip when they lost their mom. The Stoics—you know how much I love them—looked for positives in every situation. I'm paraphrasing, but Seneca would say that it hasn't been for nothing that you had such a good friend, and just because fate, or chance, or . . . whatever has taken her from you, there's no reason for the *friendship* to end. Even though Didi may be gone, a big part of her still goes on living. That's especially true in this case, with her book and everything. Keep this in mind: all those years you knew each other, all that you went through together—it's all *your* past, too, and no one can take that away from you."

Suzy's eyes are full of tears as she throws her arms around Thomas and squeezes. "Thank you. Thank you so much."

When Suzy finally breaks away, I punch Thomas on the arm. "That was pretty good. You're all right. Sometimes. And I guess that Seneca guy was kinda smart, too."

"High praise from you. I'll take it. And I'll pass that on to Seneca, too. Even famous philosophers need positive reinforcement."

Meanwhile, Nadine steps up onto a raised platform where a small table is covered with "Swallow's Eggs"—painted, egg-shaped stones glued to pieces of driftwood—that are handed out at the end of every Swallowtales to writers who have "broken out of their shells." Super corny, I know, but people love the things. Not quite everyone receives a Swallow's Egg, but it's close, so the presentation takes some time.

I'm keeping one eye on Keyheart at all times in case she decides to leave before it's time for *her* award. Even though Jordie Holloway twisted her arm, giving her no choice but to accept his terms, she's still as obnoxious as ever, rolling her eyes and sighing loudly as the "eggs" are handed out.

Finally, only one egg remains, but it is larger, mounted on a piece of marble instead of driftwood like the others, and there's an actual engraved brass plaque attached.

"We have one final egg," Nadine announces. "A very special one, for a very special writer."

Keyheart, paying close attention, puffs herself up. Her expression changes to one of confusion when Wendy Eppinger joins Nadine on the stage to present the last egg.

"Wendy, first, let me thank you again for taking the time to join us here for Swallowtales," Nadine says. "We may not be the biggest writers' conference, but we like to think we're the best, and it's all due to the generosity of professionals like you."

"Thank you, Nadine," Eppinger says. "I love coming to Swallowtail Island! Honestly, I think it's the Midwest's best-kept secret. I hope you'll invite me back for next summer."

The crowd cheers and Nadine nods enthusiastically.

Eppinger continues, "Well. If you'll excuse the unfortunate pun, this week really has been one for the books. Like a great novel, it has given us a little bit of everything:

Reflection on the past. Hopes and dreams of a better future. New relationships. Old loves reconciled." Her eyes search the crowd, landing on Howard Allam and his wife, and she smiles. Howard raises his glass to her. "Friendships, the spark of creativity, the expected, the *un*expected, conflict, drama, and tragedy. Sadly, we lost one of our own this week, a promising young writer named Didi Ferrer. For me, though, the moment that defines this year's Swallowtales came the other night, when we gathered to listen to writers read from their new works. One work seemed to stand out for its originality, its honesty, its ability to reach deep down inside us and touch our hearts. It is that work that we honor today with this final egg. The title of the book comes from John Keats, who wrote *this* line in 1819, two years before his death at the tender age of twenty-five: *My heart aches, and a drowsy numbness pains my sense, as though of hemlock I had drunk.*"

Almost everyone in the audience nods in agreement with the choice as they search out Ann Keyheart, whose usual scowl has been plastered over with a self-satisfied smile. Meanwhile, I'm rocking another version of the very same expression, for a *completely* different reason.

"And so, it gives me great pleasure to announce the recipient of this final egg," Eppinger says, holding it up for everyone to see. "The First Annual Dinah Purdy Award for Excellence goes to *A Drowsy Numbness*, by . . . Didi Ferrer!"

Ann E. Keyheart's biggest fan, the man I know only as Irwin, lets loose a resounding *Woo!* the moment the words *A Drowsy Numbness* leave Wendy Eppinger's lips. Others in the crowd join in, but the cheers quickly turn to chaos and confusion when they realize that it was Didi's name, not Keyheart's, that had been called out. As for Keyheart, she has already taken two steps toward the stage when she freezes in place, her beaming face instantly taking on an expression that could melt glass.

"I spoke to Didi's mom a little while ago," Eppinger says. "She's on her way back from Japan right now and is so sorry that she can't be here to accept this honor on Didi's behalf. She asked me to thank everyone for their kindness, and asked that I give the egg to Didi's roommate, Suzy, for safekeeping. I'm hoping that she's still here."

"She's right there," Nadine says. "Come on up, Suzy."

Suzy weaves her way through the crowd to the stage, where Eppinger presents her with the egg. "Your friend has left us with a very special gift. Thanks to the efforts led by a *very* determined young woman, I had the

opportunity to read the entire manuscript today, and I have *never* been so moved by a book. Ever. This book is going to bring happiness to a lot of people. You have my word: Didi Ferrer won't be forgotten."

Suzy thanks her, and after hugs from both Eppinger and Nadine, rejoins us. A few feet away, Keyheart turns redder and redder until she finally explodes: "This. Is. *Outrageous*. I'm going to sue you, every last one of you. You have humiliated me, *publicly*. That, that *girl*, stole *my* book. She had access to everything. I can prove it! Jordie! Where's Jordie Holloway? He can tell you. He knows the truth."

Holloway appears on cue from behind Nadine. "You're right about *that*. I do know the truth. I can state with absolute certainty that Didi Ferrer wrote *A Drowsy Numbness*, and you tried to steal it from her. You promised to help, and then you betrayed her. You never sent it to *anyone*. Lucky for me, she was impatient and sent me a query and the first three chapters. That's what brought me to Swallowtales."

"Well, aren't *we* lucky," Keyheart says.

"You see, I'm afraid I wasn't exactly honest with you earlier today," Holloway continues. "There is no Professor Struna—the man you met is a wonderful gentleman named Simon Stanford, and the short story that he supposedly kept all these years is a . . . well, I'm afraid it's an artistic *fabrication*, courtesy of *that* young lady," he adds, pointing at me. "But the thing is, you *believed* it all because you knew it was *possible*. You knew you didn't write the book. And then you admitted it."

"That's a lie! I admitted nothing! It's my book. My lawyer is going to have a field day with you. With *all* of you. Say goodbye to your precious Swallowtales and all these insipid, no-talent wannabees."

"Actually, Ann, you *did* admit it," Holloway says. "With a little help, I recorded our conversation. I'm not proud of it, but I'll admit that I was tempted to go along with your lie, just to get back in the game in a really big way. But it doesn't take a genius to see why I have to do this. The world may be a screwed up place right now, and there's a lot of nonsense out there about *facts* and *truth*, but in this case, the truth is simple: Didi Ferrer wrote *A Drowsy Numbness*. Not you. You didn't even know who wrote 'Ode to a Nightingale,' for crying out loud. We have no choice but to honor her for that. For *anyone* else to get the credit for this wonderful, moving, enlightening book would be a travesty of the worst kind. I don't know if it will stand the test of time, but I *can* say this, now that I've read the whole thing: It's the best book I've read in twenty years, and I plan to give a copy to everyone I know."

Keyheart smirks. "You do that. And I will happily accept the royalties from every one of those copies."

"I wouldn't be too sure of that," Holloway continues. "You see, a *very* clever girl named Lark sat me down and pointed out some things that lead to only one conclusion. You know, Ann, I assumed that you stealing the book was a crime of opportunity.

That after Didi's accident, you swooped in like a vulture and picked her computer clean."

The crowd has backed away from Keyheart, who stands alone, staring unblinkingly at Holloway and radiating rage. "My lawyer is going to eat you for breakfast."

Undaunted, Holloway moves in for the metaphorical kill: "But Didi Ferrer's death was no accident, was it, Ann. It was deliberate. Premeditated. *Murder.*"

Gasps, cries, shouts, and general chaos come on the heels of that last word: *Murder.* It's also, apparently, the last straw for Keyheart. Without another word, she spins on her heels and storms out, the crowd parting before her.

"Whoa, whoa, WHOA!" a man's voice booms above the crowd noise. It is Officer Pawlowski, who has just come from inside the lobby. "For the love of . . . now look here, Holloway. You can't just go around accusing people of murder in public. Let's all just settle down. Everybody had a nice week here on the island doing whatever it is you do, but now it's time for everybody to go *home.* Nobody's been murdered. What happened was a tragic *accident,* pure and simple."

"No. It *wasn't,*" I say, stepping up to be at Nadine's side. "He's right. It *was* murder. You need to stop her." I point toward to the door that Keyheart is heading for.

Pawlowski palm-slaps his forehead so loudly that everyone hears it. "You! *Again.* You *promised* me you were gonna drop this. The last thing you said to me was—"

"I said I'd keep my word," I say. "And I am. I promised to drop it if I was *wrong*, but I'm not, and I can prove it if you give me five minutes."

"Listen to what the kid has to say," Holloway insists.

"Seriously. You *need* to hear this," adds Suzy. "We owe it to Didi. She was only *twenty-four* years old. And, obviously, she was brilliant. If she was murdered, somebody's got to pay the price."

"You can't let her leave the island," I say. "Think about it. Do you want people saying that you let a murderer go?"

I find Thomas in the crowd and make eye contact. He mouths, *Are you sure?* and when I nod in response, he gives me a thumbs-up and says, *Go for it.*

Pawlowski considers his options and finally gives in. "I'm not nutty about this, but the boat doesn't leave for twenty minutes. I'll give you *five* to convince me that I shouldn't let it leave with her on it."

From the back pocket of my shorts, I take out a stack of index cards that I have prepared. "I can do that."

CHAPTER
17

PAWLOWSKI MOTIONS FOR ME TO follow him into the hotel lobby, away from the crowd that ignores his plea to just go *home* and instead seems to be heading for the bar to share their own Keyheart stories.

"Mr. Holloway, too," I say. "And Suzy. And Blake. I couldn't have done it without them."

"Fine."

As soon as we're seated around a table in a quiet corner of the lobby, I take a long, deep breath, and begin.

"Didi told me about her book on Saturday, on our way back from Big Egg Island. She finished writing it a few weeks ago, and then all *this* got started when she gave a hard copy to Keyheart to read. Keyheart read it and told Didi that she *really* liked it and was going to pass it on to her editor as a favor. A few days later, Didi asked Keyheart if she'd sent it, and Keyheart got irritated with her for being impatient. That's when Didi decided to send part of it to an agent, to see if they might be interested in it."

"Me," Holloway says. "Apparently, she had no idea that I used to be Keyheart's agent, or that we hate each other."

"Meanwhile, like Mr. Holloway said, *Keyheart* never sent the book to her editor, and never intended to," I say. "On Saturday, I was there when Didi introduced herself to Jean Morse, who happens to be Keyheart's editor. It was obvious that she had never heard of Didi or her book. And by the way, in the *year* that Didi worked for her, Keyheart didn't write a single word, even though she told everyone she was working on a book. On top of that, her last couple of books didn't sell very well, and most of the reviews were pretty bad. Basically, I think she was kind of desperate."

"She was *totally* desperate," says Suzy. "Didi said so all the time."

"From what I've heard, it seems like that's par for the course for a writer. It's a long way from that to planning and committing an actual murder," Pawlowski says.

"Maybe for most people," Holloway says. "Ann Keyheart is *not* most people."

"Remember those stories I told you out at the house?" I ask Pawlowski. "She had a way of making real enemies. And getting what she wanted. In this case, she wanted Didi's book for herself, and came up with a plan to make it happen, starting with her return to Swallowtales. She hadn't been here for years when *she* called Nadine out of the blue and offered to take part for *free* . . . as long as she and Didi could stay in the Captain's Cottage, the farthest one from the hotel. Then she orders a bunch of boxes of chocolates from Keke's Cocoas to be delivered to New York. Check with Keke. She'll have the order. Here's the thing, though: Keyheart and Didi are *both* allergic to nuts. Some of the boxes she ordered had nuts. Keyheart said she was buying them to give as gifts, and maybe she did, but she saved one box for herself—I'll explain why in a minute."

"Tell him about the EpiPen," Suzy says.

I hold up the another index card. "That's next. Actually, why don't you tell him," I say.

"I've known Didi since the first day of high school," Suzy begins, "and she never went *anywhere* without one. She always had one on her and knew *exactly* where it was. But, somehow, the day before she's leaving New York for Swallowtail Island, hers just *magically* disappears from her bag, even though the only place she went was Keyheart's apartment. She thought maybe it fell out, and of course, Keyheart said she didn't find it, but come on. It doesn't take a genius to figure out that the dragon lady took it. She tells Didi not to worry because *she* has one, and since they're going to be sharing the cottage here on the island, she'll be fine. I'll bet you anything that if you searched Keyheart's apartment, you'd find it."

"And she'd say that Didi must have dropped it," says Pawlowski. "She was there every day, right? Still haven't heard anything that sounds like real evidence."

"We're not done yet," I say. "The missing EpiPen *could be* just a fluke, but then there's her missing phone, which brings us to last Saturday, the day they arrive here on the ferry. Funny story: Before I went over to the ferry dock to meet them, I drove out to the point here to see if the ferry was on the way. As it's going by, a woman standing at the back tosses overboard what I *think* is a can of that CoffLEI stuff that everybody here drinks—you know, in the striped cans. But yesterday I realized something. That wasn't just some random woman. She had on a big sun hat with a green band around it, the *same* hat that flew off *Ann Keyheart's* head as she was coming down the gangplank to meet me. And that striped thing she threw into the lake? Suzy, tell Officer Pawlowski what Didi's phone case looks like."

"It was striped, navy blue and white," Suzy answers.

"Yup. On the way to the hotel, Didi asked Keyheart for it. Supposedly, Keyheart borrowed it on the ferry because the battery on *hers* was dead, but then I remembered that I saw her check it for messages right after we got to the cottage. Anyway, when Didi asked for it back, Keyheart admitted that she had *accidentally* dropped it overboard."

"Accident, my foot," says Suzy.

"Okay, she lost her Epi-thingy and her phone. Anybody can have a bad day or two," Pawlowski says. "I'm still not sure—"

I hold up the next index card, cutting him off. "Back to those boxes of chocolates. The number one thing to remember about them is that it is impossible that chocolates with nuts got mixed in with the no-nut kind *at* Keke's. You talked to her, right? They're not even made in the same place. Here's what I think happened. Remember the other day when I told you about the cellophane from the trash that you gave me? And the Scotch tape?"

Pawlowski nods and says, "And the way I remember it is, you were convinced that somebody was trying to kill this Keyheart lady."

"I was wrong about the *who*. I'll admit that. But I was right about the *what*. Before they left New York, *Keyheart* opened a box *without* nuts very carefully, took out some of the pieces, and replaced them with ones from a box *with* nuts. Then she replaced the wrapper, just like I said, using a piece of Scotch tape so you couldn't see that it had been tampered with. When I dropped the two of them at the cottage to get them settled in, Keyheart insisted that Didi break out the box that they had brought from New York—the one that Keyheart had tampered with. It was definitely a green box, with dark chocolate, which Didi preferred. In order to make it all look really innocent, she had *me* open them. Then *she* picked out a chocolate and handed it to Didi, saying that she knew it was her favorite kind. Dark chocolate and espresso."

"That *was* her favorite," Suzy confirms. "She was a caffeine freak. Keyheart would have known that."

"She also picked out one for me and one for herself. The whole thing was staged so that a witness—that's me—would see Didi eat a chocolate from that box and *not* get sick," I say. "Keyheart chose the pieces because she knew which pieces had nuts and which didn't. If something happened with me there, it would have ruined her plan. She made a big show of telling Didi that the rest of that box was all hers, and then she—Keyheart—took the unopened box from the welcome basket."

"Were those from Keke's, too?" Suzy asks.

"Yeah. A green box, but they were milk chocolate, not dark. Definitely no nuts."

"They wouldn't have been Didi's first choice," Suzy says. "The darker, the better."

I flip to the next card. "I left them at around one thirty that afternoon, so I can't tell you much about what happened in the cottage for the next hour. The plan was for me to come back at two thirty to take Didi someplace she wanted to go—Big Egg Island—and then to the yacht club. She *really* didn't want to go sailing, but Keyheart had arranged it with the Cheevers and told her they'd be insulted if she didn't show. The fact is, Keyheart couldn't care less about the Cheevers. What she wanted was some alone time with Didi's laptop, and now we know why. She wiped that thing *clean*. There are no Word documents, and even stranger, no email. Every single email in Didi's account is gone. Inbox. Sent emails. Folders. Spam.

Trash. All empty. Come on, Officer Pawlowski, you saw that for yourself. You have to admit that *that's* crazy."

He nods. "I admit it's not normal, but hey, you never know with people."

"That's true," I say. "But there's more. Personally, I thought it was kind of strange that Didi didn't store her documents, especially something like a book that you've been working on for months, or even years, on the cloud. I mean, everybody does that now. And everything about her life was so organized. She was super cautious about everything, so how is it possible that she didn't have a system for backing up her work? It's like the first thing they teach you about computers.

"Well, it turns out that she did, it was just really old-school. She used a thumb drive, or a flash drive, a memory stick, whatever you call it, the thing that goes into a USB port." I hold up Didi's pendant and pull apart the two *D*s for Pawlowski to see. "This was her lucky charm. She wore it around her neck, everywhere she went, and lucky for us, she never told *anyone* about it. Even Suzy didn't know. And, more importantly, Keyheart didn't know. Because it's all here, every word of *A Drowsy Numbness*, the book that *Didi* wrote."

"And Keyheart stole," Suzy adds.

"I know what you're thinking," I say before Pawlowski can object. "Keyheart's going to say the opposite, that Didi was trying to steal the book from her, but we have a recording of her *admitting* that Didi wrote it. And on top of that, she made a *big* mistake the night that Didi died. It's like they always say: there's no such thing as a perfect crime. When I dropped her off at the cottage on Saturday night, she went inside and I started back up the path toward the hotel. I remember exactly where I was when I heard her scream—the moment when she supposedly discovered Didi's body. I measured the distance this morning; it's seventy-eight yards. Walking at a normal pace, and stopping once, at 10:08, according to my phone, to send Thomas a text telling him I was on my way home, it took me almost a full *minute* to reach that spot. That's a *long* time to find Didi, who was right there in the living room. But Keyheart had work to do. I can't prove it, but I think Keyheart unplugged the cottage phone before she left for the party that night. One, when I stopped at the cottage to take her to the party, she didn't answer the door right away, so I had somebody at the hotel desk call the landline. I had my ear pressed against the door, but there was no phone ringing inside. And two, I *know* Didi was back from sailing because the Cheevers were at the party, but when Keyheart had me call Didi at the cottage, it just kept ringing, which is exactly what phones here on the island do if they're not plugged in. But Didi wouldn't have known that until she tried to use it, when she was in trouble. Remember, no cell phone and no EpiPen, so that landline was her only chance. I guarantee you that Keyheart's fingerprints are on the plug for the phone. She touched it *twice*. To unplug it and then plug it back in before I went inside."

"We can check that," Pawlowski says, paying closer attention with every added detail. "Okay, keep going."

"Well, after Keyheart screamed, I ran back to the cottage and pounded on the door. She let me in, told me that Didi was dead, and then fainted—or, at least, pretended to. You remember what she was like that night, right? I think a lot of that was an act. Anyway, I checked to make sure Keyheart was breathing, and then called 911 as soon as I saw Didi. When I got off the phone, I checked the kitchen and peeked into Didi's room. It didn't register with me at the time, but her laptop was open and I could see the wallpaper on the screen. It's a picture of an old woman waving from the ferry dock here on the island."

"That's her grandmother," Suzy says. "It was the last time Didi ever saw her."

"Well, last night, I was doing some serious thinking," I say, "and for some reason, I couldn't get that picture out of my head. Something just didn't add up, but this morning, when you let me see the laptop again, I realized it's not the picture itself, it's the fact that I was *able* to see the picture. See, the thing is, her computer is set to sleep after *ten* minutes, the screen goes *black*. So, in order for the wallpaper to still be visible when I walked in the room, *somebody* must have touched the keyboard sometime between 10:04 and 10:14, which is when I went in, which I know because of the time stamp on a picture I took in the room. It wasn't me, and it couldn't have been Didi. The paramedics said that she'd probably been dead a couple of hours.

Even if they're off by an hour, it's still impossible. There's only one answer: Keyheart checked the computer, probably making sure that Didi hadn't looked at her email. And that's it. Put all the pieces together and there's only one possible answer: Ann Keyheart *murdered* Didi Ferrer."

"And stole her book," Blake adds.

"You're sure about this computer thing, this . . . whaddya call it, wallpaper? Ten minutes?" Pawlowski asks.

"You saw the settings on the laptop," I say. "And I'm *positive* about what I saw that night. C'mon, Officer. You know I'm right. She probably decided to do it here on the island because she knows there's only one cop, and she figured she could out-smart you, make you believe it was all an accident. But you're too smart for that."

When in doubt, try a little flattery, I always say.

"*Well?*" Blake says.

"I'm gonna need you to write up exactly what you just told me," Pawlowski finally says. "But yeah, I think I've got enough to go on. To bring her in for questioning, at least."

Suzy high-fives me. "You did it, kid. Now, let's go get her."

"You three aren't going anywheres," Pawlowski orders. "I mean it. Don't interfere."

"I'm offended. We're not going to *interfere*," I say. "But you can't stop us from watching when you slap the cuffs on her."

"Fine. Just keep your distance. Slap the cuffs on her," he adds, scoffing. "*Somebody* watches *way* too much TV." He storms off toward the main desk in the lobby and asks about Keyheart.

Neil Derry, the hotel manager, tells him, "She's checked out, Officer. One of the boys drove her to the ferry dock a few minutes ago."

Pawlowski checks the time on his watch and runs for the door, shouting over his shoulder, "Call the ferry dock and tell them to hold the boat on my order!"

He leaps into the seat of his police golf cart, madly searching his pockets for the keys, when Derry comes running out of the hotel a few seconds later, waving his arms.

"Officer! Wait. Ms. Keyheart isn't at the ferry dock. One of the boys overheard her talking to some guy about the next flight off the island. He said something about Irwin Air, that the plane was ready whenever she was."

"What are you talking about?" Pawlowski says. "There are no flights. No Irwin Air. There's no planes. Now, where are my danged keys?!"

"You're wrong. There *is* a plane," I say.

"Stay out of this," Pawlowski says. He pats his uniform all over, finally digging out a keyring from the back pocket of his pants.

"No! Listen to me! It's true. We saw it land on Saturday morning. In the lake, up by Cattail Island. A *seaplane*. I *swear*. And Irwin is this . . . this *guy* who follows Keyheart around, everywhere she goes. Like a groupie. He would do *anything* for her. It must be his plane."

"There *was* an Irwin staying at the hotel," Derry says. "Irwin Jansen. He checked out an hour ago."

"What do you mean, up by Cattail Island?" Pawlowski asks me. "Can you be more precise? Like, how far up?"

"Almost to Dinah Purdy's house," I say. "There's a dock—I think Les Findlay keeps his boat there."

"I know the place," he says, checking his watch again. "Gonna take me fifteen minutes to get there in this thing." He turns the key and speeds away in the cart, shouting again at Mr. Derry to hold the ferry, just in case.

Derry hurries back toward the lobby door, unable to hide his excitement at being in the middle of something *big*. "Oh, this is *so* exhilarating," he says. "Intrigue! Here on Swallowtail Island!"

"Come on," Suzy says, pulling me toward the row of golf carts. "Let's go. I want to be there when she gets arrested."

"No, wait. I have an idea. You two go. Blake, you know the way." I toss him the keys.

"You sure?" he says.

"Yeah. I have to find . . . Pip! Pip!" I run back toward the hotel entrance and *barely* avoid colliding with her at full speed when she bolts through the open door with Nate hot on her heels.

"What's wrong? What happened?" she says, her eyes as big as her favorite cereal bowl.

"Where's Tinker?" I ask. "I need a ride—fast!"

CHAPTER
18

THE WORDS ARE BARELY OUT of my mouth when I remember how far Pip's bottom lip was sticking out only a few minutes earlier, and the reason for it: Tinker is back home, in the barn! And Blake and Suzy are already out of shouting range. I quickly text both of them, but get no reply.

"Shoot!" I say, kicking the dirt. The thought of missing the showdown between Officer Pawlowski and Keyheart is unthinkable. I *have* to get there.

"I'll go get her," Pip says. "I can be back in—"

"It'll be too late," I say, checking my phone again." Still no response from Blake or Suzy. "Need another plan. Look for a golf cart with the keys in it."

"You're gonna steal a golf cart?"

"Pip! Not now. Please, just look!"

"Where're they going?" Nate asks, pointing far up the driveway at the cart with Blake and Suzy.

"That seaplane we saw the other day—I need to get there. Like, *right now*. C'mon. Help me find a cart with the keys in it."

"I can give you a ride!" Nate says.

"A golf cart's faster than your bike."

"I'm not talking about my bike," he says. "Wait here."

I shout, "Nate! I don't have time!" but he's already racing toward the trees behind the hotel.

"Here's one!" Pip cries from the seat of one of the hotel's carts.

"Yes! Let's go," I say, and leap over a row of shrubs to join her. I jam the pedal to the floor and turn toward the driveway and the road.

"Why are we going so *slow*?" Pip asks after we've gone a short (make that a *very* short) distance.

She's right. We've both ridden in enough golf carts to know that something's wrong with the one we've chosen. "Battery must be low." According to the indicator on the dashboard, it's almost fully charged, but when I tap the glass front of the gauge, the needle immediately drops from the *F* to just barely above *E*. "No! Argh!"

As I'm debating whether to turn around and look for a different cart, a motor revs over my shoulder. It's strange enough to hear a motor on Swallowtail Island, but I'm really surprised when I spin to find Nate, wearing Pip's old riding helmet, inches away from me. It takes a moment for what I'm seeing to sink in. He's not on his bike, or a golf cart, or even a lawn mower. Nope. The crazy kid is driving a *motorcycle*, and sporting the biggest smile I've ever seen. Okay, if I'm being totally honest, it's definitely more *scooter* than motorcycle, but still.

I hit the brakes, and so does he. "W-What are you doing?" I say. "Where did you get that?"

"That is so cool," says Pip. "And so illegal."

"It's a 1972 Honda Super Cub," Nate says proudly. "C'mon. Get on. I'll take you. I've even got another helmet. I gave Suzy a ride earlier."

"Go!" cries Pip, pushing me out of the golf cart. "I can make it home in this, and then get Tinker. I'll meet you there."

I climb onto the back of the Honda before I think too much about the fact that my ten-year-old brother is driving. "You're sure you know how to drive this thing?"

"Duh. How do you think I got here? Put your feet on those black things. And hold on!" Before I even have a chance to wrap my good arm around his waist, though, he twists the accelerator. My arm cast bangs against my forehead and I almost fall off the back as we speed off.

"Be careful!" shouts Pip.

"I'm trying!" I say.

When Nate turns around to wave goodbye, he forgets that he's holding onto the handlebars and we swerve almost into the ditch.

"Oops!" he says. "Sorry about that."

"Do you know how to get there, up to Les's dock?" I ask as we approach the Lake Road intersection. "Like, the fastest way?"

"Pip's shortcut?"

"No! Do *not* take the shortcut!" Jumping over fallen trees and fences on Tinker, with Pip at the reins, is one thing. Attempting it on a motor scooter with Nate, who, as far as I know, has ridden it exactly *once* before, is a deal breaker for me. "Go left and then I'll tell you when to turn again. Remember that grass road that goes up to Nadine's?"

"Yeah, I think so," Nate says.

The speedometer says we're going thirty-five, but after months of nothing but bikes and golf carts, it feels a *lot* faster.

"Pretty nice lawn mower, huh?" he says over his shoulder.

"Where did you get this thing? Does Thomas know about it?"

"He knows I *have* it. It was in that old barn at Nadine's. It used to belong to her friend, Kira, when they lived in Africa. Nobody used it for a *looong* time. I asked her if I could try to get it running, and she said yes."

"How did you know how to . . . whatever?"

Nate shrugs. "I just do, I guess. Engines are easy. Nadine said there was nothing wrong with it. I watched a couple of YouTube videos, but mostly it just needed some cleaning."

"And a spark plug," I add. "You must be some kind of

mechanical genius. I don't know anything about that stuff."

"It's not that hard, really. There's—"

"What about, you know, the *law*? Like, no cars or motor-cycles, or even scooters, *remember*? And never mind that, you're only ten years old!"

"Nadine says it's okay to ride it as long as you don't go on the roads. You have to stay on your own property," he says.

"Um . . . Nate? We're *on* a road."

"Yeah, I know, but I finally got it running this morning and I couldn't wait any longer to try it out."

"So, Thomas doesn't know you're—"

"Uhhh, not really."

"That's what I thought. Turn *there*," I say. "Right after that big maple tree."

"You sure?"

"Positive."

He slows and makes the turn, and then says, "Uh-oh."

"What? Oh." A hundred yards ahead of us is the Swallowtail Island Police golf cart with Officer Pawlowski at the wheel.

"What should I do?"

"Go. Fast. As fast as you can. Go around him before he has a chance to—"

"To what? Shoot us?"

"Geez, you sound just like Pip! He's not gonna shoot us. Just go!"

"Okay, here goes."

This might be a good place to mention that a 1972 Honda Super Cub is not exactly the fastest thing you've ever seen. But it is pretty quiet and a lot faster than an electric golf cart, so a few seconds later, we've caught up and are ready to pass. As Nate makes the move to go around him, Pawlowski's head swivels around in total surprise. His eyes meet mine as I look over Nate's shoulder.

"Hey! You can't . . . Stop! Right now!"

I let go of Nate for a second and put my hand to my ear as if I haven't heard, and almost fall off as we swerve left and then right onto the narrow, grassy path that starts where the gravel section of the road ends.

"Keep going!" I shout in Nate's ear.

Pawlowski rants, "That's illegal! I mean it. Stop! Daggone it!" He pounds the dashboard of the cart, cursing us as we zoom ahead.

Meanwhile, my goldfinch charm has bounced out of my shirt. With my good arm clinging tightly to Nate, I reach up with the other and wrap my fingers around the tiny charm. I squeeze it once for luck and tuck it back in, thinking of Pip and Tinker and the last time I was being chased by that same golf cart.

"It's all good," I say to Nate. "Don't worry about him. He's always yelling at me about something."

"He looked pretty mad."

"He'll get over it. I *am* trying to stop a murderer from getting away, after all. I can't help it if I get there first."

"Why doesn't he get something faster than a golf cart?" Nate asks.

"Maybe you should suggest that when he finally shows up," I say.

"Ha! No thanks. I'm staying away from him."

"That line of trees is the start of Nadine's farm," I say. "Get back on the paved road. The trail's too rough. It was okay for Tinker, but this thing will never make it." A quarter mile past Nadine's, the trail converges with the road, which heads north, more or less following the shoreline all the way up to the old breakwater and Rabbit Ear Point. We're not going quite that far, though, and I scan the water for signs of movement as we scoot along on the little Honda. There are a couple of small boats across the channel, tucked into the cove on the south side of Cattail Island, but no sign of a seaplane. I'm about to give up, thinking that we're too late, that we've missed them, when somewhere ahead of us, an engine roars to life.

"That's it!" I cry, crushing Nate in my excitement. "It has to be."

"I. Can't. Breathe," he says.

"Sorry. Keep going. I owe you one, little bro," I add.

As we come around one last bend in the shoreline, the dock, and then the plane, come into sight. It's still tied to the dock, across from Les Findlay's sturdy workboat. And there's some *excellent* news—Les is there on the dock with Irwin and Keyheart.

I wave my arm and shout, but he can't hear me over the sound of the airplane's engine.

Irwin helps Keyheart into the cockpit, and then shakes Les's hand before climbing through the door and pulling it closed behind him. Les then gives the plane a mighty shove, spinning its nose around so that it's pointed toward open water and Cattail Island.

Nate squeezes the brakes and I slide off the back before we come to a complete stop. We run to the end of the dock with the plane's engine roaring even louder. As it glides away, slowly picking up speed, the propeller churns up the water and sends a wall of spray at the three of us.

Irwin turns the plane south, and when he does, I have a clear view of Keyheart. She waves and then she *blows a kiss* at me, which feels a bit like she's smacked me in the face with a mackerel.

This isn't over.

"Hey, you two," Les says when he turns around and sees us. "Pretty sweet, isn't it? Nineteen forty-seven Republic Seabee. My old man had one just like it. First one I've seen in thirty years, I'll bet."

"I don't care what it is. We've got to stop them," I say. "Come on. Police are on the way. And this time they're not after me. It's *her*." I jump from the dock into his boat and wave him in.

Two things that I love about Les Findlay are that he doesn't treat me like a kid, and he doesn't ask too many questions. Without a word, he hops into the boat and starts the engine.

Nate, fearless as ever, jumps in next to me, still grinning like mad.

"You sure?" I ask.

"Yeah. Are you crazy? I'm not gonna miss the best part."

"Put these on," Les says, tossing life jackets to us.

"Hold on tight," I say, struggling to get my cast through the arm hole of the life jacket.

"Get the bow line," he says. I unwrap the line from the cleat and he shifts the engine into reverse and backs away from the dock. "So. You have a plan, or you wingin' it?"

"*Totally* wingin' it," I admit. "Can't we just . . . get in front of him so he can't take off?"

"Maybe. If we get there before he starts his run. Hold on," he says.

Nate and I almost fall backward off the center seat as the boat lurches forward. Irwin's plane, meanwhile, approaches the bottom of Cattail Island.

"They're turning around," Nate says.

After completing the turn, the plane comes to a complete stop, rocking slightly in the choppy water, the engine quiet, the propeller barely turning.

"What's he doing?" I ask.

"Being a good pilot," Les answers. "Going through his

checklist. Flying a Seabee's a little more challenging than driv-ing a golf cart. You screw up, you die. Right now, he's checking his fuel, his flaps, the wind. He has to take off *into* the wind, that's why he's facing this way."

We draw closer and closer, and I find myself gripping the railing on Les's boat so tightly that my hand aches.

"What did she do, anyway? The one you're all after?" Les asks.

"She killed a girl named Didi Ferrer. And stole something from her. All for money. And to be famous."

Les shakes his head. "Fame and fortune. Get you every time."

Suddenly the Seabee's engine roars back to life, revving louder and louder as the propeller spins faster and faster.

"Too late to get in front of him," Les says. He spins the wheel and heads for the plane's tail as it picks up speed. "I have an idea, but we don't have much time, and it'd be a heckuva a lot easier if you had two good arms. Might need both of you. Either that or one of you drives the boat."

"I can help," Nate says.

"That's the Nate we all know and love," I say. "Agreeing to something before you know what's involved."

"Open that forward hatch," Les says. "There's a long piece of line—rope—inside. Good. Need you to tie one end of it to the ring up by the bow. You know how to tie a bowline?"

"A *what*?" I ask. We're twenty-five yards directly behind the Seabee, and the spray from the propeller is pelting us.

"I know how!" cries Nate, crawling forward to join me. He takes the end of the line, threads it through the bow eye, and ties a knot that I've never seen before.

"Good job," says Les. "Now listen carefully, 'cause you're only gonna have one shot at this. First thing, make a loop, about a foot around, in the other end of that line. Use a bowline again. When he starts to lift out of the water, I'm going to get us right underneath him, okay? You'll see a little wheel on his underside, maybe eight or ten inches around. As soon as you can, you reach up and slip that loop around the wheel, and then run back here with me. And hold on, 'cause it's gonna get a little crazy. Got it?"

I nod as Nate ties the loop and holds it up for Les to see.

"That's good. Here we go. Remember. Stay. In. The. Boat!"

I don't know how fast we're going, but with the wind and spray from the propeller, it feels the way I imagine sticking my head out of a car in a rainstorm at eighty miles an hour must feel.

"When I reach up to do it, hold on to my belt," I shout in Nate's ear.

MICHAEL D. BEIL

"No! I should be the one," he says. "You hold on to me."

"No way!"

"Yes! I have two hands. You only need one to hold on to me."

I hate to admit it, but he's right. "Okay. But don't do anything crazy."

He smiles. "Little late for that, doncha think?"

"He's starting to lift!" Les shouts. "Get ready!"

"We're ready," I say.

As the Seabee struggles to break free from the water's surface, the tail rises first. With less drag, the plane accelerates suddenly and for a moment, it looks like we've lost them. But Les pushes the throttle all the way forward and we slide under the tail, and . . . there it is! A small wheel, exactly as he described.

"That's it! Tie it on!" I yell at the top of my lungs.

Nate leans forward over the bow, the line in his hands. With my left hand, I have a death grip on his life jacket, while my right arm, in the cast, swings around, helping me keep my balance in the bouncing boat.

I hold my breath as he reaches up and slips the loop around the wheel.

"Yes!" I scream, pulling him in to me. "You did it!"

At the moment he releases the rope, though, we bounce on a wave, creating just enough slack for the loop to fall off the wheel and drop into the water.

298

Nate reacts in an instant, pulling the line back in as fast as he can until he has the loop in his hand again. Meanwhile, the Seabee rises higher and higher in the water. For a few endless seconds it is like a water-skier, skimming across the surface, trying to build up enough speed to go completely airborne.

"One more chance!" Les shouts as we inch forward once more beneath the tail. Nate reaches up, but his hands and the loop of rope are still six inches from the wheel, and he can't reach any higher. "Lift me up!" he cries.

In the next split second, a million things go through my mind, and most of them involve me explaining to Thomas exactly how I dropped his son over the side of a boat going fifty miles an hour.

Luckily, I don't have enough time to *really* think about all the bad possibilities, and I do exactly what he says: with my one good arm, I grab him around his knees and *toss* him into the air at the exact moment the Seabee skips over one final wave and lurches upward.

In one quick motion, he wraps the loop around the wheel a second time and shouts, "Got it!" as I let him fall into the boat on top of me.

"Hold on!" Les screams as forty feet of line uncoils. When it reaches the end, we lurch violently, with Nate and I tumbling forward as the line becomes tight enough for a high-wire act to perform on. As we clamber toward the back of the boat, somehow the line—and Nate's knots—hold, and we're no longer beneath the Seabee—suddenly, we've become an anchor, dragging Irwin and Keyheart back to Earth. The extra drag from Les's boat is simply too much for the Seabee. It settles back down into the water, a boat once again.

Les grins like a fisherman who has landed the catch of a lifetime and musses Nate's hair.

"You kids are something else. Where'd you learn to tie a bowline?"

"Pip taught me. She uses it to tie up Tinker," he says. "It's good because no matter how hard Tinker pulls on it, she can always untie it."

"That's it in a nutshell," says Les. "Everybody oughta know how to tie one."

"What do we do now?" I ask.

"Sooner or later, he'll realize that he's not going anywhere with us attached. Doesn't have much choice. Might as well head for the dock."

It's clear that Irwin hasn't given up, and I can't help smiling when I picture the scene inside the Seabee's cockpit. "I would *not* want to be Irwin right now. You have no idea how crazy that lady is. I'll be she's telling him to head for that hole in the breakwater."

"He loves his plane too much to try that," says Les.

Ahead of us, the Seabee slows and turns toward the dock, where a crowd is gathering. Officer Pawlowski stands at the end, arms crossed and head down. Running toward the dock is

Suzy, with Blake at her heels. Two more carts are just arriving. First is a Cheever Construction cart with Owen at the wheel, and Gabby and Pip squeezed into the seat next to him. And in the other, Thomas, Nadine, and Jack.

My heart misses a couple of beats when I see Thomas, but mostly I'm relieved by the thought that he didn't see the worst of it. "Maybe we don't tell Thomas *exactly* what happened out there," I say to Nate.

He looks up at Les, who nods and says, "I think that's very wise."

"You think I should *lie*?" Nate says.

"No, but maybe you . . . leave out a few details," I say. "It's for the best. Especially for Thomas. If he knew, he'd never sleep again. It's bad enough he's gonna find out about the motorcycle thing."

"Oh. Yeah. Forgot about that," Nate says. "It was worth it though."

I high-five him. "Totally. I still can't believe you kept it secret."

Finally the Seabee reaches the dock and Irwin kills the engine as Pawlowski and Suzy fend it off and attach the dock lines.

"Guess it's safe to untie us now," Les says, and Nate goes forward to undo his knot.

"See?" he says, holding the line up for me to see. "Even after an *airplane* pulled on it."

"You two okay?" Thomas asks.

While Les backs us into his space on the dock, I give Thomas the thumbs-up, which immediately puts him on guard. He knows that I never use that gesture when I really mean it. Other than being soaked and our hair tangled from the wind from the propeller, Nate and I actually do look just fine—especially compared to the *last* time I got off Les's boat. Together, we still have four working legs and three working arms—the same number we started the day with.

Pawlowski pounds on the cockpit door. "Open up. And keep your hands where I can see 'em."

Irwin climbs out first. Pawlowski looks him up and down and shakes his head. "Have a seat over there. Don't go anywhere. I'll talk to you later."

Keyheart follows a few seconds later, muttering about being surrounded by incompetent *idiots*, who can't even fly their own planes.

"Ann Keyheart, I'm arresting you for the murder of Didi Ferrer," Pawlowski says, spinning her around and marching her down the dock. "You have the right to remain silent . . . "

"Oh, *shut up*," she rants as he continues reading her her rights: "I haven't done anything. I will sue you and everybody on this island. That book is mine. *Mine.* Come *on*. Who's gonna believe that a book *that* good was written by a total *nobody*? Didi and that *holier-than-thou* attitude of hers. Whatever happened to her, she had it coming. Thought she was *sooo* smart. So *smug*."

"Do you understand your rights?" Pawlowski asks.

She opens her mouth to respond, but stops momentarily when she sees me standing between Nate and Nadine. "You're first on my list, Lana. Why don't you go someplace and . . . be *tall*, you circus freak."

"What does that even mean?" I say. "And it's *Lark*. Not Lana, or Lucy, or Lebron. You know, you *almost* had me fooled. When I heard all the stories about how terrible you were to Howard Allam and Wendy Eppinger—"

"Don't forget your pal Jordie Holloway," she says, smiling horribly. "I ruined his career, too."

"It made perfect sense that they would try to kill you," I say. "Every one of them had the motive. They had the means—those boxes from Keke's are everywhere. It's even possible that they could have figured out a way to switch the chocolates and get them into your room. But in the end, it was all about greed, and maybe a little jealousy. You couldn't *stand* that Didi wrote a book that's better than anything you could ever even *hope* to write, so you just had to do something about it."

While all this is going on, Jack and Nate kick a soccer ball back and forth, but one of Jack's passes sails over Nate's head and rolls straight toward Pawlowski. When he bends over to pick it up, Keyheart grabs the gun from his holster and starts waving it around.

"Everybody back up!" Keyheart says, snarling and spitting like a rabid dog. "Irwin! Get that sad excuse for an airplane ready to go. Maybe this time you can actually get it in the air."

"Here we go again," says Les, oddly calm for somebody in the presence of a gun-waving maniac.

"I don't think so," I say.

Pawlowski, still holding the soccer ball, says, "Everybody, just do as she says. Give her plenty of room."

"That's right," Keyheart snaps. "Nice and easy. Back up, everybody."

I stand my ground and mentally measure the distance between Keyheart and me. Twelve yards, give or take a couple of feet. Penalty kick distance.

"Give Nate his ball," I say.

"What? Oh, yeah," says Pawlowski.

Here's the thing: when it comes to soccer, Nate and I have a real connection. We always seem to know exactly where the other is on the field and have an uncanny ability to anticipate the next move without a word being spoken. So, at the moment Pawlowski releases the ball, Nate and I make eye contact. The slightest nod from me sets things in motion.

I take a small step toward him as he taps the ball in my direction.

One more quick glance at Keyheart to calculate the angle and distance, and then one, two, and . . . my right foot swings backward and then, with every brain cell focused and every atom of my body behind it, flies forward, striking the ball cleanly, imparting the perfect amount of "bend."

It rises, spinning and curling toward the upper left-hand

target on my practice goal. This time, though, the target is the venom-spitting head of my once-upon-a-time-favorite author.

In perfect unison, everyone sucks in their breath, and time slows as every rotation bends the ball harder and harder to the left. Like a goalkeeper who's been caught off guard and knows she's beaten, Keyheart's eyes widen as she realizes there's no escape from four hundred and fifty grams of whirling rubber about to tattoo the name "Wilson" on her forehead.

Ironically, if it had been a penalty shot, I would have been denied the goal because the ball hits her squarely in the face and rebounds, flying over my head and landing in Les's boat.

Keyheart, meanwhile, does a perfect imitation of a tree falling in the forest.

Timberrrr!

CHAPTER
19

IT'S PAST MIDNIGHT WHEN I finally collapse onto my bed. Pogo acknowledges me by briefly lifting her nose from the pillow and then placing one paw against my side. Across the room, Pip sleeps soundly, her face glowing in the pale blue moonlight. A westerly breeze lifts the curtains at the sides of the French doors, setting the carved-bird mobile above me spinning. I reach over to Bedlam's cage and lift the sheet.

"G'night, Bedlam."

"Sweet dreams," he whispers in Mom's voice.

There's a quiet knock on the doorframe and I turn to find Suzy standing there. "Hey. You're still awake," she says.

"Yeah. I'm still a little wound up."

"Not surprising. I, uh, just found this," she says, showing me the copy of *Little Dorrit* that I'd found with Owen's help.

I jump from the bed. "Omigosh! I forgot that I put it in your room. I meant to tell you, but there was so much going on. Did you look inside?"

She nods. "It's . . . incredible. Where did you—"

"It was still there, in the house on Buckeye Street. Didi's grandma's house. I had a little help. Owen Cheever's family owns the house, and he got us inside."

"You have to keep it, you know," Suzy says.

"I-I don't know. It's not like a sweatshirt."

"It *belongs* here—on the island, I mean. Didi finally brought it home. Look, I talked to her mom about her stuff—she's all about what Didi would have wanted, who *she* would have wanted to have things. She said it was all up to me. Her parents *are* getting the rights to her book, and that's enough. They're not exactly the most sentimental people you'll meet."

"But the nightingale came from her *grandmother.*"

Suzy hands me the book. "And now it's yours. Whatever the story is with those two birds and the books, you're the right person to decide what to do with them. But I think they belong on Swallowtail Island. Now, go to bed. I don't know about you, but I'm gonna dream about my last breakfast with you guys. Thomas promised waffles with real maple syrup and I can't stop thinking about it. Who knows when I'll get to eat like this again."

Thomas must have started cooking at five in the morning, and goes all-out for breakfast. I follow Suzy into the kitchen. Platters of food cover every horizontal surface. Waffles, pancakes, bacon, sausage, scrambled eggs, hash browns, and bowls of fruit. On the stove, still more is cooking on the griddle that covers two burners.

"Geez, Thomas. Did you invite the whole island for breakfast?" I ask.

"Nobody goes away hungry this morning," he says. "Even Nate, our own little Evel Knievel."

"So, how much trouble is he in?" I ask. "'Cause, I mean, he kind of saved the day. Keyheart would have gotten away if we hadn't been there."

"I'm still not sure where she thought she was going," Thomas says. "Canada? They'd turn her over in a second. I still haven't decided on the punishment yet. Lucky for you both, Officer Pawlowski is willing to forget the whole thing— Boys! Breakfast!—provided he never sees that scooter on the road again." He sets a pitcher of maple syrup on the table and motions to us to sit.

"This is even better than my dream," says Suzy. "And my dream was pretty spectacular."

"I told him he had to make an *extra*-special breakfast," Pip says, hugging Suzy, "to make sure you come back."

Suzy guides Pip into her seat. "You can count on it, kiddo."

"Sit, everyone. Eat!" Thomas commands.

We do as we're told and stuff ourselves until we can eat no more.

When we have pushed back from the table a few inches, Jack gives Suzy a box containing a small wooden swallow, carved by a local artist. "It's from all of us," he says. "But Pip and Thomas picked it out."

"It's perfect! I love it. Thank you guys," she says.

"We thought about a box of chocolates from Keke's," Blake says, "but, you know . . . "

"Yeah, probably not," Suzy says.

"Consider yourself an honorary Heron-Finch-Emmery," Thomas says. "You're always welcome. We'll keep your room ready."

"You guys are too nice. I mooch meals and a place to stay for a week and you give *me* a gift . . . *and* invite me back."

"That's what friends are for," Jack says.

Suzy musses his hair. "You know, for somebody so young, you're very wise." She plants a kiss on his cheek, turning it bright red. Then she turns to me and says, "And, speaking of *friends*, when is your big date with that cute kid? The one with the hair?"

I try to shush her before she finishes, but the blood is already rushing to my face and the damage is done.

"What?! Lark!" Pip cries. "You're *not. Owen Cheever?* Ewww."

"That's *gross*," says Nate. "He's such a loser."

"Sorry. I forgot it was a secret," Suzy says as I press my warm, red forehead onto the kitchen table.

"It's *not* a date," I say. "I'm not allowed to date. Thomas said so. "We're gonna watch a stupid movie. At a campground. Outdoors."

"Don't forget, you're getting pizza, too," says Blake, earning a death-stare from me.

"Hmm. I'm no expert, but pizza and a movie sounds like a date to me," Thomas observes, enjoying every second of me being uncomfortable.

"Yeah, it kinda does," Suzy agrees.

"Aaagh! It's not a date!" Desperate to change the subject, I point to the clock on the kitchen wall. "We're gonna be late, Suzy. We have to get to the ferry."

"Afraid you're right," she says. "I'm gonna miss you guys. Come here. Hugs!"

She gets a hug from everybody—even Blake, who's not usually much of a hugger.

While Thomas loads her bag and guitar into the back of an Islander Hotel golf cart, which they kindly let us borrow one last time, I say, "Be right back. Have to grab something from my room." I run up the stairs, peek inside my backpack, and throw it over my shoulder.

Suzy says, "Bye, guys!" and waves as I toss the pack in the cart and we rumble down the drive.

On the road between the little harbor and town is the Duck & Drake, which is advertised as a bait shop but also sells a wide assortment of snacks, drinks, and mystery novels, especially the kind that are a series of ten or twenty (or more) books. The owner is a retired English teacher and avid reader, and in front of the shop she recently installed a Little Free Library, one of those "take a book, share a book" boxes that looks like a tiny house.

"I need to stop here for a second," I tell Suzy. I pull the cart into the grass parking lot, reach behind my seat for my backpack, and dig out my once-prized copy of *The Somewhere Girls.* "Don't think I'll be needing this anymore. The crazy thing is that it *is* a good book. She's a really good writer. Why did she have to . . ."

"You and your friend Les nailed it. Greed. Jealousy. Fame and fortune. Powerful stuff. Forget about her. Thanks to you, people are going to remember Didi Ferrer. And they're going to get to read *A Drowsy Numbness* . . . with *her* name on the cover."

I open the tiny door and place the book on the bottom shelf of the box, squeezing it between *A Year in Provence* and *Night Train to Lisbon*. There's a book I haven't seen before about taking care of horses on the top shelf, so I snag it for Pip, who believes that there's no such thing as too many books about horses.

"Feel better?" Suzy asks when we're back underway.

I nod. "Yeah. I do."

"I'll bet you're ready for a nice, quiet week. You don't have much time before school starts, do you?"

"Don't remind me. New school. New team. New friends. New *everything*."

"Don't sweat it. You're practically a celebrity. Everybody on the *island* already knows you. The rest of the country is going to when all this really hits the news."

"You really think people *care* about this?"

"Are you kidding? A famous writer kills her assistant and steals her book—a book that publishers are now *fighting* over—and then gets caught by a one-armed, *really* tall, twelve-year-old girl and her adorable motorcycle-riding brother, who *somehow*—and, by the way, I *definitely* don't believe a word of that fairy tale you told Thomas—ties a rope to the getaway seaplane while they're going fifty miles an hour in a boat driven by a Vietnam vet? And then, when the murderer grabs the cop's gun, you *flatten* her with a soccer ball to the head. Yeah, nobody's gonna like *that* story." She grins, and then I see her eyes get really big when she looks toward the ferry dock. "Whoa. What the heck is going on there? Stop here. Seriously. I'll walk the rest of the way."

All around the ferry terminal, packs of reporters and

producers are setting up cameras in an absolute frenzy.

"Are all those—"

"Reporters," Suzy says. "If I were you, I'd turn around and vamoose. Go home and don't answer the door or the phone. Let them talk to the cops, and Nadine. She used to be a reporter, right? She'll know how to handle it. I'm gonna sneak around the side and hope nobody has a picture of me." She climbs out of the cart and grabs her bag and guitar. Then she throws her arms around me and squeezes. "Thank you. For everything you did for Didi."

"Text me, or, uh, call me, okay?" I say, fighting back tears. "Geez. It has been one crazy week."

"You can say that again," she says, letting go of my hand. "I'm gonna miss you, kid."

She takes a few steps and then, still walking, looks back over her shoulder at me. "One more thing: Give that Owen kid a chance. He seems okay."

Suzy is now the second person to tell me that. A couple of weeks earlier, when I compared Owen to Steerforth, David Copperfield's troubled, ill-fated friend, Dinah suggested that maybe Owen is not a lost cause and that maybe I'm just the person to help him find the right path.

You want the GHT? I'm not so sure. I just don't see myself in the "saving Owen Cheever" business. Yeah, I'll watch the movie and get a pizza with him because I promised, and I don't break my promises, but once that's over, I'm done.

With a river of reporters streaming toward the Islander Hotel, I can't very well drive past them in a golf cart with the hotel name in big letters across the hood. Instead, I turn around and head back toward the Roost. I can return the cart later, or even better, I'll get Blake to do it.

On my way home, I'm cutting through town when I see a woman stopped at an intersection, straddling a bicycle and staring at a map of the island. I'd guess that she's fifty-five or so and dressed in jeans and a crisp white blouse. She's also obviously lost, because she's spinning the map in circles and squinting to read street signs. When she sees me approaching, she waves and smiles broadly.

"Good morning," she says, waving. "Beautiful day, isn't it?"

"Hi. Uh, yeah. It's nice."

"Can you help me? I'm looking for Buckeye Street, and according to this really *awful* map, it should be right *here*. But the sign says Hickory Street."

"Buckeye's that way," I say, pointing behind me. "It's really this street, but it's kind of tricky, because *this* part is called Hickory. Don't ask me why. C'mon, I'll show you."

I wheel my bike around and she follows me until I stop at another intersection and point up at the sign.

"Buckeye Street," she reads. "Thank you. This is all a stroll— or a ride, I suppose—down memory lane for me. It's my first time on the island in . . . *forever*. I lived on this street when I was a little girl, but only for a few years. *That's* the house, I think."

This time I'm the one doing the following as she pedals slowly down the street, stopping in front of what is now a very familiar house to me.

"Oh, yes. This is it. Number twenty-two," she says. "It was yellow when I lived in it."

The hair on the back of my neck comes to attention and I'm speechless as she drops her bike in the grass and stares up at the house.

"You . . . lived here? Number twenty-two Buckeye Street?"

"I did, indeed. A long, long time ago." She steps toward me and holds out her hand. "Hi, I'm Barrie Francis."

For a few seconds, I'm struck completely dumb, and I must look like a complete idiot to her.

"Are you . . . okay?" she asks when it becomes clear that I have lost the ability to speak. "I've never said this to anyone in my life, but you literally look like you've seen a ghost."

I nod to let her know that I'm okay. I swallow, and stare. And finally, I remember how my tongue works. "Barrie. Francis. Really?"

"Okay, you're officially freaking me out a little right now," she says. "But yes, that's me."

"You wrote a letter," I start.

Her hand flies to her mouth. "Omigosh. You must be . . . Lark?"

"How do you know that?" I say. I can feel my pulse pounding at my temples.

"I got an email from a friend of yours, an Owen . . . Cheever. I'm not sure *how* he found me, but he did. He told me who he was, and *where* he was, and said that you had found something that belongs to me. I swear, I've never done anything like this, but I got in the car at four o'clock this morning and drove all the way from Williamsfield, the other side of the state. Came over on the first ferry this morning. I was intending to email Owen, but I just had to see the old house first."

"Owen Cheever found you," I say quietly.

Okay, universe, I get it already.

"And from the look on your face, I take it he didn't tell you," Barrie says.

I shake my head. "No clue. It's all right. I mean, I'm glad he did. I'm just . . . surprised. It's been a *really* weird week."

"I heard little bits and pieces from people on the ferry on the way over. There was some kind of book festival, and a girl was murdered? Is that true? It seems hard to believe. It's so peaceful here."

"It's true," I say. "And that girl, and you and me, and my mom and her best friend, Nadine, we're all . . . connected, sort of. I can explain it, but it's gonna take a while. Can you come with me, out to my house? You can put your bike on the back of the cart. We need to make one stop, though, to pick up Nadine. She has to be there for this."

She agrees, shrugging and smiling. "In for a penny, in for a pound, as they say."

After leaving Swallowtail Island at the age of eleven in 1976, Barrie Francis lived in thirteen houses in eight countries over the next seven years. Her father's job with a defense contractor took him to Europe, South America, and even an island in the South Pacific, and his family followed along every step of the way.

"And you've never been back here?" Nadine says.

"Thought about it a few times," she says, "but something always came up. I suppose I was a little bit afraid. My memories of the island are all so wonderful, so perfect. I didn't want to take a chance on spoiling them. When that email came, though, from someone on Swallowtail Island . . . something seemed right about it."

"This is my house," I say, turning into the drive. Pip is brushing Tinker, and the boys are kicking the soccer ball back and forth when I park in the shade under a tree in the backyard.

"It's like something out of a movie," Barrie says. "I can't believe it's real."

Thomas opens the screen door to the kitchen when he hears me pull up. "I thought you were going to return the . . . Oh, hi, Nadine," he says, adding, "Hello," when he sees Barrie.

Nadine handles the introductions, and Thomas offers everyone coffee while I run upstairs, returning ten seconds later with *The Pickwick Papers* and *Little Dorrit* behind my back.

"What's going on?" Thomas asks.

"Remember that letter in the paper you showed me last weekend?" I say. "About the girl who brought the bird in the book to school for show-and-tell? This is her! The actual girl, not the one who wrote the letter to the paper."

"No kidding," Thomas says. "How did . . . never mind. Go ahead with what you're doing."

"First, let me just say that there have been some *coincidences* the past few days on Swallowtail Island," I say. "Like, a *lot*. And then you showing up today, standing there and looking for Buckeye Street . . . to tell you the God's Honest Truth, I'm a little freaked out by it all. I keep telling myself: remember the birthday problem."

"Oh, that thing where you put twenty-three people in a room?" Barrie says. "And there's a fifty percent chance that two of them have the same birthday. That's a good one."

"I can't believe you *know* that," I say. "Although this week, I shouldn't be surprised."

"I'm a math teacher," she says. "I *love* stuff like that. Anything to make it real for kids helps."

"Okay, this first," I say, handing her the note she wrote in 1976, begging whoever discovered the secret inside *Little Dorrit* to keep it safe for her until she returned.

"Oh, my," Barrie says, recognizing her own handwriting from more than four decades earlier. "I feel like I'm going back in time. I remember writing this as clearly as if it were—" She stops short when she sees the book in my hand.

"Believe it or not, it was still in your old house, in the library on the second floor."

She takes the book from me, rubbing her hands lovingly over the leather binding. "*Little Dorrit*. Charles Dickens."

"Go ahead, open it."

Smiling, Barrie lifts the cover and runs her fingers over the faded green ink of the stamp from Crackenthorp Books and below that, the handwritten inscription indicating that the book is from the library of T.P. & P.C. According to the letter I received from Mr. Crackenthorp, that is the name of a now-defunct women's club in London—The Procne & Philomela Club.

"I wish I could bottle the feelings I'm experiencing," Barrie says. "Or at the very least, that I was clever enough to put them into words." She turns the pages—one at a time at first, and then faster and faster until the tip of the nightingale's wing appears through a hole in a page. "It's actually here. How can that be?" More and more of the bird appears as she continues turning pages. When she reaches the center, she gently removes the nightingale from its nest and cradles it in her hand, stroking the enameled back as if it's a living thing. "It's as beautiful as I remember. I'm stunned that you found it, but . . . *how* did you? Where?"

"The funny thing is, the bird and the book, they weren't together. They hadn't been for a long time. It's just dumb luck—"

"Or fate," Nadine interjects.

"Right. Or fate. I actually found the bird first. Or, to be more accurate, it found me." I proceed to tell her the short version of Didi's story—how she had taken the nightingale from her grandmother's house (which, before that was *Barrie's* old house, and before *that*, Nadine's grandmother's) and how the guilt had tormented her for all those years, and then how she brought it with her when she finally returned to the island for

Swallowtales, where she was going to sell her novel and bury the past once and for all. And how, after her death—her *murder*—Suzy and I found it in her things, and I immediately recognized it as the companion to the silver swallow that Mom had found in a copy of *The Pickwick Papers* about thirty years ago.

I then show her *that* book, opening it to reveal the swallow inside, with its stunning blue-green iridescent back.

"And look, it's from the same bookstore in London, Crackenthorp's, and has this same writing about the T.P. and P.C."

"How did they end up on Swallowtail Island?" Barrie asks.

"At the beginning of World War II, when London was being bombed, Crackenthorp's sent them to Captain Edward Cheever, who was a friend. I wrote to Mr. Crackenthorp, and he—well, his son, actually—told me that. But he didn't know anything about the birds. Only that the books themselves weren't valuable."

Nodding, Barrie says, "Edward Cheever's house is the museum now, right? I remember bits and pieces of his story."

"Somewhere along the line, between the forties and the seventies, the two books got separated. *Little Dorrit* ended up in the house on Buckeye Street, where you first saw it, and where you left it."

"Edward Cheever may have given it to my grandfather," Nadine says. "They were good friends. Some years later, probably when the Cheever family was cleaning out the captain's old house, *Pickwick* ended up in a junk shop, where Lark's mom found it."

"Anyway," I say, "once I saw Didi's nightingale and heard her story, I just *knew* that *Little Dorrit* was still there. That's where Owen Cheever, Captain Cheever's great-grandson, comes into the story. His family owns the house, and he got me inside. And . . . there it was."

"And somehow Owen found me," Barrie says. "I guess that's the world we live in, though. It's hard to be invisible. I'm really glad he did. That truly is an extraordinary story. That poor girl. Carrying around that guilt all her life and then finally coming back, and . . . it's like one of Shakespeare's tragedies."

"Starring Ann Keyheart as Lady Macbeth," Nadine adds.

"I suppose the question is, now what?" says Barrie. "After what it's been through, what it meant to that girl, I-I can't take it away from here. It belongs on Swallowtail Island. It belongs *to* Swallowtail."

"I have an idea," I say. "What if we donated them to the Cheever Museum? I mean, that's where they belong, so everybody can see them. It's where they came from, kind of. They *were* Edward Cheever's, at least for a while."

"You're sure about that?" Nadine says. "It's incredibly nice, and thoughtful, but . . . "

"Me and the Cheevers. I know. We have a *complicated* relationship," I add for Barrie's benefit.

"Well, count me in," Barrie says. "It's a lovely plan."

"We can include your letter, too," I say. "And we'll have to write something about Didi, too. She's an important part of the story."

"I'd be happy to help you with that," Nadine says. With a glance at the two books on the table in front of her, she adds, "Call it a hunch, but something tells me that we haven't heard the last about these birds."

I spend Saturday afternoon with Dinah, drinking sweet iced tea and talking about the events of the past week. It is a perfect day for sitting on her porch; warm but not hot, with a ten-knot breeze from the southwest. A hundred or more sailboats with spinnakers of all colors flying parade past on their way from Put-in-Bay to the Southeast Shoal Lighthouse in the Pelee Passage, where they will turn south and head for the finish line just off Perry's Monument. I hadn't realized it before, but Dinah has begun to take the place of my old therapist. She may be ninety-two, but she "gets" my confused, adolescent brain, and I'm totally comfortable talking to her about almost anything.

"Are you still keeping a journal?" she asks. "You haven't mentioned it in a while."

"Yeah, but I haven't written a word all week. I have some serious catching up to do. This hasn't exactly been a normal week."

Dinah shakes her head slowly and then says, "I'm very sorry that you've had to see the very *worst* of human nature up close. First, the Cheevers and their shenanigans, and now this Keyheart woman. Goodness. I despair of what you must think of mankind, but I *promise* you, there are still good people in the world. I have known many. Promise me that you won't give up on us."

"I haven't . . . yet," I say, smiling. "Thomas gave me this poster of an old Peanuts cartoon. It's Linus saying, '*I love mankind . . . It's people I can't stand.*' For a while, it was kind of true, but now . . . I don't know. I mean, yeah, there're the Gilbert Cheevers and the Ann Keyhearts, but then there's you, and

Nadine, and Thomas. And geez, Pip *alone* gives me hope for humanity. Seriously, if they figure out a way to clone that kid, the world would be a better place in a *minute*."

"Well, I'm only an old woman, but I happen to think that her big sister's pretty special, too. Now, let's talk about what we're going to read next. Something hopeful. Something to *inspire* us. And make us laugh a little. Maybe some Gerald Durrell or James Herriott. No! Wait, I have a better idea. It's time you met Cassandra Mortmain and her family. I think you'll love them. There's a copy on the shelf inside. Why don't you bring it here, and we'll get started today. It's called *I Capture the Castle*."

Only one chapter in, and I'm already feeling better about the world, though I can't help smiling nervously when I return home and find Thomas in the moth-eaten, ragg wool sweater that he calls Big Red. I'm afraid there might be a little of Cassandra Mortmain's father in him.

"It's time I started painting again," he says when he sees me staring at a hole in the left sleeve. "And you know . . . "

"You need Big Red for inspiration. Right. Good luck with that."

"How about you?" he asks, checking his watch. "What are you wearing tonight?"

"What am I wearing . . . omigosh! I almost forgot." Owen. Movie. Pizza.

"Remind me where, exactly, you're going for this not-a-date? And what's the movie?"

"It's at the campground. I guess they show movies outside. It's some space . . . *alien* thing," I say. "The *Third* . . . something something. Sounds kind of stupid."

"You know, if you really don't want to go, you don't have to. But it *is* just a movie. It's not like anything's carved in stone."

I'd been only half listening, but caught the last part, the "carved in stone" bit. "What did you say?"

"I was saying that it's only a movie, not a lifetime commitment. You might have a good time. Do you need any money?"

"I-I dunno."

Honestly, I have no idea how this works. Is Owen paying? Are we splitting it?

"Grab a twenty from my wallet just in case. I take it he's coming to pick you—"

Before he can finish, there's a knock at the kitchen door.

Thomas and I look toward the door, and then at each other. Neither of us moves. The house is so quiet that I hear the clocks ticking, the dust mites crawling in the carpeting, the paint drying in Thomas's studio.

In my mind, I travel back in time one week. There's Didi, the first time I saw her, coming down the *Niagara*'s gangplank with Keyheart's bags. A moment later, we're together on Big

Egg Island, her fingers tracing the outline of a swallow carved in stone. There she is once more, on the way to the yacht club, rubbing her special *DD* pendant between those same fingers.

And then.

My hand goes to the goldfinch charm hanging around my neck as I think about what Mom told her that day, literally a *lifetime* ago—about the universal desire to make a mark on the world, to be remembered. There's no doubt in my mind that Mom left hers. A week earlier, I might have said that Pip and I were her version of the carved swallow on Big Egg, but I'm starting to see that we're just the tip of the iceberg. She left her mark on Didi, too, and who knows how many others. And Didi, in turn, left hers on me, and Suzy, and many more to come, I'm sure, when *A Drowsy Numbness* is published.

It's time, I say to myself. Time for me to start making my own mark on the world. I don't what it's going to be, but if Mom and Didi—and the Stoics—have taught me anything, it's that there's not a second to waste. No waiting to be pushed out of the nest for me; I'm going to leap into the world with everything I have and not worry about what everyone else thinks. And at this moment, that means pizza and a movie with Owen Cheever, who is pacing nervously on the porch outside the kitchen door.

He knocks a second time and without another moment of hesitation, I open the door.

Acknowledgments

BEFORE I BEGIN TO THANK the many wonderful people who have had a part in the creation and/or marketing and publicizing of The Swallowtail Legacy, I feel that a word about writers' conferences and those who take part in them is in order. As someone who has been on both sides of the table, as an attendee and on the faculty, I can say with utmost confidence that the character of Ann E. Keyheart in no way represents my actual experience. Without exception, I have found the writers, editors, agents, and others on the faculty side of the table to be incredibly generous with their time and talent, and honest but gentle with their criticism. And on the flip side, I remain in awe of the courage it requires for aspiring writers to share their work, to put it out there for the world to read. So go ahead and sign up for next summer's Swallowtales (or WordFest, my other favorite fictional writers' conference, chronicled in Michael Chabon's *Wonder Boys*); you'll be glad you did.

Now, on with the important business, in which I extend my sincere and eternal gratitude to:

Bethany Buck, Editor-in-Chief at Pixel+Ink, for always knowing exactly where the manuscript needs "a little more of this, and a little less of that" or a good nudge in another direction. I'm looking forward to many more visits to Swallowtail Island, and I'm grateful that you'll be on the ferry.

Sara DiSalvo, Publicity Manager at Holiday House, for creating and following through on the amazing publicity plan for *Wreck at Ada's Reef* that gave me so many excellent opportunities to talk to so many great people. And Michelle Montague, Terry Borzumato-Greenberg, and Mary Joyce Perry, thank you all! Everything about my experience with Pixel+Ink and Holiday House has been far above and beyond my wildest expectations.

Gretchen Mills and Teresa Ramoni, early readers who continue to astound me with their brilliance and insights. I've said it before, but I'll say it again to both of you: I hope I can return the favor one day!

As always, the wonderful Rosemary Stimola and everyone at the Stimola Literary Studio for taking care of me in so many ways.

A belated thank-you to Hallie Ephron, who really should have been thanked in the acknowledgments of *Wreck at Ada's Reef.* As the instructor in a mystery writing seminar at the Yale Writers' Workshop, she convinced me to stick with middle grade and to let Lark tell the story. Check out Hallie's books and the fabulously entertaining *Jungle Red Writers* blog that she writes with several other mystery authors.

And finally, my family (as Lark might say, "the whole fam damily") for your unending understanding, love, and support.

About the Author

In a time not long after the fifth extinction event, Edgar Award–nominated author MICHAEL D. BEIL came of age on the shores of Pymatuning Lake, where the ducks walk on the fish. (Look it up. Seriously.) For reasons that can't be disclosed until September 28, 2041, he now lives somewhere in Portugal with his wife Laura, cats Bruno and Maisie, and Kit, a rambunctious English Setter. He still gets carsick if he has to ride in the back seat for long and feels a little guilty that he doesn't keep a journal.